INSIPID

BANAL. LIFELESS AND COLORLESS

CHRISTINE BRAE

I will never forget this time, that place
Your touch, your face.
The way my heart felt so brand new
You lit up my life in so many ways.

I will always remember **You.**

PROLOGUE

My mom is always there for me,
Her support makes me be the best I can be
She's the one who knows me best.
She comforts me when I'm depressed
She listens to what I have to say
She makes my problems fade away
And though we have our share of fights
In the end she makes everything all right
There are also times we don't always agree
But that's okay because I know she will always love me
Her faith is so strong, her love for me so great
I'd go crazy without her, my mother is my soulmate!

 Mother's Day 2004

TODAY MARKS THE third anniversary of the day I died. The setting sun skates across the water surrounded by the orange sky streaked with alternating layers of blue and white and yellow. The water is still and calm with only tiny rolls of waves washing upon the shore. If I looked far enough, I can see her standing at the end of the universe. I can feel her presence close by. I can hear her sweet singing voice next to me. How many times have I imagined what it would be like if I saw her again? Soon, now. Soon.

I walk sideways along the shore where the water meets the sand, farther and farther from any sign of life. Away from judgment, from condemnation. From things that remind me of the mess I've made. My hands are full, my steps are heavy. But my heart… it's open. It's free. I've done what I could to apologize for all the hurt I've caused them. I've said the words to tell him just how much I love him. Without me, I know they will all be forced to move on.

I stop in the middle of nowhere, ready to finish what I came here to do. In my left hand is one single flower. A calla lily. Simple and understated, but meaningful. In my right hand is a little box with breathing holes and a chirping sound emanating from it.

Let me sit down for a while, I say to myself. Collect my thoughts. Remember why I'm here.

I sit for what feels like hours, but in the scheme of things, I know that it's only for a minute. Slowly, I open the box with the bird in it. The swallow, so tiny, but whose wings are strong and powerful, cowers along the edge of the box, shaking and afraid. I take a deep breath and touch its head with my little finger. Is that what a feather feels like? I'm shaking. I'm sick. I don't think I can do it. How can something so small scare me so much? How can something as docile, as insignificant as a bird, cause me to change my path every time I come across it? Another deep breath as I lift it gently, my fingers lightly enclosing it before I place it on the palm of my hand. Its scraggy little feet feel like pin pricks on my skin.

There. That wasn't so bad now, was it?

I laugh out loud as I raise my arm up in the air, tossing the bird up high, watching it fly far away from me. *Ha! Take that!*

The tide creeps up. The tiny box washes away as I stand up to complete my journey.

The water is dark. My feet feel cold. With the flower clasped in my hand, I move forward. Slowly, surely. I step upon the sand until I can no longer see my feet.

I flinch and jump up in surprise. Something rubs against my legs. Seaweed wraps around my toes. I close my eyes and keep moving. My last fear. Fear of the bottomless unknown that is part of every life. This will be over soon.

Beyond my comfort zone and into the ocean I go. Deeper and deeper until the tide pushes me forward and my feet can no longer anchor themselves on the sand.

I close my eyes and pray. I pray for forgiveness, but most of all I pray for those who will be left behind.

As the tide carries me further away, I delight in the numbness that the cold brings to my skin. The muffled sound of the water in my ear. The overwhelming, heartfelt feeling of closure.

Floating, floating, floating away filled with so much peace.

PART I: FALLING

"Not knowing how to think
I scream aloud, begin to sink
My legs and arms are broken down
With envy for the solid ground
I'm reaching for the life within me
How can one man stop his ending
I thought of just your face
Relaxed, and floated into space"

"Into the Ocean" by Blue October

ONE

Seasons

WHAT DO THE seasons mean to you? To some people, they are a part of every waking day, times of the year that are taken for granted. To others, like myself, they make up the chapters of one's story. I've always been one to mark my memories by the passing of the seasons. Somehow, the look of the clouds, the skies, the temperatures, the way the rains fall, the colors of the grass—in my head, I've managed to align them with the major events in my life.

I found love in the summer and then lost it in the spring. I cried myself to sleep in the winter and froze my heart with the soft tumble of the snow.

They say that youth is wasted on the young. But the truth is that life doesn't come at you just because you're young and inexperienced.

Life happens at every moment.

It doesn't wait, it doesn't hold back. It charges at you,

builds you up, allows you to soar to the highest of heights and gives you a taste of the beauty of living. The trick to all this is knowing not to sit back, that complacency is the enemy lurking in every corner.

One day, it will return with a vengeance to break you. It will render you lifeless, alone, and out of control. It will plunge you into the deepest, darkest recesses of the soul and it will cover you in darkness. You will be lost and alone. Everything you have ever believed in will disappear in an instant.

Like every wintry day when the sun fails to shine and the cold chills you to the bone, when the biting wind eats at you and no amount of shelter can save you from the frigid emptiness, you will lose hope. You will choose to stay inside, clamoring for every bit of warmth to survive. But as the days get longer and the nights fade faster, you will lift up your head, and one day catch the sun peeking through the clouds.

With every ounce of desperation, it will fight its way through the murkiness and one day rise up, never to be beaten down again. With every spring comes new life, a blossoming of death into an understanding, a calmness, a peace. You will smile again, you will hear yourself laugh, you will shed the weight of the clothes on your back. All this in time to welcome that glorious, inevitable summer.

Without the cold, the piercing pain, and the loss, there can never be joy. We need the winter to truly enjoy the gift of the summer so that by the time the autumn comes upon us, we are ready. We are prepared. We transition into sadness once again, knowing that these days are limited. That there is hope within the seasons. That change is imminent and that happiness is only a few crazy moments away.

When I was nineteen, I had my whole life's plan ahead of me.

And now, at forty-two, I don't know who I am.

My name is Jade and this is my journey. Welcome to the seasons of my life.

TWO

The Road

"GOOD MORNING, JADE," Noelle, my secretary greets me, a little too cheerily for a Monday morning.

"Hey, Noey. Let me drop my things off and stop back to look at today's schedule." I slow my gait down briefly to make eye contact with her before reaching into my purse for my keys and shuffling on towards my office. I feel a sense of relief as I open the door and shut myself in.

These are my gates, this is my fortress. The one right thing I have accomplished in my life.

This is the day I have been dreaming of since I knew that I wanted to submerge myself in a career dominated mostly by male players. And yet, a profound sadness fills my heart as I make my way to my desk and lay my purse on the table. I remove my coat and scarf and hang them on the back of my door, looking around at the wide expanse of the space as I return to my desk to take a seat. My

Executive office has wall to wall windows, a rectangular glass desk dwarfed by the openness of the room, a conference table facing a large presentation screen, and a small glass lamp stand. The size of the room as well as the all glass décor make it cold and empty. There are no pictures; the ones in my old office were removed almost two years ago. The walls are painted white. Blemish free, stain free, lifeless white. The holes in the walls that held pictures from a former executive have been cleaned up and filled in. It is a brand new office, meant solely to remind me of my brand new life. I move around the room with a cadence that feels so routine, so mechanical. I sit at my desk, remove my boots, put on my high heels, retrieve the portable mirror, brush out my hair and touch up my eyes. *Someone used to call them his emerald eyes. His lush, verdant pasture. His respite. To me, they're just two more things to worry about in an aging face.*

I lift myself out of this trance as soon as I notice Noelle standing timidly outside my door through the opaque glass interspersed through the solid walls.

"Hi, come on in." I open my door and slip into one of the seats at the conference table. I motion for her to come closer and point at the chair next to me. "What do we have going on today?"

"First things first," she says proudly, "I had them clear all the flowers and plants that were delivered outside of your office this morning."

"Where'd they all end up?"

"We redistributed them around the floor. Some of them were placed in the lobby. All the cards are on your desk."

"Thank you. I know it's a weird quirk of mine, but—"

"Totally understand. Your allergies. No need to explain." It's what Noelle does best—pretending to make sense of what's come over me. "Well, today's the day after all," she starts out, "the press release will be out at 9:00 am and the Executive Team would like to do a champagne toast right after it goes live. Warren wants you in his office at 9:30 where you will be answering questions from a handful of reporters. Your name and bio will be shown on all thirty television screens across the floors."

"Ugh. Seriously?" I groan, still queasy about all this publicity behind my promotion.

"You deserve this, Jade. Revel in it. The first woman Executive Vice President on the Board of Directors. It's an honor for me to be working for you," she argues, choked up with emotion.

"Thank you, but I've been acting in that capacity for quite some time now. Nothing is going to change. I'm still the same person that started here ten years ago. And the only reason I accepted this new role is because Warren wouldn't stop hounding me about it. And of course, now that I can devote my time to this, I think it will be good for me as well." I refuse to let my mind wander towards the thoughts that would remind me of my life's trade off. *Bad for good. Nothing for something. Heart for soul.* I panic when it dawns on me that the press will be here any minute. "Do you think I need to call my stylist to make sure I look all right?"

"Oh my God, no! Look at yourself. You're so well put together, as always. You look great today, no need to worry about that. It's gonna be a cinch. Think of all the other magazine photo shoots you've done in the past few years," she maintains consolingly. "This will be a breeze."

"You are always so kind to me." I reach out to touch her hand. "Tell me what's next."

"Well, your dad called too. He wants you to call him back as soon as you can. You then have an 11:30 lunch appointment with representatives of MT Media Group."

"Who are they?" Somehow, this name doesn't ring a bell.

"They're the media company that we're going to be

representing as they go through their merger with Global Technologies. They're tentatively scheduled to be in town for two weeks to review the merger plan with you."

"Okay. Is that it?"

"That's basically it for now. You're back in those system implementation sessions for the rest of the week."

"Story of my life." I chuckle.

As soon as Noelle steps out, I walk towards the far corner of the room and dial my father's cell phone number. I sit on the floor right by the corner window with my knees up under my chin. I work on the floor a lot, a habit that followed me through from my college days.

An unexpected voice comes through the receiver. "Jade, darling, how've you been?"

"Hi, Mama. Is Dad there?"

"Yes, we're just finishing up breakfast. He left his phone on the dining table and just quickly stepped into his office. I'll ask Concha to bring the phone to him after we chat for a bit. How are you?" Her accent is thick and stilted but warm and laced with character. She's the rock of our family. The epitome of the woman behind the man.

"I'm good. Just crazy busy with work. How have you been feeling lately? I'm thinking of coming up there in a few weeks, as soon as soon as Dad finalizes the closing date for the new building."

"Can you make it for a couple of days so we can spend some time together?"

"Of course. I would love that. I'll let you know the dates. Sorry, I have to run to another meeting. Can you please have Concha give Dad the phone?" I deliberately try my best not to sound like I'm brushing her off.

"Okay, hija." Just when I expect to hear my dad's voice, she has an afterthought. "Jade?"

"Yes, Mama?"

"Did you do what we spoke about the last time? Are you seeking help? Talking to someone?"

"Not yet, I've been too busy, but I promise, it's on my list." I follow this assurance with a nervous giggle.

Her tone is somber and soft. "Okay, I love you. Keep me posted." I hear loud footsteps as she instructs the maid to get my father.

"Hi, Jadey." Finally, my token of comfort.

"Hi, Daddy. Noelle said you called."

"Yes, I did. Have you read the contract I emailed to you to get you up to speed on the building purchase? What do you think?"

"Yes, I reviewed it. So far so good. I've asked one question about striking a clause for recoverability and am waiting on it. I just told Mom I would come home for a few days for the signing, so please keep me posted on the dates. With work and all, it's so hard to take days off."

The loving tone of my mother calling to my father and then the sound of crinkling paper can be heard in the background. I picture them in the warmth and sunniness of our home, their love and support such a sharp contrast to the cool and aloof setting I am in.

"Honey, the press release was just faxed over by the office! Your mom and I are so proud of you. I know I've always given you grief about joining our company. After all, this will all be yours when we're gone, but I get it now. You've accomplished so much for yourself. Congratulations! Your mom and I will make a transfer to your account as our little gift to you. Buy something. Or better yet, how about that Evoque that you've had your eye on for a while?"

"Oh, Dad. You really don't have to. I don't need anything."

"Honey?"

"Yes?"

"Please be okay."

"I'm trying, Dad. I love you and Mama so much. See you soon. And don't worry about the contract. I'll handle it."

I don't wait for him to respond. I press END on the call knowing that I would need a few minutes to contain my desperate urge to get sick before the press shows up for the interview.

THREE

Flash of Light

"LET'S ALL LIFT up a glass to the newest, and probably the smartest, member of our circle! Congratulations, Jade Richmond!" Warren, the President of the company announces excitedly. "Gosh, Jade, you don't know how happy I am to have you finally join us."

"Thank you, Warren, Dave, Mark, Tim and Skip. I'm honored to be a part of your team," I answer, as we all take a sip of our champagne. My appointment makes the Executive Team six members strong. Even though I've been unofficially a member of the team for a while, and my responsibilities won't be changing, the acknowledgment still fills me with pride.

Warren allows the press to swarm the conference room for a few minutes. It no longer surprises me that most of their focus is on taking pictures of me and commenting on my outfit. Noelle had issued a statement earlier to limit the types of questions to be asked of me, but still they persist.

"Ms. Richmond, how have you been since—"

"No personal questions please," Noelle breaks in sternly.

I follow up with a general statement, hoping it will help to redirect their queries. "I'm very excited about this new role. As you all know, Warner Consulting has been working on expanding its global presence over the last few years. We successfully launched our European presence last year and this year we plan to bring the Asian Pacific market into our fold. After all, we are a Fortune 500 company that's quickly making a play to be a Fortune 100 company," I say confidently.

They ignore my statement and continue with their thirst for personal information. Like vultures circling around their prey. *Don't break, I remind myself. Don't give in.*

"Ms. Richmond, does this increased responsibility serve as an outlet for—"

"I said *no personal questions*, please." Noelle protectively lifts her arms up to halt their progress, her narrowed eyes warning them that she'll stop any further questions if this trend continues.

Fifteen minutes of small talk and I'm ready to retreat back into my shell. I make a lame excuse about a previously scheduled conference call and scurry back into my office. The official press release Noelle mentioned earlier is waiting for me on my desk. I lean against my chair as I read the words corporate affairs wrote for the entire world to see. My life in a few sentences.

"Jade is a true master of her craft and has worked diligently to build a seamless and compliant operational process that has allowed the company to grow and prosper over the last ten years. Her excellent collaboration skills have also allowed our company to gain its reputation in the field of financial consulting. Jade strives for perfection in everything she does and holds an extremely high degree of personal integrity and dedication to our company."

Right there, I decide that I am truly happy. My life had taken the worst turn and has found itself heading back and falling into place. The past is past. I have everything I need now, I convince myself. The two people who had my heart are gone forever. It's time to live in the present, enjoy what I've always had. This job. My travels. My parents. My success.

So why can't these tears stop flowing?

I peer up from my desk to find Noelle standing by the doorway, staring at me.

"Jade?" Apparently she's called my name a few times. "Are you okay? Would you like me to come back in a few minutes?"

I swivel my chair around and quickly wipe my tears. "Oh, no need. What can I do for you?"

"Your 11:30 lunch appointment is here. Thirty minutes early. I've asked them to sit in the conference room and also informed them that you might not be able to see them until the scheduled time."

"I'm free now. Give me a few minutes and I'll be right out to greet them. Who are they?" I ask, unsure whether she would notice that I knew she had told me this before.

"The two men from MT Media. For the merger?" she responds patiently.

"Oh yes, them." I reach over a pile of papers to pull out the folder she gave me this morning so I could prepare. Lucas Martinez and Leigh Taylor are the MT Media principals. We're going to assist them in the due diligence process for a merger they're considering with a global tech company, which means it could turn out to be a long and grueling process. Weeks, maybe months. It's all part of the job, I remind myself as I straighten up my skirt and peer at the window to check my appearance. People often tell me that I look at least fifteen years younger than my actual age. My auburn hair is thick and wavy just like my father's and my dark green eyes are straight out of his German gene pool. I'm not tall at all, just 5'4", but with long legs and a lean waist. I got my skin from my Puerto Rican mother, flawless and wrinkle free. At least for now.

After a few seconds of making sure that I have all the details in my head, I collect my materials and walk down the hallway into the designated conference room. I'm not one for quick comebacks and ad lib conversations. I'm methodical and analytical, and I need to process and plan before every business meeting I attend. Somehow, I don't feel as prepared for this as I should be and so I take a few more minutes to gleam through my notes before leaving the confines of my workspace.

"Hi!" I say warmly, extending my hand out to the first man by the door. He looks like a model right out of a GQ magazine, blond with thick, wavy hair. "I'm Jade Richmond, so nice to meet you."

He takes my hand and shakes it firmly. "Leigh Taylor. Pleasure to meet you, Jade."

"How was your trip here? Did everything go okay?"

"It was a long flight, but no delays. Thank you for asking."

"What hotel are you staying in?" I ask, trying to start a conversation.

"We're at Trump Towers for now. We'll probably move to a more affordable hotel depending on our length of stay. Let me tell you, it's great to be catching the tail end of the summer in Chicago."

"Yes it is! You actually came at the perfect time; the heat isn't as overpowering as it was a month or so ago. Indian summer in Chicago is something everyone needs to experience."

As Leigh and I exchange business cards, I see him through the corner of my eye. He remains standing in the background, silently watching me interact with his colleague. He doesn't approach me; he waits in observance until my conversation comes to an end before he glides across the room to shake my hand. He's remarkably attractive.

His deep brown eyes draw me in as soon as I come face to face with him. A chill runs through my body as he grips my hand firmly and holds it for a few seconds longer before introducing himself.

"Lucas Martinez, Ms. Richmond. A pleasure to meet you as well." His rich baritone voice, coupled with a crisp Spanish accent, is music to my ears.

"Hi, Mr. Martinez. Call me Jade. I was just telling Mr. Taylor over here—"

He interrupts before I can finish. "I know, I heard. I was right here watching you. And please, call me Lucas. First names here, as we will be working together for a few weeks."

I turn to him and smile. Once again, his eyes bore into mine and I back away, afraid to admit what's going through my mind. "Anyway, I'm here to take you to lunch. Do you have any preferences as to the type of food you'd like to try?"

"Not really," Leigh chimes in. "We're pretty much open to anything."

"There's a quaint little Italian place a block away from our office. Would that be all right with you?"

"Yes, of course," Lucas responds, with a gallant sweeping movement of his arm. "Lead the way."

FOUR

Jumping In

"I HAVE TO warn you both, these heels have a mind of their own. They don't allow me to walk very fast. I can either meet you there or you can casually stroll down the street with me," I offer jokingly.

"I think we will happily take our time to enjoy the sights on our way to the restaurant," Lucas answers with a sideways smile.

I can't help but grin back.

The walk is quiet and uneventful. Both men try their hardest to limit their pace to keep up with me. We loiter along the river, speaking animatedly about the beauty of the city. I regale them with my people watching stories from my office window twenty-three floors above the ground. I'm pleased at the way I am able to elicit a few laughs from them along the way.

"The water looks almost light blue today," Leigh observes. "The bright sun actually makes it look quite stunning, with the reflection and all."

"Really? It looks the same to me as always. Algae green." I smirk. I really don't see the beauty he's talking about. What I see is the same unappealing green river in front of me day in and day out. It's filthy and murky and filled with dead people. People who were dead even before they killed themselves. I force the morbid thoughts to the back of my mind and paste on a smile as we meander over to our destination.

The restaurant is packed for a Monday but thankfully Noelle has called ahead, ensuring that we're seated immediately.

We're shown to a booth and both men end up sitting across from me. I try my best not to stare, but I can't help noticing everything about Lucas. His shiny brown hair is neatly cut, short on the sides and slightly thicker on top. Clean to the top of his ears, no sideburns. His deep set brown eyes sparkle with dancing flecks of amber and gold. They are earthy, muddy, dark, and warm yet impenetrable. His cheekbones are high, his nose fine and narrow. His jaw is a perfect V shape, lined with a rough shadow of stubble, and his lower lip is fuller than his upper. That's where his lopsided smile comes from, I decide. Leigh's features are the opposite. While Lucas is dark and mysterious, Leigh reads like an open book. Lucas is tall and shadowy and strong, Leigh is all blond and blue-eyed pretty.

"Is this your first time in Chicago?" I ask both men after we place our orders.

"I've been here a few times, but I believe it's Lucas' first time here," Leigh responds before taking a sip of his drink.

"That's correct. This is my first time here and I'm enjoying it more and more," Lucas chimes in.

"What have you guys been doing since you arrived?"

"Nothing much. I've been so jet-lagged that I've stayed in for the past few nights. But Mr. Single over here has been around quite a bit," Leigh teases.

Lucas laughs and takes it all in stride.

"Where are your families from?" I continue to prod.

"We're both living in Southeast Asia for now; my wife is from there," Leigh explains, pausing to take a sip of his water. "But I'm originally from Boston and Lucas here grew up in Barcelona."

"Southeast Asia is pretty far from Spain. How did you end up in that part of the world, Lucas?"

"My mother is from there. We moved when she wanted to retire with family. I received my graduate degree there and found the perfect niche for my media business. Leigh just joined me as a full partner a few months ago." He looks at me with a curious glint in his eye. "Tell us about yourself, Jade," Lucas urges, watching me as both men fall silent, waiting for my response.

"There's nothing to tell. Born and raised in San Francisco, working in Chicago. German father, Puerto Rican mother. Stanford School of Business," I rattle off as if it's the most uninteresting background in the world. "I'm more interested in hearing where Mr. Single has been going for the past few days. Which places have you checked out?"

He laughs emphatically, as if trying to lighten up a question that might uncover a secret. "Nowhere important. Just places around Trump Towers. Any recommendations?"

"Unfortunately, I'm not the right person to ask. I don't go out much, if you can't tell. Too old, too tired. Noelle from our office is more your age. She can help you out."

"She just called us old, man." Leigh turns to tap Lucas on the shoulder.

"No! I said I was old, not you!" I argue, afraid that I've insulted them.

"Well, if you're old, we're old too?"

"Okay. Let's just get this straight. How old are you guys?"

"I'm 33 and Leigh is 35."

"Enough said. I'm almost ten years older than you."

"What the f—" Leigh blurts out, stopping himself just in time. "I mean, sorry. You must be joking. You don't even look our age. You look younger than us!"

"Thank you," I smile, "but you don't have to suck up to me for anything."

"We're not!" Lucas scoffs. "Truly. I agree with Leigh. You look like you're in your twenties. So many women must be jealous of you."

The waiter arrives just in time for me to ignore that last statement, and thankfully, the rest of lunch is spent on small talk. These men have impeccable manners. I know it's the culture; they dine with the routine of royalty from the old world, with its aristocratic etiquette—changing plates after every course, spooning their food instead of shoveling. Once in a while, Leigh or Lucas chimes in with their disbelief about my age. The thing is, I've gotten used to it; I hear it like a broken record over and over again, so much that I cringe every time age becomes a subject in any group conversation. *"So and so, how do old do you think Jade is? Jade, tell them how old you are!"* You'd think it's a good thing, but more often than not, human nature's propensity for envy and competition makes it more of a bothersome attribute, particularly in a world where men still rule the workplace. Not only am I the illustrious "woman in a man's world," I'm apparently a youthful-looking one to boot.

Later on in the afternoon, I lead them back into the conference room which will be their home for the next two weeks. Roughly fifty binders are spread out on the table, all full of documents that need to be reviewed together before putting the merger plan in place.

"Make yourselves comfortable in here, gentlemen. Feel free to use the phone and all the other facilities and equipment while you're here. I'm only two doors away, so please let me know if there's anything you need from me. I assume you'll be looking everything over and asking me questions as we go along?"

"That's the plan," Lucas responds.

I nod my head before turning around to walk back to my office.

"Jade?" At this point, I still don't recognize whose voice it is that calls to me.

I swing back towards the table, where they've now chosen their places, two seats apart, both with their backs to the glass wall. Lucas stands up and starts leading me towards the door.

"Is it okay if I get your cell phone number in case you're out of the building and I need to ask you a question?"

"Of course," I say, "Is your cell number on the card that you gave me?"

"Yes it is. Use the one that ends in 03."

"Let me program it on my phone and I'll send you a text."

"Sounds good, thank you."

I address both men as I reach out my hand to shake theirs. "Welcome again. I'll see you both tomorrow."

A few hours later, I'm still thinking about him. I stare blankly at my phone for a few minutes before making the move that I somehow know is going to change my life. I'm like a high school girl with a silly crush, the only difference being that this girl is a 42-year-old woman and the boy is a much younger man.

I send him a text message.

Jade: *Hi. It's Jade. Just wanted to let you know that I've left for the day. Have a good evening.*

The phone dings back immediately.

Lucas: *Thanks for letting us know. Goodnight, Jade.*

FIVE

His Story

I ARRIVE AT the office early the next day to prep for an all-day learning session about the new financial system our company is about to implement. No one is at the office when I arrive at 7:00 am, not even Noelle. I luxuriate in the silence of the before and after hours, when my mind is clear and unencumbered by the crazy events of each workday. With my door closed, I sift through my desk and search for the necessary files for review before the meeting. My mind is so filled with thoughts about the day's presentation that at first I forget about our foreign visitors in the conference room next to me. Noelle reminds me about them with a phone call at 9:00 am to ask me whether we should be catering lunch for our guests. I instruct her to go ahead and arrange for their meals while they're here and drop by the conference room on the way to my meeting.

"Good morning! How are you?" I greet, addressing Leigh, too shy to look in Lucas' direction. All I notice is that he's wearing slim dress pants that highlight his strong, long legs.

"Good morning, Jade," Leigh answers while Lucas looks up from a blueberry muffin.

"I'm in a full day meeting, but please email or text if you need me. Noelle has you set for meals for the duration of your stay. I assume you'll just continue reviewing the documents in the binders?"

"Yes, that's what we intend to do for the next few days," Leigh concurs.

Lucas continues to munch away on his muffin. His relaxed demeanor is in direct contrast to the nervous reaction I have towards him. I have to consciously steer my eyes away, determined not to look in his direction.

"Okay, well, have a great day, gentlemen." I nod confidently before turning around to leave.

"Jade, wait up." Lucas chases after me while frantically wiping his mouth with a napkin. "I might have questions for you tonight. May I just come to your office and discuss after your meeting?"

"Yes, of course. My meeting ends at six, so I'll be free after then."

"Oh. Well, I don't want to keep you here too late," he counters, running his hands through his hair.

"No worries. I'm normally here catching up on work after business hours," I assure him, giving him a smile and walking away before I say anything more. I'm normally adept at separating business from personal feelings, but this time it feels unnatural to me; somehow my mouth wants to start rambling uncontrollably.

Nine hours later, Lucas shows up at my door carting two black binders in his arms. He uses his free arm to knock softly on my wall to catch my attention.

"Hi, Jade. Is this a bad time? I can come back when you're free."

"Oh, no, this is fine. Would you like me to go to the conference room so I can answer Leigh's questions as well?"

"Leigh's gone for the day. His son is here visiting from school."

"Oh. Okay. Please have a seat," I offer as I stand up to join him at my conference table.

He leafs through the tabbed pages in one of the binders and opens it up to a specific page.

"This one," he says, pointing. "How were the calculations made? Did we factor in the gross value of assets? Can we get a copy of those documents?"

"Yes, of course. Let me send that to you via email," I suggest as I grab a pad and pen. "Let's go through all your questions so I can send them all at the same time."

We spend ninety minutes discussing methodology and results. He constantly challenges my inferences to a point where he begins to get on my nerves. Not that I'm fazed by his questioning—his analytical abilities actually impress me. *So young. So sure of himself. So black and white. No broken lines. I like his principled outlook.*

Lucas writes a few more notes before gently pulling the binder away from my hands. "I think I've challenged you enough for one evening," he states cockily.

"That was a challenge?" I chaff back in his face. "I thought it was a healthy discussion."

He gets up to gather the binders and start his trek back to the conference room. "Thank you for your time."

I shrug my shoulders, watch him strut away, and take a few steps to retrieve my coat. I'm not going to overanalyze his completely cool demeanor. Just as I walk out of my office, I notice him coming back in my direction.

"Hi again." He smiles sheepishly. I feel the warmth coming back.

"Hi."

"Peace offering," he says softly, looking like he doesn't know what to do with his hands. He finally keeps them busy by tucking them inside his pants pockets. He looks like a runway model striking an easygoing pose. "I wanted to know if you would like to grab a quick bite downstairs before you leave."

"I'm not that hungry, but I was on the way to the Pantry across the street to get a pop."

"A pop?" he asks, turning his head quizzically, as if I've just spoken some foreign jargon.

"Sorry. A soft drink."

"That sounds good, is it okay if I join you?"

"Come on. I'm buying." I tilt my head in the opposite direction, motioning for him to follow me. We take the elevator down in silence and he follows right behind me as I lead him towards the outside of the building.

It's another perfect summer evening; the stars are out and there is no wind. Lucas and I sit on the lower steps of the building and share a bag of Cheetos while sipping our cans of Coke. He reaches into his pocket and pulls out a pack of cigarettes.

"Smoke?" he offers.

"Sure," I oblige as I take one from the pack. *What am I doing? I haven't smoked in years.* "Do you smoke a lot, Lucas?"

"Actually, I don't. This is my stress reliever. I'm a runner."

"So am I! That's funny. Does that mean we're both stressed out?"

"Definitely. We have the perfect excuse to let go for a little bit." He flashes me a smile as I lean over to him for a light.

LUCAS SHOWS UP at my office at 8:00 pm every evening that week, coat in hand, ready for our nightly jaunt to the little grocery across the street. During the day, we act like colleagues, speaking to each other only about business, working on the merger proposal together. Leigh remains part of the team, acting more like the senior partner in this engagement and leaving Lucas on his own to ask the questions and draft the responses. We spend the evenings together as friends, but we share more than a Coke and a bag of chips. We share stories and experiences, with one cigarette quickly turning into two or three. He does most of the talking, I do most of the listening. Over the past few months, I've learned to keep my thoughts and feelings to myself. No one wants to hear about a lonely woman and her sad life, especially when it looks so perfect and fulfilled from the outside. Although I never forget the age difference between us, conversations with him are comfortable and easy.

"What's your story, Lucas? How come you don't have a girlfriend?"

He doesn't answer me right away. Sometimes I think it's because he translates his thoughts first into words and then into another language. "I'm still recovering from something that happened recently. I got in the middle of something against my better judgment." I begin to sense a tinge of discomfort from the way that his body shifts in the opposite direction.

"What happened? You can tell me," I say, before changing my mind. "Only if you want to, of course."

"I thought I was in love with a woman who was divorced from her husband. She ended up going back to him. I kind of knew how it would get resolved, but I jumped in anyway."

"What was she like?"

"She was captivating; we hardly knew each other. I met her at a time when she was lost and alone. She's actually the best friend of

Leigh's wife. He is very close to her. She remarried her husband last year and they just had their third child."

I listen without any interruptions, nodding along as he waxes poetic about their relationship, watching him gesture with his hands as he speaks. After a few minutes, I notice that we're both holding our cigarettes with orange powder caked on our fingers. I let out a laugh as I hold my fingers up to his face. He takes them and swipes them across his pants before doing the same thing to his.

"I'm sorry," I say, to both his story and the fact that he now has orange streaks on his pants. I heedlessly reach over to brush the stains off—his thighs are rock solid.

There's a peculiar silence between us before he quickly reaches over to take my hand. He lets it go as soon as he catches me glancing around uncomfortably, and continues the conversation with an air of nonchalance. "Don't be," he says bluntly. "That's what life is all about. Leaping in against what seems like obvious odds against you. Taking chances. You'll never know if you don't try."

"I guess you have that luxury when you're young."

"Oh, here we go again. Why do you always attach age to everything?" He holds my gaze and silently challenges me not to look away. "Those eyes of yours. I can tell that there are things you want to share with me, Jade. They're like pages of a book just waiting to be turned."

"There's nothing to tell. Life goes on and I'm living it the best way I can." It's time to make another attempt to change the subject as I try to avoid any eye contact with him. "Tell me about your family. How are they? How many siblings do you have?"

"I'm the oldest son in a family of four kids, two boys and two girls. My parents have been married forever. My dad drives my mom crazy; she's much younger than he is." He enunciates that last sentence before he continues on. "We're a little bit more liberal I think, culturally, about love and marriage and free expression."

"I've heard about that Latin/Spanish cultural macho male thing," I tease.

He wiggles his eyebrows mischievously. "Don't you forget it. Did you hear the one about us being the best lovers?"

SIX

Leather

I ARRIVE AT the office Monday morning with a brand new haircut. My long hair has been trimmed and layered, and for the first time in forever, my nails are painted red. I also had a three-hour session with my stylist, which meant thousands of dollars in new and updated outfits. I justify my new efforts by thinking of him as a new friend, someone removed from my current life with a refreshing outside perspective. I hardly see Lucas during the day, but feel comforted with the knowledge of his close proximity to me. Things are going so well with the proposal that they think they might wrap up by the end of this second week. Whatever it is that's happening now has a looming end date in my mind.

Lucky for me, my first meeting includes my close friend and co-worker, Leya Markland. A meeting with Leya is the best way to start the work week. We've been friends since I first started at Warner Consulting. She works in Operations, so we're removed enough

34

from each other to separate our personal and professional lives. We're complete opposites in looks, but we share the same work ethic and devotion to the company. Leya is a jeans and t-shirt kind of girl, creative, artsy, and casually alluring with a breezy personality, frank and honest and to the point. Her blonde hair, blue eyes, and height reflect her Nordic heritage, and I often feel so tiny standing next to her, even in high heels. Leya calls me out on everything including my brand name shoes, my purses, and the fact that I hardly repeat the same outfit twice. She keeps me honest. Maybe that's why I'm afraid to bring her in on my latest secret.

"Good morning, Ms. Richmond," Leya greets me with her usual one liner before occupying the place next to mine at the conference table.

"Hi."

"Psst!" she whispers entirely too loudly for my taste. "Where's my friend and what did you do to her? The woman next to me is wearing leather pants and her nails are painted red."

"Ugh. Too much? It's too much, isn't it?"

"Yes. Too much for the men in this office. You look hot! I mean *caliente*!"

"Shhh!" I slap her arm playfully as other people file into the room.

"Hot guy alert!" Carissa from Finance says as she points to the men in the room across from my office. "Jade, you're so lucky. Everyone on this floor is swooning over those guys. Especially the dark-haired one."

"How old do you think he is, 30?" Mandy from the same department chimes in.

"Someone looked him up on LinkedIn. Very accomplished. He's single too," Tori from Operations declares with authority.

"How do you know that?" I ask, finding myself secretly miffed and defensive.

"Facebook!"

"Okay, okay. Settle down," I say, biting my tongue from telling them to stay away from Lucas. "Sorry about that digression, folks. Whose meeting is this?" I inquire testily, eager to change the subject. Thank goodness that was enough to deflect everyone from that bizarre conversation.

The meeting lasts for forty-five painful minutes. The women in attendance all seem intent on watching the men in the conference room across from us. My insides are gloating at the fact that we share a secret no one can touch. And then I feel guilty about the women in this office who are single and available and desperately looking for love. Life is funny that way—the more you seek, the less you find.

After the meeting is over, I bring Leya over with me to meet him. Leigh has stepped out of the office to meet with people from another department.

"Lucas, meet Leya Markland. She's our Director of Operations. Some of the statistics in those reports were prepared by her team."

His eyes light up as he immediately saunters over to stand next to me. "Pleased to meet you, Leya."

"Hi, Lucas. How is everything going?" For a few seconds, Leya actually turns on the charm and warmly reaches out to shake his hand.

"Everything went better than we expected. In fact, we'll be wrapping up things by Friday." I detect a tinge of sadness in his voice as he turns his attention towards me despite the fact that he is speaking to her.

"Oh. Well, not that I'll be happy to see you go, but I'm glad that our proposal is acceptable to you. Have a safe trip home if I don't speak to you again before Friday."

I take hold of her elbow and lead her away from him. Leya pinches my arm as soon as we're out of earshot.

"Oh my God!" she squeals. "That guy wants you. He was eye fucking you the whole time. You and your leather pants!"

"Ley. Stop. Aside from the fact that he's young enough to be my son, he's leaving in three days!"

"Stop with the exaggeration! You weren't having children when you were nine, Jade. Oooh. He can be your Same Time Next Year guy!"

I shove her into the elevator before she could say another word and wave sweetly at her as the doors come to a close. I whip out my phone as soon as she's gone and fire off a text to Lucas.

Jade: *Check your security settings on Facebook.*

I LIVE FOR the evenings alone with Lucas as our routine continues for the next few nights. Conversations over Cokes and chips under the sky and the stars, wrapped up in the warm Chicago breeze, with Lucas sitting next to me on a cement ledge outside the building somehow couldn't be more perfect. Our personal interaction consists of little touches, tiny nudges, and penetrating gazes when a point needs to be made. To the outsider, it might come across as a little telling, but to us, it's just what we've grown accustomed to.

"Did I tell you that I was engaged briefly?" he asks one soggy Wednesday night three days before his planned departure.

"No, you didn't. What happened?"

"I cheated on her. I can't seem to stay faithful to anyone. My travel brings about so much temptation and most of the time, I give in. I'm a shit, aren't I?"

"Yeah, pretty much," I admit without looking at him.

His flippant demeanor disappears and his look turns serious. "Jade, why do you think some marriages don't last?"

"I think it's because people are constantly changing, forever growing," I reply quickly. I know the answer to this one. "It takes a lot of work to keep in step with someone else."

"What are your parents like?" He dips his hands into my bag of pretzels and crunches away.

"I'm an only child, so my parents are my world. My dad is my best friend. My mom keeps me grounded." *That's all the information I'm willing to divulge for now.*

"How did you get so driven? Did you always know that you would devote your life to your career?"

I feel insulted, like a major loser. "Do I give you the impression that I don't have a life outside of this?"

He touches my thigh lightly before casually stressing his point. "Jade. You're here until midnight every day."

"How do you know that it's not only because you're here?" *Did I really say that?* "What about you? There must be so much pressure on you to keep up with the business."

"Yes, actually. The business skyrocketed prematurely, and I couldn't handle the pressure to keep up. I'm better now, but for a while there, I was seeking out things to help me cope."

"Things like what?"

"Drugs. Alcohol. Socially, of course, but still. I knew it would only keep me afloat for a while." Lucas rolls the pretzel bag into a ball and shoots it straight into the trash can. He reaches into his pocket, pulls out his pack of smokes, and hands me one.

We stay quiet for a few minutes, taking sips of our Coke,

puffing on our cigarettes. He finally breaks the silence.

"Can I ask you a question?"

"Sure."

"Am I crazy, or do you do your best to avoid flowers at all costs? Every time we walk across the street, you seem to avoid walking by the flower boxes on the sidewalk."

"Allergies. I'm paranoid. I don't want to get sick. They get pretty bad."

"Ah." I can tell he doesn't believe me because he nods his head exaggeratedly.

"Now it's my turn to say something." I look at him with a pointed smirk on my face.

"Go for it," he responds as he inhales a puff of smoke.

"You need to use more contractions in your sentences." I let out a laugh as I nudge him with my elbow. "You sound so formal all the time."

"I totally agree with you. And you would think that with all the traveling I do in this country, I would have picked up on your American slang by now," he says, genuinely amused by my statement. "So you are going to be my teacher, okay?" He accentuates the word "are" to mock me.

"Okie dokie." I follow this up with a wink. He throws his head back and laughs.

While we relish what's left of our drinks and watch a flurry of cars drive past us on the bridge, the comfortable silence is back.

"So, you think that people can really outgrow love?" he asks suddenly, turning towards me with a serious look on his face.

"Life is a crazy combination of phases," I say diplomatically. "We all go through different stages in life, and all handle them in many ways. Some people can handle the bullshit and some emerge from it wounded and scarred. As people change, their feelings change too. Sometimes, love doesn't survive that war. Sometimes, it dies. Food for thought, Lucas."

"Words of experience, I'm assuming?"

"Yes. Something you have yet to learn." Quick one-two punch. Just in case he forgets how young he is. Compared to me, that is.

"So much wisdom, Ms. Richmond," he says with a laugh. "I'm going to ignore that last comment. Let's go back to those scars. Are you ever going to open up to me about them?"

"Never!" I joke, leaning into him so that our shoulders are touching. "Hey, look, let's have a contest. The one who can make the best smoke circles wins."

THE NEXT DAY, I decide to sneak in a run along the lakefront before going into the office. I have a monthly membership at a gym by the marina for locker and shower space on days that I run outside before work. The morning turns out to be a bit balmy, so I figure a quick four miler will be sufficient to help me let out some steam. I take a different path than most runners, running the back way along the water rather than the scenic route. My thin white tank top with a built in bra is almost still too hot to wear on a day like this. The last mile is grueling. It takes every bit of energy for me to soldier on despite being lost in my thoughts, enjoying my music. Even before I slow down for a walk, I hit the stop button on my Garmin watch, excited to see that I still made good time despite the slower pace. I cool down briskly, reminding myself that the earlier I get to work, the sooner I'll be able to see him.

Him. *He* is standing right in front of me, wearing a gray sleeveless tech shirt and black running shorts, with a circle of sweat centered on his chest. We have the same neon-colored brand of shoes. It makes me laugh.

"I saw you out at the mile two marker but thought I would give you time to finish," he starts. "How was it?"

"Bad. Those late nights at the office are taking a toll on me," I reply jokingly. "Never mind the cigarettes. Are you heading back?"

"Do we have to? Can we cool down with a short walk? It's only 7:30."

"Sure." We trudge on slowly along the cement path towards the starting point. I look around worriedly, prepared to turn the other way the minute we see someone from the office.

"Relax, we're just running together." *He reads my thoughts. How does he do that?*

"I know," I respond defensively, stopping in my tracks when a large group of birds blocks me from moving any further.

Lucas keeps going until he realizes that I'm no longer walking alongside him. He turns around with a questioning look, about to open his mouth to speak.

"Birds. I can't," I say, standing there helplessly. "Don't shoo them this way, then they'll all start flying towards me!" I shriek, backing away, terrified as he begins to approach me.

He circles around them until he's back at the place where I stand. To my astonishment, he lifts me up and slings me over his shoulders, running through them and flapping his arms.

"Lucas! Put me down! What are you doing?" I giggle, bouncing up and down in his arms.

"I'm protecting you from the birds!" he reminds me as if this is totally normal, running and keeping a firm grip on my legs at the same time.

A flash of light sparks the corner of my upside down eye. "Luke! Did you just see that lightning? It's going to rain! We'd better head back!" I cry, my words bouncing disjointedly as I'm jostled up and down. The birds are long gone but I'm still enclosed in his arms.

"First the birds and then the rain. Jade! Is there anything you aren't afraid of?" He runs effortlessly for a few more feet and then stops to put me down. He looks around and turns to me seriously. "Okay, the coast is clear."

The clouds choose that moment to open up and the raindrops fall like buckets of water. We're soaked in a matter of seconds. For some reason, we find it extremely funny, bursting into laughter at the same time.

"So much for that!" He snags my hand and we run for what little shelter there is, the drinking fountain shed, which has a little awning that extends a few inches past the structure. I'm not surprised that there's no one there. People must have sought more dependable refuge once the lightning started to hit.

"Look at my hair!" I exclaim, running my fingers through my thoroughly flat head.

"Jade. That's not what I'm worried about," he says as his eyes darken and his look changes. I follow the direction of his gaze to find my shirt soaked through and totally transparent.

"Oh my God, Luke!" I wrap both arms around my chest in embarrassment, but his eyes never move.

His hand gently reaches out to wipe the drops of water from my cheek, slowly trailing downwards towards my crossed arms. He bends his head down and growls provocatively in my ear, "I'm dying to touch you."

I don't know what comes over me. I drop my arms to reveal myself and allow his eyes to rest upon me for a few seconds. "Lucas, we have to go. Please. The merger. Too much at stake. For you. For me." I can't say the words. I can't be here anymore. I'm dizzy with arousal.

"Okay." He quickly fusses with the hem of his shirt as he lifts his arms to remove it. "Put this on, please."

I slip the shirt over my head, trying not to think about how good it smells. "Thank you. I'll see you at the office?"

"Yes. I need to cool down a bit. Go ahead."

"See you later," I whisper, reaching out to touch the gloriously rugged stubble on his face before turning on my heels and running back to the locker room.

SEVEN

Panic

THE NIGHT BEFORE his last full day at the office, I wake up in the middle of the night in a panic. I've had these attacks before, and my doctor has given me many ways to deal with the cold sweats and shallow breathing that accompanies these onslaughts. As I sit up on my bed to switch on the light, my thoughts are filled with memories of the past two weeks. I feel apprehensive and anxious. All I can think about is the fact that I'm never going to see him again. Ever. I feel sad and displaced, overwhelmed with the familiar feeling of loss and profound emptiness. I can't explain it and all I know is that I don't want the morning to come.

Needless to say, the sleepless night takes a toll on me the next day. I can't shake this feeling of melancholy. Nothing feels right. I'm tense and agitated. Many times during the day I walk past the conference room to catch a glimpse of him pacing around the table, organizing his binders, packing them up in boxes. I don't make an effort to stop by to engage him in conversation. In fact, I avoid him the entire time, making sure to keep my door closed as a sign that I don't want to interact with anyone. I've never felt this way before. The need to have him in my life, even if just as a friend... this connection, this longing... it's completely foreign to me.

Later on that evening, I sit on the floor and stare out the window. I haven't spoken to him all day. I don't know how to approach him, how to say goodbye. I hear the converging sound of footsteps, but I don't move from where I am. Quietly, he enters my office and shuts the door behind him. I watch him come closer from the reflection on the glass.

"Jade."

"Do you ever wonder what their stories are? Those people crossing the bridge, walking back and forth across the river?"

"I don't know, I don't have this view from my office," he says lightheartedly.

I don't say anything and we let a few seconds of silence pass between us.

He sits down on the floor right next to me. "Where do we go from here, Jade?" he asks sadly, stretching his legs out in front of him and leaning back on his arms.

"We finish the report and go on with the merger." I turn to face him. "You'll go on to earn fifteen million dollars from this and be a very rich and happy man."

"I don't want you to worry about us. It's not over. I'll be back."

"I'm not worried."

"Yes, you are." He moves next to me and puts his arm around my shoulder. "You're not alone anymore. I'm here."

I resolve not to give those words any credence. They can't be anything more than empty promises. There's no use in prolonging this. Whatever it is.

"I don't need you to feel sorry for me."

"Oh God, do you think that, really?" he says in irritation. "You really don't know, do you?"

"Know what?" I ask, taken aback by the change in his attitude.

"How enthralling you are, Jade. How intriguing and soulful and utterly sexy you are. You don't see what other people see in you. That's what makes you so special. You don't use this—" he pauses to sweep his arms up and down as if tracing me from head to toe, "as leverage. You see it as a burden when it shouldn't be."

"So you're psychoanalyzing me now, young man?" I say in a stern but amused tone. I want him to remember our age difference. *This will never work.*

"Jade?" he mutters, tilting my head upwards so that our eyes are locked together.

"Hmm?"

"I'm going to kiss you now." His lips touch mine ever so lightly at first, increasing in pressure as he firmly holds my head in place. As I open up willingly to him, they turn heated and overpowering. "You are so enticing," he whispers, lightly tucking a strand of hair behind my ear before holding my face in his hands.

For the first time in years, I forget that I'm broken. I feel shiny and new. Loved and desired.

If only for a few brief seconds.

I know right here and now that nothing will ever be the same for me. I've ventured into new territory. The high from a touch that cures the deepest of wounds… it will never leave me. I will never recover from this.

"Luke, stop!" I cry out, jerking my head back to release his hold on me. "The deal isn't done yet. We can't do this."

It takes him a few seconds to catch his breath. "Okay, okay," he concedes, looking to the floor, his breathing still heavy. "I realize that our professional relationship is still ongoing until the final report is issued. And so to accommodate your vehement request, I'll refrain from touching you again. But…" he gently lifts me up off the floor to carry me over to my desk, seating me on the edge and standing between my legs, "I'm going to make sure that you know what I've been wanting to do to you since the morning that we met." He peels off the scarf around my neck and throws it on the floor. Slowly, he unbuttons my blouse expertly with one hand, taking his time, watching for my reaction.

I look away and hold my breath, afraid to move a muscle. I feel the cool air of the room on my skin as he snakes his hand underneath me to unclasp my bra. I close my eyes as he lifts it up to expose me.

"Every part of you is perfect," he croons as he slides my blouse off my shoulders. "The other day. In the rain—"

He pushes me further back with agonizing caution until I'm supporting myself with both arms and my legs are dangling off the desk. With one quick swoop of his arm, the desk is cleared of everything that has made up my life for the past two years. Piles of papers are now scattered on the floor around his feet.

"What's this?" he asks as his thumbs lift up my chin and caresses a purple line around my neck, right above my collarbone.

"Thyroid surgery," I volunteer willingly.

"Hmm. It doesn't look like stitches," he murmurs to himself as he plants tiny kisses along its jagged line. "My God, you smell like heaven."

A mixture of emotions runs through me, excitement and panic at odds with each other. *Past and present are going to collide. How will this end up?*

He diverts his attention to the only item that's left on the table, a combination pen/ highlighter, oval in shape and thick in width. He begins to trace the blunt end of the pen down my neck, outlining my breasts and circling towards my stomach, until he reaches my waistband. He undoes my pants and pulls them down swiftly, letting out a gasp as he sees what I'm wearing.

"Oh, God, Jade." He guides my hand and slips it into the fine lace that leaves little to the imagination. "Touch yourself, Jade. Imagine that it's me touching you. It excites me to imagine myself inside you. Watching you will be enough for me for now. I've been watching you, delighting in you for two weeks." He moves my hand up and down, back and forth, for a few seconds. "Make yourself come. Come to my voice, to my words. I want to have you. And I will. Mark my words. This," he says, pushing two fingers inside me, his dusky eyes turning up in a hint of pleasure when I gasp in surprise.

"Is." He does it over and over again, increasing in intensity with every touch.

"Not." As he utters this last word, he moves it faster and faster until I arch my back and place my other hand over his.

"Over."

"Lucas!" I gasp, shaking from the force of my climax.

"Come, baby, come," he heaves in my ear before muffling my cries with his mouth. He holds me until our breathing slows down somewhat. I hear the loud sound of ruffling paper as he mindlessly steps on the sheets that are creased and crumpled all over the ground.

I feel exposed and embarrassed, lying limp in his arms like I've just run a marathon. I haven't felt this helpless in so long. He's got me under his spell that I don't even remember where we are or how we got here. I am swept up in so much emotion that I don't want it to end this way. I don't want him to leave without being able to touch him, without being able to please him like he did me. While the consequences of our actions flash in my mind, all my concerns quickly dissipate as soon as I look up into his face.

I jump off the desk and kneel down on the floor to pick up the debris that is the aftermath of what we've done, the symbol of our chaotic relationship. If nothing else, maybe I can put some order to it.

"I'm sorry," he says as he bends down to help me collate the torn and wrinkled pages of the documents that have defined my life until tonight.

"Don't be." I turn emotionless and robotic. I'm on a mission to clean this up as reality now begins to brutally take over. "Go ahead and finish packing your stuff up. I'll run down and get us some food," I offer, refusing to look at him, fixated at the wreckage in front of me.

He nods his head dazedly, the look on his face showing me that he, himself, is still processing what just happened between us. He lets go of my hand and pauses to say something, but decides otherwise and reluctantly walks away.

I can't help but smile when I notice the pen sticking out of his back pocket.

EIGHT

Passing Through

LUCAS: *GOOD MORNING*

Jade: *Hi.*

Lucas: *I can't stop thinking about last night*

Jade: *:)*

Lucas: *Are you okay?*

Jade: *Yes, of course I am*

Lucas: *Are you at the office yet?*

"Hi." He strides in just as I'm about to respond to his text.

"Hi."

"Are you sure you're okay?"

"Yes, I am. Are you?"

"I don't want to leave." *But he has to.* "Leigh is back for the conference we're having at 10. He's been visiting another client while in town. I want to spend time with you before my flight this afternoon. I'll come back after our meeting, okay?"

"Okay. Lucas, about last night—"

He intentionally ignores me, standing by my desk with his hands on his hips. The tone of his voice transposes, turning disconnected and businesslike. "Jade, after I leave here, it might be best that you don't know what my next steps are regarding the merger so you remain uninvolved going forward. Given what happened between us, it allows you plausible deniability. Is your phone a work phone?"

"Yes, is yours?"

"Yes. We shouldn't talk about work when we're on personal time. Don't tell me what you're doing, what you're working on, and I'll do the same."

"Yes, that makes sense." I know just how to lighten up the mood between us. "I think I'm going to call you 007. Secret Agent."

It works. A huge grin crosses his face and his eyes begin to smile again. "Ha! I like that. And which Bond girl do you want to be?"

"Anyone but Moneypenny."

"Why not Moneypenny? She's not technically a Bond girl, but I like her. The other women came and went with each new movie, but she stayed a constant in his life. Besides, you're hotter than any one of them because you're real!"

He turns pensive all of a sudden and brushes his hand against mine. Quickly, I pull away since the door to my office is wide open.

"I'll see you at the meeting," he mumbles as he walks out the door.

Two hours later, we're lined up along a large conference room table, the representatives of MT Media on one end of the table and the Executive Team of Warner Consulting on the other, for a closing meeting to discuss next steps now that the plan has been drafted.

Lucas starts out by thanking our staff for a job well done. "I especially want to thank Ms. Richmond for accommodating us while we worked on the draft. She went above and beyond what we expected of your firm. Her studies and proposed plan of action were like nothing we have ever seen before." His deep brown eyes never leave mine. They drill a hole straight into my heart. No matter who addresses him, no matter whom he speaks to, he keeps his eyes on me.

I nod my head in acknowledgment. "Thank you, Mr. Martinez. It was a pleasure working with you."

More small talk ensues. It's interesting to see him in action. His charm and easy demeanor have everyone eating out of his hand by the time the meeting is over. More than anything, he comes across as compassionate and considerate. He is respectful of the older executives and seems genuinely excited to be working with all of us. After we all stand up to leave, Leigh commandeers his attention with strict instructions, "Lucas. We're out of here in ten minutes."

"Bro, our flight doesn't leave till five!" He sounds panicked, worried. He lifts his brows and shakes his head, as if trying to deny what Leigh has just said.

"I scheduled another meeting with the lawyers at their office. We'll proceed to the airport from there. Pack up. We're heading out."

Everyone stands around to listen to their conversation, each of us concentrating on his reaction. Lucas glances at me, his eyes attempting to communicate something I don't register. I'm too caught up in my own misery to help him out with his. *This is going to be our goodbye. He and I in the midst of ten other people who have no clue of the chaos that we have willingly started together.*

He remains standing by the doorway as people file out one by one, watching for me, waiting for me. When I reach the point next to him, he leans over discreetly, his voice sad and angry at the same time. "I'll call you from the airport."

I mask my face with a veil of professionalism. "Lucas," I say, "it's been a pleasure working with you." I extend my hand to shake his before turning my back and walking away.

By the time I get back to my office after stopping over to update the other team members, he's gone.

I try to convince myself it's all for the best. It can never go anywhere. Two weeks of my life shouldn't be too hard to shake off.

LEYA AND I are stuck in a four-hour planning session for the rest of the afternoon. Although I feel sad, I begin to realize that occupying myself would be the best way to cast aside what had happened in the last two weeks. I'm actually excited at the prospect of leaving the office on time today. *Where will I go? Shopping? To the gym?* At exactly four o'clock in the afternoon, the table starts to shake. It's my phone, vibrating like mad. I turn it over to check out who's calling.

Lucas.

Leya eyes me suspiciously. "Who is it?"

"No one. Keep going." I push the phone away from me. "Steve, what were you saying about the graph that you just put up on the screen?"

It rings again. This time, I pick it up and hold it up to my face while watching his name and phone number flash across the screen. I feel like I'm in high school. *Let him go into voicemail. I want to record his voice on my phone.* And he does.

The third time it rings, Leya's evil eyes look irritated. "Someone is obviously trying to reach you. Go ahead and take it."

I roll off my chair, grab the phone and mouth an "Excuse me" to the rest of the group while walking out the door, ducking into an empty cubicle adjacent to the meeting room.

"Jade Richmond."

"Hi."

I close my eyes, willing the passage of time to stop here and now. "Hi."

"I'm boarding soon. I promised I would call."

"You didn't have to. I know you were probably trying to get to your meeting."

"We didn't have a meeting. Fucking asshole just wanted to get me away from you, I think."

"Seriously?" I glance from side to side to make sure that no one is listening to me.

"Yes. Anyway, I wanted to thank you for everything you did for me while I was there. I think our trip was a success."

"Glad to be of assistance."

"I'll call you from my destination, ok?"

"Okay. Safe travels."

"Take care, Jade. Talk to you soon."

I check his voicemail message hurriedly, like a child tearing open a present whose content, although known, is the one thing he's been waiting for all his life. Somehow, I've immortalized his voice in a little metal box to remind me that he was here with me once.

"Hi, Jade. It's Lucas. Just wanted to let you know that I'm at the

54

airport. I'll call you as soon as I arrive home."

I listen to it twice before deciding that I'm being absurd.

I never make it back to the meeting. I sit in my office in a daze, wondering what had really happened in the past two weeks. So many people have breezed in and out of my professional career, and Lucas certainly isn't the first attractive man I've worked with. I don't have a clue as to why this feels different, why he affects me this way. All I know is that I want him to be the one to change my life.

NINE

Mind Games

LIFE GOES ON. Meetings, late nights, travel. The season changes from summer to fall. Warm breezes are replaced with cool, crisp winds blowing leaves all around the city. With the season's transformation, he is right here with me. His calls and texts are a constant; a call at least once a day, sometimes two or three texts at a time. Funny ones, simple ones, ones just to let me know that he's around... as if he wants to assure me that I'm not forgotten. We never discuss many personal things, mostly small talk about anything and everything.

007: *Hi. I just arrived in Buenos Aires.*

MP: *Have a fun Brazilian weekend.*

007: *What?*

MP: *Brazil. Have fun.*

007: *Buenos Aires is in Argentina!*

MP: *Oh. Oops.*

It takes him a few weeks to send me a work related email. The guilt of what we've done hits home as soon as I see his name surface on the notification box. It feels like a careless intrusion into my professional life, threatening to burst out in the open and eventually take us both down.

From: Lucas Martinez
Sent: Monday, October 21, 2013 1:58 AM
To: jade.richmond@warnerconsulting.com
Subject: Follow up on Open Items

Dear Jade,

I hope that this email finds you well. This is to confirm that the following items remain open until further notice of completion from you:
• signed document related to the net valuation of securities as of planned purchase date
• schedule of liabilities to be settled at purchase date

MT Media expects to be able to return back with a response as soon as we receive the final figures from you.

Thank you and warm regards,
Lucas Martinez

I'm not even done reading the email when a text message comes through from him.

007: *Hi. Sorry about that email. I know it sounds so formal.*

From: Jade Richmond
Sent: Monday, October 21, 2014 8:58 AM
To: lucas.martinez@MTMedia.com
Subject: Follow up on Open Items

Dear Lucas,
Thank you for the follow up. Please be informed that we are working on getting you the data that you need as soon as possible.

Best regards,
Jade Richmond

MP: *Hi. I know, it feels weird.*

007: *I just got your email. I love it. Best regards, ha!*

MP: *Where are you?*

007: *I can't tell you.*

MP: *Oh, I forgot. Sorry for asking. Wait, no. You told me last week!*

007: *I know. That was a slip on my part. What does your week look like?*

MP: *I can't tell you.*

007: *I should have known that was coming. :)*

ONE MONTH HAS passed since he left. Due to the time difference, his texts arrive sporadically, but always around a certain time of day. I'd be lying if I said I didn't look forward to them.

007: *Ms. Richmond, are you there?*

MP: *Yes, Hi.*

007: *Can I call you?*

MP: *When?*

007: *Now.*

MP: *LOL. In meeting. Give me five minutes to get out of it.*

I walk out of any meeting to take his call. It doesn't matter who it's with—clients, peers, staff—he's suddenly my first priority. Sometimes I block my calendar in the afternoons, knowing that he will be calling. Our conversations are short, always about little things, never about anything of substance. Perfect. I've decided that I'm addicted to his voice more than anything. It doesn't matter what we talk about, I listen, I laugh, I tell him about my day. We never mention the merger. As far as we're concerned, things are happening around us, but we're no longer involved since the final report had been issued.

007: *Stopped by a temple while here in Thailand. The monk tells me I need to use my heart more instead of my head.*

MP: *Did you tell him you didn't have a heart?*

007: *Very funny. I told him to go fuck himself.*

MP: *You did not.*

007: *:)*

MP: *Oh my God. You did.*

LEYA, UPSET WHEN she realizes that we have yet to celebrate my promotion, organizes a get together one Wednesday night after work at the bar located right next to our office. Coming from a company with more than 3,000 people in the same building, we could walk into this bar alone and end up with 50 other people that we know, so I'm not sure why she had to actually organize anything. True to form, I show up an hour late for my own party. I've disciplined myself well enough not to leave the office until I complete all my work, so a presentation that's due the next day keeps me from arriving on time.

I see Leya as soon as I walk in, waving frantically to get my attention. "Jade, over here!"

"Hey. Who's here?" I ask as I remove my coat and lay it on the empty seat next to me at the bar. I glance around to see whether I'm able to recognize some familiar faces. There are just too many of them, employees from different departments, making it difficult for me to pick out anyone in particular. So I find myself waving at people from every corner of the venue. Might as well cover all my bases by making sure that I'm consistent with my friendliness.

Leya and I have mostly male friends, probably because the women at work are younger than us, intimidated by us, jealous of us. Early on, we'd tried to assimilate ourselves into social events with the women from our office, but because of our friendship, we never really made the effort to go beyond casual acquaintances. My position in the company also plays a large part in this isolation. At this level, people are either in awe of you or hate your guts because of the tough decisions you make to prioritize the interests of the company. Whoever said life was lonely at the top wasn't kidding.

"Steve, Mike, and Eric are getting drinks, and there are a few people from Strategy at the table across from us. The women from Research are approaching." She motions towards them with an inconspicuous tipping of her head.

Melanie and Debbie, leggy brunettes with too much cleavage, approach us with drinks in hand.

"Hey, Jade," Debbie greets, taking an embarrassingly large swig of her wine.

"How've you been?" Melanie asks. "Heard there was some hot guy on your floor for two weeks."

I laughed at her comment. "Hot guy who?"

"I was at that closing meeting," Debbie puts in. "There were definitely fireworks going on between him and Jade!"

"Jesus, Debb. What have you been smoking? He was a colleague here to finish up with a merger. Besides—"

Leya interrupts my oncoming tirade by lightly pinching my arm. "Jade, lets saddle up to Tom the bartender and ask him for our drinks."

"Great idea," I agree as we slide down the bar to catch Tom's attention.

"Hey, Tom, two Moscow Mules, please!" Leya orders for us. "You were a little defensive over there," she says, carrying our cold copper mugs to seats at the end of the bar. "What's up? Spill."

"Nothing," I answer, staring straight down into my drink. *If I myself can't figure out what the hell is wrong with me, how on earth will I be able to explain it to her?*

"Jade. It's me. You can tell me. It's not like I don't know what was going on," she whispers. "Sarah from Planning actually made a comment about it the other day. She asked me point blank what the deal was between you and Martinez. She said she was on the floor late one night and and saw you and him deep in conversation in the conference room."

"It was work related!" *My career! Everything I've accomplished up until now. If this gets out, it could all be over for me.*

"She acknowledged that. She said you were poring over some documents, but that the electricity in that room was off the charts."

"She's making shit up. Please, Ley! Shut those rumors down! Shit like that will ruin everything we've worked so hard for. It will bring this company to its knees!"

"Jade," she shoots me a warning look, "let's talk about you."

"I miss him."

"Did anything happen when he was here?" I've obviously

spiked her interest. She's staring at me, eyes narrowed, intent on reading the expression on my face.

What does she think she is? A human lie detector?

"Did I sleep with him? No."

"Okay. And that's good?"

"I don't know."

"Jade! Please, no one word answers! Talk to me!" she exclaims, thumping her drink on the bar in apparent exasperation.

"I miss him, Ley, but he's nothing to me. He doesn't know anything about me, he doesn't really make an effort to know me. I can't even call him a friend."

"Liar," she says, looking straight at me.

I glance downwards to avert her eyes. "I wasn't ready to say much," I admit.

She starts to get excited. "Did you do anything with him, I mean physically?" she whispers.

"He touched me… he kissed me."

"And?"

"And nothing. That's just it. It's all in my mind. I don't know what anything means. He texts three times a day, he calls every few days. I feel vulnerable and exposed, Ley," I yield to this fact, feeling like I'm one step from banging my head on the bar, but grateful that I can talk to someone about everything. "I wait for those calls, those texts. And I don't like the fact that I do. I miss his nothingness in my life. His face. His voice. Is there even such a thing as nothingness? Missing something that's not even tangible, something I can't define?"

"Did you tell him about—"

"No. He's like this young kid who just talks about himself. He asks about me once in a while, but I never go into real detail. I'm entranced by what he tells me, though. It was nice having a new friend…" I trail off, leaning back in my seat and nodding my head to Tom for another drink.

"Maybe it's the newness, Jade. Maybe he's a new and welcome addition to your life after everything you've been through."

I shrug my shoulders casually. "Nah. He was a fling. It's over. I'll be okay. I just need to get him out of my head. Maybe not take his calls or texts. Maybe just move on with my life here."

"It's not that easy, Jade. You know that. Once you got physical, it took this "fling" on to a whole new level. And I must tell you— you've been smiling a lot more lately."

I don't let the comment sink in. The smiles don't mean a thing; it would never work out. Nothing good can ever come of this. It was a distraction and it's over. Women my age don't have flings, and they don't have heartbreaks either.

Or do they?

"I'm not going to jeopardize my job or my position in this company for this 'fling,' Ley. Trust me on this. I'll be fine. Now let's go back to those people or else someone will complain about my being unsociable by the time we return to work tomorrow morning."

I don't give her time to react as I hop off the bar stool and scoot away.

TEN

Wishing and Waiting

FALL IS SLOWLY fading into winter. Not only am I feeling lifeless and mundane, but everything else around me is dying too. The trees, the leaves, the grass. No more flowers, less and less birds (though those are blessings). The resplendently rusty colors of the season are no longer visible to me. Life, it seems, is going south for the winter. It's a slow day at the office with only one meeting in the morning. I had Noelle block my afternoon to allow me to review the merger papers and complete my final report. I take a short break and decide to call my best friend, Olivia, a painter who hails from Boston. Regal, charming and incredibly smart, she's the ultimate embodiment of a creative mind. Her mood swings and artistic outbursts all contribute to the eloquence and poetry of her works. She's outgoing and outspoken while I'm more reserved and systematic. She taught me how to be spontaneous, I taught her how to trust.

She answers the phone right before it goes into voicemail.

"Sorry, I was vacuuming the house."

"Again? You were doing that yesterday."

"I know. I just can't stand it when there's fluff on the carpet." She pauses. "Or anything else, for that matter."

I let out a forced chuckle. "How's the art exhibit going?"

"Almost ready."

"Let's do more tax planning okay? I know that this show will be another hit and we need to plan to put away some money for taxes next year." I judiciously make a note on my pad to look into some stocks for her to invest in.

"Okay. But guess what?"

"What?"

"I bought another Louis."

"Which one? I did too!"

"No way! Really? I just bought the Artsy Diamante. Blue."

"I beat you. I bought the Limited Edition Graffiti." I scroll through my camera roll and send her a picture of my newest baby.

"Jade! You said you would save money for our trip!"

"I know... but I figured if I can't have Lucas, I can just have Louis."

She laughs heartily at my statement. "True. Makes sense. Louis will never hurt you. He makes you look and feel good."

"Exactly," I concur with a giggle. *She makes me feel better already.*

"So are we set for our trip? It's in three weeks."

"Yes! I'll email you the flight confirmation and hotel is done too. Five star Ritz, baby."

"Are we flying with the plebeians?"

"Nope. First class."

"Perfect. I love you. Are you getting better?"

"I'm fat and old."

"No, you're not. You know you're gorg. Don't just make up shit so I feel sorry for you. Stop it."

"I'll stop," I say, not wanting to prolong this conversation. "See you in three weeks?"

"Yup. Hey, Jade? Have you checked in with our friend yet? You know, the one you should be talking to at least once a week?"

"No, I haven't. Been busy." I can feel my nose growing. The truth is, I haven't been able to register my thoughts on anything lately, let alone open up to someone else about my most recent stupidity.

"There's no excuse. You know you need to keep in touch with him. Will you promise to do that as soon as you hang up with me?" I hear her walking away from the speaker phone. This is so her, unable to stay in one place for very long.

I sigh heavily. "Okay, Olivia. I promise."

"Okay. I have to finish my vacuuming. Talk later!" She hangs up without giving me a chance to respond.

Reluctantly, I search for his name and phone number in my Contacts directory.

He answers the phone immediately. "Hello, Jade."

"Hi. I'm sorry I haven't been calling. Work has been horribly busy, and I've been having a really tough time."

"It's okay. Just try to call me more often. It's important that you keep your connection with those who can listen to you. You've been through so much—"

"I met someone!" I burst out with elation.

"You met someone where? Who?" He sounds confused.

"I'm trying to figure things out. It's not right. Well, it's probably just all in my head."

"I'm sure it's not just in your head. But regardless, follow your heart, Jade. You've left it alone to survive on its own for so long. Give it some well-deserved love."

"Thank you. Promise I'll call you next week."

"Okay, until then, I pray for you every day."

The phone beeps with an incoming call. I guess I'm not going to get any work done this afternoon.

"Hi!" I hear myself say. *That isn't my voice. It's a fake sing-song tone, winded and too ardent. This isn't you, Jade.*

"Hi. How are you?"

"Good. And you?" *I'm missing you terribly, I want to say.*

"I've got great news. I'll be in Chicago next week for an emergency meeting. We're working on a campaign for the Christmas season. I'll be there for a few days… might be intense, all work and late nights, but I want to sneak at least one night to see you."

"I would love that."

"Will you stay downtown so we can go out? Dinner or something?"

"Yes."

"Stay with me?" *Yes, yes. I want to.*

"Hmm. Maybe not, but I'll take a hotel close to yours. Tell me where you decide to stay." I pause for a second and add, "Can you try to stay far from this office? I don't want us to be seen together."

"Got it. Yes, of course. I'll text you my hotel as soon as I book it."

"I can't wait to see you," I reveal mindlessly.

"Me too. See you soon, Jade."

ELEVEN

Song and Dance

THE CHILL OF the November air seeps through my legs as I walk briskly towards the office dragging my suitcase behind me. This is it. The first day of our week. Or the week that he's here. And I'm an idiot for wearing a dress in this cold weather. I packed as if I was going on a long trip, mocking myself whenever I remembered that I was just going to be taking a hotel in the city. I've been waiting for this week for so long. I missed him. Whatever part of him I missed, I have yet to figure out. I've completely abandoned my original plan of staying away from him. When he called me about his upcoming visit, I just couldn't pass it up.

My phone rings right as I struggle to get my suitcase through the revolving doors that lead to the office lobby.

"Hi! Are you here?" I squeak excitedly. No holds barred this week. I need to show him just how much this time together means to me. I've completely shocked myself when I realize that I'm following my heart. For once. Lord help me. I've never done this before.

"I am. I'm actually a block away from your office. I can see you from the window."

He's kidding, of course. I roll my eyes and shake my head as I delay getting in with the rest of the employees. "What hotel are you at?"

"The W. And you?"

"Lucas! That's right across the street from my office! Didn't we agree that you would find a hotel that's farther away to avoid being seen?" I exclaim under my breath, acknowledging the people around me with a slight nod of my head.

"Jade, Barcelona is a smaller place and I don't even get seen there. Relax. Everything will be fine. You worry too much. Where are you staying?"

There's no point in arguing with him. I'm too enamored to think clearly. "Across the street from you on the opposite side."

"Oh yes, I know that hotel. Cool. You're getting good at these secret missions," he teases. "So I'll call you later?"

"Yes, call me later."

The morning drags on as people shuttle in and out of my office. Questions. Issues. Complaints. Everyone seems to want to unload on me these days. I sit at my desk trying to concentrate and attempting to direct my attention to the piles of papers in front of me.

Finally, it's lunch time. I unhook my purse and don my coat, zigzagging through the maze of cubicles until I reach the elevator bank. I'm feeling quite excited as I take a ride to the ground floor where Leya is waiting patiently on one of the marble benches scrolling through her phone.

"Ready?" She smiles as she gets up to follow me out the door.

We find ourselves at a swanky lingerie shop called La Perla on Michigan Avenue. Pat, my personal shopper, is waiting by the counter with a sly smile on her face.

"I'm ready for you," she says as she leads me to the fitting room. "So what's with the emergency need to purchase some undergarments?"

Leya can't help but release a wicked laugh.

"Nothing," I reply. "Just ran out of good stuff to wear." I blush hotly at my lame defense.

"I'll be out here, Jade. Get busy." Leya takes a seat in front of the fitting room while I draw the curtains. I look at the outfits that Pat has laid out for me. Lace lingerie in all colors, some bodice-type full length slips, wireless bras, bustiers, nightgowns, underwear. I try on the different colors and styles. The one I can't stop staring at myself in is a corset-type outfit in a gorgeous plum color. I peek out from between the curtains and motion for Leya to come inside.

"Holy shit, Jade! Are you sure you're 42? That body. You are smoking hot!" Leya exclaims. "He's never going to stand a chance with that one. Sold!" She laughs heartily.

Leya's thundering voice causes Pat to come barging into the fitting room.

"You think?" I slip another see-through nightie over my head. "What about this one?"

"That's definitely you," Pat declares proudly. "It brings out the color of your stunning eyes."

That settles it. Flattery gets Pat everywhere, and I walk out of that store with a thousand dollars in beautiful outfits and a priceless infusion of self-confidence and hope.

By six o'clock that evening, he hasn't called. I stay in the office, not knowing whether I should go to my hotel to freshen up or remain there in case he wants to see me earlier.

Who am I kidding? I can't work.

I find myself glancing at my window repeatedly to check out my reflection in the glass. *Why would he want to hang out with someone as old as me? I don't blame him for not calling. Maybe he's changed his mind.* Two hours later, I finally give up. I take my suitcase and trek to my hotel feeling stupid and rejected.

He doesn't call.

I order room service, drink two glasses of wine, and fall asleep.

I'M CRANKY ON Tuesday morning. All-out, full-on temperamental. Everyone stays as far as possible from me at work. I keep my door closed for most of the day to complete a pressing project. I want to schedule a trip back to La Perla to return everything I purchased the day before. *What was I thinking?* I start to analyze everything that has transpired between where we are today and his phone call about his upcoming visit. *One night? He was going to try to see me for one night?*

I muster up all my energy to think clearly about this situation. Where have I been for the past few weeks? I need to get a grip on this now. It ends right here. I'm too old for this shit.

Or not.

"Hello?" I answer on the third ring.

"You're mad."

"No, I'm not. Why should I be?" I fiddle with my pens and doodle on the pad of paper in front of me.

"We ended up working until past two and I didn't want to wake you in the middle of the night. I couldn't break free to sneak a call without everyone being in the room with me." His voice is gentle and conciliatory.

"That's fine," I reply, though my tone is in direct conflict with my words.

"Well, it's not. I can't take being this close to you without seeing you. I'm going to wrap up by eight this evening. Where would you like to meet?"

"Why don't you just finish what you're doing and I'll see you some other time?"

"What? No, Jade! Tonight. Please see me tonight," he insists.

I pause for a few seconds. So much for ending this.

"Okay. Nine?"

"Where?"

"Somewhere far away from this office."

"Why don't I meet you at the place a block away and we can just decide where to go then?"

"Sounds good. See you later."

DESPITE ALL THE outfits I brought over with me for the week, I decide not to bother changing into something more appropriate. I'm wearing a casual pair of leggings, a long sweater, and some flat riding boots. All he's seen me in are work clothes—even those leather pants that one day were matched with a business jacket—so this one should turn him off, I tell myself. The fact that I'm not going to get all gussied up to see him puts us in the friend zone.

The bar across the street is unusually dark and full of people. By the time I arrive, he's standing by the door, waiting for me. I want to run into his arms, but obviously, I don't. All I can think about is the fact that there might be people from work who will recognize us.

"Hi." He steps forward and kisses me on both cheeks.

"Hi."

"You look gorgeous. Your hair is longer." His face is close to mine, just staring into my eyes and holding his gaze frozen on me. His right hand carefully reaches out to touch the side of my head and he takes a lock of hair and twirls them between his fingers.

"Old," I state, suddenly very conscious of the lines on my face, the wrinkles around my eyes. Maybe I shouldn't have smiled so much when I was younger. I'm certainly paying for that now. I try to deflect his attention by looking away.

"You're timeless. Ravishing," he whispers as he brushes his nose against mine.

"You look great too," I say, meaning it more than anything I've said so far. He's still as gorgeous as ever. I suddenly feel inadequate, small and insignificant next to someone like him.

He laces his fingers in mine and leads me through a labyrinth of booths full of people as he searches for an empty space.

"I thought we were going to go somewhere else?" I ask nervously.

"I can't wait to sit next to you and catch up. Don't worry, it's dark. No one will see us. And to be honest with you, it's too fucking cold to walk outside," he rebuts confidently, pulling me to sit at the last booth by the corner.

The view of the city from this rooftop is mesmerizing. He hunkers down next to me and we both shed our coats. He immediately holds me by the waist and pulls me closer to him.

"Hi," he murmurs, skimming his nose against my neck. I close my eyes and take the time to feel his lips against my skin. "Take this off, it's in the way," he commands as he tugs on my scarf.

"No. I'm freezing. And Luke, there are people from work here!" I stiffen up and pull away slightly.

He gives me a bothered look. "Let's order some wine. That

might relax you a bit." He motions for the server to approach us.

She's blonde and young and perky. She hands him the wine list and he takes forever to look it over.

"Their wine is shit here," he grumbles. "They're cheap."

"Just pick one, Luke. It doesn't make a difference to me. Let's order some appetizers too. I'm starving," I say, a bit impatient about the way he's taking the menu so seriously.

He hands it back to the server immediately. "Your Spanish wines are limited. Please just bring us the best bottle of Rioja that you have and one of each of the dishes on the list of the small hot plates." He turns away from her dismissively and snatches my hand.

Our server doesn't leave. She continues to stand at the same spot, gaping at him. "Oh! Are you Spanish? I love that accent of yours! It sounds so sexy."

He completely ignores her and strikes up a conversation with me until she walks away. I don't even have time to roll my eyes at him before she's back. And this time she brings a friend with her.

"My friend here speaks Spanish," she says in her high-pitched cutesy voice. "She can translate for you if you need her to." Her friend nods in agreement and giggles at the same time.

"As you can see, I speak perfect English," he responds tersely. "And we're kind of in a hurry, so can you please just get us our order? You're both making my girlfriend here feel very uncomfortable. She's about to fly at both of you and scratch your eyes out."

"Luke!" I squeak, delivering a light swat on his thigh. He covers my hand, brings it to his lips, kisses it, and returns it back to where he wants it. I keep it there. The tension between us is so evident that it frightens the servers away. They disappear in a matter of seconds and soon they're nowhere to be found.

"Jealous?" he teases.

"No. Why should I be?" I joke back. "But I do want to warn you that those two aren't going to be getting a tip from us tonight."

He laughs heartily at my comment. *There go those lopsided lips and that sexy, husky laugh.*

"I knew it! God help those who mess with Jade Richmond!" he declares as he scoots his body down, stretches out his legs, and rests his head on my shoulders. Slowly, he leans in to plant tiny kisses along the side of my chin, trailing along until he teases my lips with a slight brush of his. The energy in the bar is turned up drastically when the DJ starts to play dance tunes. We sit in silence for a while until he stands up and takes my hand. "Dance?"

"No thanks."

"Oh, come on. It's Pitbull. We have to."

"Pit who?" I joke with a puzzled look on my face.

He rolls his eyes but doesn't respond. Gingerly, he pulls me by the hand until I find myself following him on to the dance floor. We move together. I keep up with him. He looks so young, so full of energy. He gawks at me, surprised at the fact that I can dance. The floor is so crowded that I lose him for a minute. There are two men surrounding me, dancing with me, but I don't pay any attention to it. I keep dancing. I'm lost. In every sense of the word.

He finds me and makes no qualms about hooking me by the waist and pulling me close to him. "You're so sexy I can hardly stand it," he gushes in my ear. "And you can move."

"Hip hop dance classes are the best for cardio! You should try it!" I yell through the loud music. Just as those words leave my lips, I'm hit with a flashback of the life I used to have. *I would give up this night with him to go back to the beginning.*

"What's the matter, MP?" he asks as he pulls me close, nestling my head on his shoulder. We're slow dancing to a hip hop song, but the tune that plays in my head is one I don't care to hear.

"Nothing. I was just thinking about how much I missed you, Double O," I whisper.

"I'm here now," he answers. "I'm sorry I stayed away for so long."

TWELVE

Unfinished Business

I SPEND MOST of Wednesday morning recounting a play by play of what happened between us last night. We spent a few hours watching the view of the city, talking, laughing, catching up on our lives on opposite sides of the world.

"Enough about me, Jade. Tell me about you. Your family. Your life."

"There's nothing to tell, really. I plan to take some time soon to see my parents. My dad is in the middle of another acquisition, so I've been helping him with that in addition to everything else that's going on."

"An only child, huh? Did you have a lonely childhood? I know I can't imagine my life without my siblings. Our house was always full of activity when I was growing up."

"I kind of like being by myself. I didn't really have anyone else so it's not like I knew what I was missing."

We both started stifling our yawns by 2:00 am. It was time to call it a night. We both walked out of the bar, quietly smirking as he wrapped himself around me when we passed by the two servers who ogled him all night.

We stood by the train tracks across the street to share a cigarette before addressing the inevitable.

"Take a cab with me, Jade. I'll drop you off at your hotel." He kept his arm around me before taking my hand and waving his free arm in the air to hail a taxicab.

"Don't be silly. My hotel is right there." I pointed at the glaring neon light right across the street from us. "I'm just going to walk."

He pulled me towards the door as the cab stopped right in front of us. I stepped back and released his hand. "No, Luke. It's okay. I'll walk. You get in and I'll talk to you tomorrow."

He let out a sigh, looking right into my eyes. He didn't say anything, but the expression on his face showed me that he wanted to say more than just goodnight. "Okay. If you insist. I'm not going to force you into anything. Goodnight, Jade." He leaned over slowly and planted a quick kiss on my lips.

"Bye, Luke. Thank you for such a fun evening," I said as I turned around and walked away.

I'm kicking myself. Our hotels were so close to where we were that I know the cab ride was going to be the start of something. I wanted it to happen, I was just too naive to see that as it was taking place. I pick up my phone to call him, figuring he must be getting ready to break for lunch.

He answers on the first ring. "Hi."

"Hi. Did you get back okay last night?"

"No, I was accosted by those hot young servers and we spent a wild night in a threesome."

I let out a forced laugh. "Good for you." I gather up the courage to proceed with the reason for my call. "Hey, about last night. I'm sorry I didn't get in the cab with you."

"It's okay. I wasn't going to force you to do anything."

"No, it's me. I'm so clueless sometimes. I've never really done this before so I didn't quite understand what was happening..." I let out a slight pause before gathering up the courage to say it out loud, "but I do now."

"You do what, now?"

"I want to see you. Are you at lunch? Can we meet at your lobby in a few minutes?" My tone is low and seductive. This statement has so many meanings, but I no longer care at this point. The problem with wanting someone so badly is that you put yourself out there, oftentimes at the risk of rejection. I'm so consumed with these indiscernible feelings that I don't even think of the consequences of my actions.

"Jade," he says with a sigh, "why are you doing this to me now? You know I would love to, but the client is waiting for me. We're having lunch with their underwriters."

"Oh." I try to hide the disappointment in my voice. "Okay. Go, don't be late. We'll talk later."

SIX O'CLOCK. STILL no word from him. I don't know what to think about anything. I'm beginning to wonder whether I've scared him off. Maybe I came across as some neurotic, desperate woman. I feel foolish and stupid, so I turn off my phone and bury myself in a myriad of open items. An hour later, as I trudge down the long hallway on my way back to my office from the pantry across the street, I see my old friend, Matt, from one of our divisions in Ohio.

"Hey, stranger!" he greets me excitedly. "How are you?"

"I'm great, Matt! What are you doing here?" I ask as he reaches out to give me a hug.

"Just got out of a sales meeting. Where are you off to?" His trademark smile and wavy blond hair makes me remember how many hearts he broke when he was assigned to the Chicago office.

"Oh, nowhere. Back upstairs. Trying to finish a report due tomorrow," I lie. *I'm inexplicably at the beck and call of some smug guy who thinks I'm sitting around waiting for him to call. And I'm ashamed to admit that he's right.*

"Can I buy you a quick drink before you retreat back into your cave?" he asks, his fingers encircling the crook of my arm. "It's been so long, we have a lot of catching up to do."

"Oh, hell, why not? One drink."

No more waiting.

Matt and I go way back to when he was on the sales force in Chicago. We traveled overseas together, sometimes for weeks at a time, and so I missed his friendship when he was transferred to Ohio a few years ago. He's my age and divorced with two children. He and his ex-wife have an amicable relationship, which makes him very active in his family's life. His marriage was a casualty of the life of a road warrior. He lives alone now but is never outside of a relationship.

We decide to walk to a different bar, blocks away from the office. No matter where you go in this town, the nightlife is hopping. We sit at the bar on a dead end corner where there's nothing else next to me but the bathroom wall. Matt walks away for a few minutes, only to return with my usual drink and a whiskey straight on the rocks for him.

We catch up on his life in Ohio. He's seeing three women but misses the settled life that he had with his wife. He tells me that he wants back into his marriage. He realizes that what matters are his children and what he hoped would be a best friend and lover that he could come home to at the end of every day. It's heartbreaking to hear him speak only because he embodies most of the misgivings I have in my own life. By my third drink, I've grown quiet, partly because I'm starting to feel my emotional exhaustion and partly because the bartender has spiked these drinks so much that I'm feeling lightheaded.

"He's not worth it. If he's making you feel this miserable, he's not the guy for you."

"What are you talking about?" I feign innocence.

"Jade. I can see it in your eyes. Which are still as expressive as ever, by the way," he teases. "I can see how sad you are. What's going on?"

"I'm just tired of feeling this way. It's been a rollercoaster of emotion for me, and I think it's all in my head."

"What's in your head?"

"That he's even interested in me."

"Oh, holy hell. Who wouldn't be interested in you?"

"Stop it. I'm serious. I'm so much older."

"And? So? Has anyone told you that you look 20?"

"Matt. Please. I really don't feel like talking about it."

"Jade, listen to me. Whatever you're feeling right now, if it's making you sad and unhappy, then you shouldn't pursue it. I've never known you to be like this. You've survived years and years in your career without falling for the millions of passes men have made at you. I watched it when we were traveling together. I used to think, 'Wow, this woman. She's just so put together. She can take care of herself.'"

"I know," I acknowledge sadly. "Maybe it's age. Maybe I'm getting old and sappy and needy. Look at me, I can't even hold three drinks together."

"Well, first of all, you're not a drinker. And for some reason, this dick is getting to you but he doesn't deserve you. Move on. Don't give him the benefit of doing this to you."

"Matt?"

"Hmm?" he responds as he motions for another drink.

"Do you think I'm going to die without ever feeling the way that I felt when I first fell in love? Do you think there's such a thing as being too old to want to feel that way?"

"Oh, no." He takes my hand in his and lovingly caresses them with his thumbs. "No. We're not too old. But we're old enough to know that superficial love always carries an expiration date with it. Sometimes you get so caught up in the here and now, the instant gratification, that it blurs your vision and prevents you from seeing things as they truly are. Everything fades away with time. When all is said and done, the loud noise of all that excitement and passion will eventually quiet down. The trick is to keep the music going. My wife, Michelle, she's the music that's been in my head all this time, I just didn't take the time to hear it."

"That loud noise. It reverberates in my ears every waking hour of the day. I can't shake it off." I laugh, embarrassed at my own admission. "And about Michelle, tell her. Tell her exactly what you just told me."

"What keeps you going?" He makes my confession sound terribly irrational. After all, it's a little bit unusual for someone to affirm that the source of her stress is also the object of her devotion.

I don't hesitate to respond—I have my answers. "He makes me feel young and alive. One happy moment with him trumps all the tears and stress of the times I spend without him. It sounds crazy. I think I've totally lost it."

"Ask yourself this. Do you see a future with him? Are you even in love with him or is he merely filling a gap left behind by the events of the past year?"

"I honestly think both answers are No."

"Okay, then how 'bout this one. Will he do anything for you? Will he put his life and career on the line for you?"

"No. I don't believe so," I concede dejectedly.

Our conversation is interrupted by the ringing of my phone. I don't answer it. I let it go to voicemail. It rings again and I ignore it. On the third ring, Matt presses the green button and places it against my ear. I glare at him and take the phone from his hand.

"Yup."

"Jade, where are you?"

"Out."

"Out where? I'm packing up to meet you."

"Who said we were going to meet tonight?" I say defiantly. "I'm busy."

"With whom?"

"Matt. My friend."

"Who? Where?"

"I'm out, Lucas. I'll call you tomorrow." I hang up the phone, but of course, he calls back.

"Lucas, I'll call you tomorrow!" I exclaim without a greeting.

"No. I'm coming now. Where are you?"

"I'm at—" I start to giggle. "I don't know. Where are we, Matt?"

Matt rolls his eyes and says into the speaker, "Wacker and Wabash."

"Yeah. Here," I sneer.

Ten minutes later, Lucas comes strutting into the bar. He dodges his head from side to side, trying to spot me. A smile lights up his face as soon we lock eyes.

"That's the dude?" Matt asks. "He looks like a fucking model and you're still too pretty for him."

"Well, that's what the chicks at the office said about you!" I taunt affectionately.

Lucas circles around the bar as if he's marking his territory. He stands directly behind me and kisses the top of my head, slipping his fingers through my scarf and stroking my neck.

"Well, I guess this is my cue to get going," Matt says, his a warm smile coupled with a concerned look in his eyes.

"No!" I squeak. "Stay for another drink!"

"I think you've had enough," Lucas interjects, apparently amused at seeing me so animated. "I'm here to take you back to your hotel." He centers his attention on Matt, who stands protectively next to me, waiting for me to give him permission to leave.

I stand up to wrap Matt in my arms. I'm truly going to miss my friend. I think this run-in and his advice was just what I needed. "Thank you for everything," I whisper into his chest, noticing that Lucas continues to look at him with interest.

"Take care of yourself, my friend. And be careful," he whispers back.

Lucas helps me get into my coat. By the time I'm buttoned up and ready to go, Matt is gone.

THIRTEEN

Resignation

I STUMBLE BACK to the hotel with Lucas by my side, holding me up. "I'm fine," I tell him, trying to put some space between us.

"Jade. Let me take you upstairs. I'll leave you at your door." I don't say anything. I move ahead, knowing that he's following right behind me.

"Wait. Where are my keys?" I fish through my purse, removing bit by bit of what's in there, swishing my hand around, desperate to feel the elusive key card which is nowhere to be found. "Oh, wait. It's in my pocket!" I laugh as I slip it into the slot.

He follows me inside the room and picks up after me—first lining up my shoes on the mat, then grabbing my jacket, which I flung on the floor, and my purse, which fell from my arm as soon as I stumbled in the door.

"Gosh, I have to pee so badly," I say, leaving him standing in the hallway acting as a coat rack and a purse hanger.

He's sitting calmly on the edge of the bed when I emerge a few minutes later.

"Thanks for taking me home. I'll be fine from here." All of a sudden, I'm feeling a swirl of emotions. I'm angry, and frustrated, and I want to cry because nothing has turned out the way I hoped that it would. He reaches out for me as I move past him. I twist my body around so his hands slip off my waist. "We have two more days left, Lucas. When am I going to see you again?"

"I don't know," he says solemnly. "We have to talk."

"I'm in no position to talk right now, as you can plainly see," I counter. I boldly take a seat on his lap. He immediately wraps his arms around me and I place my head squarely on his shoulder. "I'm tired and I just want to go to bed."

"I know, baby. I'm sorry this visit didn't go as well as we both hoped. The merger's not done yet and I don't want you risking anything. There's just too much to lose from your end."

I lift my head up to look at him.

"Those eyes. They drive me crazy, Jade. You just don't know how much I want to be with you."

"Then why didn't you make an effort, Lucas? Why didn't you go out of your way to see me more while you're in town? I can't believe that I booty called you at noon today. I'm so embarrassed! Do you even know what a booty call means?"

He chuckles as he gently moves to cradle my face in his hands. "I've watched enough American movies to know what that means."

"Yeah, rub it in. I don't find you funny."

"Oh, Jade. All this work for the merger. What happens isn't just going to affect you or me. Your office, my business. They're all riding on this transaction. I'm putting in all this effort to make sure that it goes through. And then we can decide what to do as soon as this is over."

"And here I am thinking that you would throw it all away for me," I say bitingly.

He drops his head down and responds somberly, "If you only knew."

"I'm kidding, Luke," I say, sounding quite annoyed. I try to lighten my tone but he doesn't hear me.

"What we have, Jade," he murmurs, "it's no laughing matter to me. I didn't plan it, but here it is. And I wish that the situation was different. I wish I met you under other circumstances."

"It is what it is," I respond. I think about what Matt had said, how Lucas will never give up anything to be with me. *Unlike everything that I was willing to give up for just a single moment with him.* "And now, I just want to go to sleep." I stand up and make my way to the side of the bed. "Show yourself out, Lucas." I don't wait to see what he does or where he goes. I lay my head on the pillow and immediately pass out.

"UGH!" I MUTTER as the phone rings at exactly seven o'clock in the morning. My wake up call. Time to get up and start another sad day at the office. "Shit! My head!" I croak as I grab my temples with both hands. I hear a low-pitched grumble and affix my eyes on someone sitting up next to me. "Nice glasses," I say, realizing that Lucas never left. He's leaning against two pillows on the headboard with a Mac on his lap, typing quietly away on the keyboard. "You didn't sleep? Why are you still here?"

"First of all, I'm still jet lagged. But more importantly, you looked so cute all curled up and asleep, I just couldn't leave you." I see the glint in his eye through the eyeglasses resting low on his nose.

"Seriously, Luke. What are you still doing here?"

"I have to leave today. I have to be at O'Hare by 10:00 am."

"What? Why? I thought you would be staying until the weekend."

"Leigh called. He said that the papers are all drawn up and we have some glitches that we need to address right away."

"Oh." I sit up and lean against the headboard while he sets the laptop on the floor beside the bed. I can't deny the look of disappointment in my eyes as the tears threaten to fall down my face.

"Jade. Don't, please." He pulls me close to him, holding my head to his chest and tenderly stroking my hair.

My God, Jade, get a grip. You're showing your weaknesses. What the hell is the matter with you?

"I'll miss you," I whisper through my tears.

"Look, I'll take care of whatever needs to be done right away and then I'll be back, okay? Two to three weeks tops. I promise. Nothing will change between now and then. This is just the beginning for us. And I'll call you. Every day."

At this precise instant, I feel like a little child desperately looking for affection. Or a mistress, clamoring for any little time she can get with her married lover. *How did the tables turn so quickly? When did I become this person?*

I reach out my hand to caress his face. "I'm saying goodbye now, Luke. I'm going to take a shower and get ready for work. Please. This time, see yourself out."

I slide off the bed, but he takes hold of my hand to stop me from walking away. With his other arm, he gently guides me back towards him, lowering me onto his lap. Slowly, he pulls my face to his and kisses me. I give in for a moment to savor the feel of his lips. They're filling every single void in my heart and I hardly even know who he really is. This man is going to break my heart all over again. I peek through my eyelids to watch him get lost in our kiss. His luscious eyelashes, his eyes, his nose. If I keep this up, I'm never going to walk away. Just as our tongues meet, I break away.

"Jade."

"I still have so many questions to ask you," I say disappointedly.

"Ask me." He plants another kiss on my lips and then lightly trails the tip of his nose down my neck.

"What car do you drive? What do you do on weekends? Do you have a dog? Where do you like to shop, what do you cook when you're at home—"

He laughs despite remaining honed in on my neck. I can barely hear his muffled response. "Silver 2014 Carrera, surf, work out, work, no dog, Versace and anything stir fry."

"Hmm." I giggle. "Interesting."

He takes the lightness in my tone as permission to continue his intention. He begins to unbutton my blouse.

"No, Luke. No more. I can't do this. Please know I'm not asking for anything from you. You don't have to give me any guarantees. I went into this knowing that it was never going to work. Just know that you have made me feel so much more than I have in a long time. Leave this room knowing that. I'm not going to pretend that you don't mean anything to me because you do."

"This isn't over. Why are you speaking to me like it is?" His face looks pained and for once I want him to say more, but he doesn't.

"Because whatever happens between now and the next time we see each other, I just want you to know that I'm thankful for the time we spent together. Goodbye, Luke." I plant a soft kiss on his forehead and will myself to mean it.

"Is that really what you want?" he whispers sadly.

"It's what needs to happen." I turn my back to him and slowly walk away.

FOURTEEN

Wraparound

BY THE TIME I opened the bathroom door, he was gone.

That was two weeks ago. I haven't heard from him since.

I finally land at the Hong Kong airport and wait for an hour for Olivia's flight to arrive. We both took direct flights from our respective home cities. I pick her out of the crowd easily—long, flowing dark hair, tall and slim and so very stylish. Her outfit stands out among the well-dressed business people and vacationers. She's wearing designer clothes in the latest style—a camouflage top with gold pants and black boots. Already there are men flocking around her, fans and strangers just wanting to breathe the same air that she does.

"Hi!" We crash into each other excitedly. "I missed you!" I say as my tears flow freely.

She smiles warmly as I swipe my eyes to dry my tears. "Jade, don't cry. I'm here now. We're going to have lots of fun."

"I know," I sniff, self-consciously. "I'm just so glad to see you."

Two hours later, we find ourselves walking up and down the streets of the Tsim Shua Tsui shopping district, an area in the city filled with street markets and designer shops. The Hermes store is practically empty except for us and two other patrons and we take our time placing our names on the waiting list for one of the new styles we're hoping to score during our stay there.

"I don't know, should we do it, Jade? I'd have to sell a few paintings to pay for this." I'm lost in my thoughts and so I don't hear a word she says.

"Jade?" she repeats testily. "Are you here?"

"Oh, sorry. What did you say?"

"Seriously? It's not like you to be so disengaged while we're shopping. Tell me right now. What's bugging you?" She tries on a matching belt and scarf and takes a selfie in the mirror.

"Nothing, I'm fine."

"I'm going to seriously impede your air supply with this scarf if you keep this up." We both do a double take and look at each other. She's crestfallen, her hand quickly rising to cover her mouth. "Oh God. I'm so sorry. I didn't mean that," she muffles apologetically through her fingers.

I shrug my shoulders. "It's okay. I know."

"What's with you, Jade?"

"I haven't heard from him in two weeks."

"Wait a minute. You told him it was over."

"I know. I guess I just didn't expect him not to at least try to get in touch with me."

She shakes her head at me, and I know it's because she sees how ridiculous I'm being. "Where is he now?"

"I don't know, at home, I guess."

"Call him. Take me out of this misery. Call him now."

"You think I should?"

"Jade! Call him! It takes two to play this game. Stop assuming; you're driving yourself nuts. If you miss him, then make the move. Call."

I take my phone out and walk away from her as she moves towards the counter. I dial his number.

"Hi, Jade! How've you been?" *Okay, good sign. At least he's not avoiding me.*

"Hi, Lucas. How are you?"

"I'm well, thank you. And you? Are you in Chicago?"

"No, I'm in Hong Kong with my friend Olivia."

"Oh wow. Hey, listen. I've been wanting to call you but wasn't sure whether or not I should, plus I've been so swamped with working on some stuff over here. I'm actually out right now, can I call you later?" There's noise in the background. It almost sounds like voices on a speaker or microphone.

"Sure, yes."

"Okay. I'll call later. Promise."

I hang up the phone and walk back towards my friend. "He's busy."

"Did he say he would call back?"

"Yes, but—"

"Jade. Stop. He'll call back. In the meantime, let's pay for our stuff and look for a place to chill for a while."

We walk around for another hour, checking out the sidewalk shops, leisurely waltzing in and out of the tiny stalls, aimlessly searching for items to purchase. I absentmindedly pick up a few more scarves to add to my collection.

"How many of those black and white things can you have?" Olivia derides me as she holds a bright orange one up to my face. "Here, why not this one?"

"Get that ugly thing away from me. It's blinding my eyes!" I squeal, turning away and walking further down the alley towards the next row of stores.

"Finally!" Olivia exclaims as she points excitedly across the street at a Starbucks. "Now we can have our coffee break!"

We find the perfect two-top directly in front of the store window, she with her venti latte and me with my grande caramel mocha.

"What's happened to you?" Olivia asks with a genuine look of confusion on her face.

"I don't know. I'm just all over the place, I guess." I stare out the window, afraid to catch her gaze. "I think I'm officially infatuated."

"Well, get your head out of your ass! You're a smart, beautiful, confident, high level executive. You're badass, don't forget that. Why are you allowing some 33-year-old dude to affect you like this? You're going all puppy over him, and you're not a puppy, Jade. You're a tiger. Or in this case, a cougar." She shakes her head abruptly in aggravation. "Or whatever animal you want with sharp claws. What is it you really want from him?"

"I don't want anything. Well, not in that way, I guess. I miss our conversations, his messages, his texts. I miss him."

"What exactly do you miss about him? You haven't really told him much about yourself and from the looks of it, you've been sustaining yourself through phone conversations and messages."

Two of my closest friends in the world just refuse to leave this alone. I'm beginning to think that Leya and Olivia have secret conversations about me. I'm comforted by the fact that they don't really know each other; but I realize that these two polar opposites seem to have the same opinion about him. That says something.

"You know me, Liv. I've been traveling with men all throughout my career. Not once have I ever been attracted to anyone. Not once have I mixed business with pleasure. It was instant with him. As soon as I saw him standing by the corner of that waiting room, I fell. He's so hot."

"Aha!" She chuckles. "I think that's it. You're lusting after this guy. Why don't you get him out of your system? Fuck it out of him, Jade. Our being here lays out the right opportunity. Call him again. Invite him to see you. I'll go away for a night if you need me to. It's a two hour flight away. Either you fly there or have him fly here. I'll fully support what you decide to do, because the way you are now is going to ruin you, your career, and your self-confidence."

I remain silent, seriously planning the scenario that she had just presented in my head.

My phone rings.

"Hi," I answer nervously, walking away from the table.

"Take your time," Olivia mouths to me as she settles into her seat.

"Hi. Sorry about that. I was at Leigh's house. He was making me listen to his new speakers. How are you enjoying your vacation?"

"We're shopping." I laugh. "I just wanted to say hi. I haven't heard from you for a while. How've you been?"

"Well, thank you. And you?"

"Great, thanks."

"Jade—"

"Lucas, is everything all right with us? Are you upset with me? I miss you."

"I miss you too so much. I just wanted to give us both some space since we're in the final stages of the merger. After seeing you in Chicago, I thought it best to wait until the issue was completely closed."

"Oh, that. Somehow you keep on going back to that." I catch myself as I raise my voice.

"I'm trying to protect you, Jade. You also told me to leave you alone."

"I'm a big girl. I don't need protecting. What I need is…" I stop to change my approach. "So, I have an idea," I say in a hushed tone, attempting to sound seductive. "Why don't you come here to see me? We can spend a few days together."

"Ugh!" He sighs loudly. "You won't believe this!"

"You're right. I won't." *Why do I even bother?*

"I leave for Costa Rica tomorrow! Another business deal we're trying to close."

I feel faint. And humiliated. Again. "Oh, that's okay. Not a problem at all. I just wanted to throw it out there. Well, listen. We're in the middle of a line at Starbucks and I have to pick up my order, so I'll let you go. Talk soon."

"Wait, Jade. Can I call you later to catch up?"

"Sure. Later."

Olivia surmises what transpired from the look on my face as I return to our table and saddle up next to her. "At least he called back. It means something that he called back."

"I guess. But he won't see me."

She opens her mouth to say something but doesn't. Instead, she sighs resignedly. "I was going to defend that fact that he's working and that trip was probably all planned out weeks in advance, but I decided that regardless of his reasons, he's not worth it. Your second booty call and he declines it. I'm so sorry, Jade." She leans in to try to pull me close, but I put my hands out in front of me to signal that I'm fine. She wraps her arm around me, forcing me to lean my head on her shoulder, whispering soberly while holding me tight. "I'm sorry. It's going to be okay."

"I'll be good. Let's just have fun for the next few days. Have you noticed how these Asian and European men look so different? Their clothes just look so good on them, so sexy and fitted, unlike the daddy jeans people wear in the States."

"It's because we're in the highest fashion district in this city! What else would you expect?"

We stand up from our seats and quickly make our way back into the streets. I loop my arm in hers as we step back out into the crowd, ready to take on the shopping universe one day at a time.

FIFTEEN

Chiberia

I FIND MYSELF smack in the middle of the wrath of winter in Chicago. There is a phenomenon called the Polar Vortex sweeping the Midwest and East Coast, blanketing us with negative temperatures coupled with a few feet of snow. Schools are called off in most areas and everyone is walking around in puffy coats and ski masks. What a perfect analogy for the state of my heart. Cold, empty and barren once again. And like the millions of people entrapped in this dark season, I accept the fact that it's a part of my life that's here to stay.

"Welcome back!" Noelle greets me exuberantly as I walk through the reception area two weeks after my trip. "You look rested and ready to take on the world."

"I probably should have taken one more vacation day to recover from my vacation," I say as I take a pile of pink message slips from her desk. "How've you been, Noey?"

"Good. It was relatively quiet around here while you were gone. That's good, right?"

"Yeah. Quiet is great. What's on the docket for today?" I fidget around for my office keys while I wait for her to walk me through the day's schedule. My life is one big Franklin Planner. Bookmarks, dates, tasks and tick marks.

"Nothing except a meeting with Warren as soon as you can. He just arrived in the office and wants to see you after you've settled in."

"Okay. Please let him know that I'll be there in a few minutes."

I shut the door to my office and get started on my routine once again. I smile at the reflection I see in the glass. The trip to Hong Kong was a success in terms of clearing my head. Olivia and I spent two weeks away from family and friends, just the two of us. My dad wasn't too happy about my absence at their annual Christmas party, but my mom worked her magic and convinced him that this was a much needed break for me. It took me about two days to wipe my mind clear of Lucas and the fact that he wasn't willing to see me while I was there. It forced the facts upon me – until that point, I guess I was secretly harboring a hope that he would fight for me, that he would ignore what I said and try to patch things up between us. So in essence, this time it felt like the official end of the line for us. My heart was hurting and I cried for an entire day. But I know that this is for the best. The shopping and the eating and the constant happy banter between Olivia and me... it was all wonderfully therapeutic.

Sometimes, the head just needs to win over the idiocies of the heart.

The door to Warren's office is wide open, but he looks like he's in the middle of crafting a very intense email. He hunches his shoulders as he angrily bangs on the keys in front of him. I knock softly on the open door to try to get his attention. He turns around, perturbed at the interruption, but his expression changes as soon as he sees that it's me.

"Jade. Come in." He stands up and walks towards one of the leather couches in the middle of his office. I take a seat directly across from him. "How are you? How was your vacation?"

"It was great, thank you. It was so nice to be in warmer weather for a few days," I smile as I cross my legs and lean back. He stands up again to shut the door for some privacy. He has a serious look on his face that shows me this meeting won't be a good one.

"I wanted to speak to you about something that happened while you were away."

"Oh?" I say. "What is it?"

"For some unknown reason, Mr. Martinez confided in someone about seeing you while he was here in Chicago a few weeks ago. It seems that you had dinner with him?"

I try to keep a straight face despite the lump in my throat. Do I deny this? My mind flashes to the texts and messages. And pictures. Yes, pictures. Don't ask me why. I couldn't help myself. Even after he told me that he couldn't fly over to see me, I maintained some contact with him and sent him pictures of our time there on impulse.

He betrayed me. Why would he tell anyone this?

"Yes, I did see him while he was here. We did have dinner."

"Just once? Did the invitation come from him?"

"What does it matter, Warren? What's going on?"

"Well, word got around and now the partners are concerned about our fraternization rules. I'm sorry to have to ask this, but is anything going on between the two of you?"

I let out a forced laugh and roll my eyes. "No! We're just friends. The final report was done by then."

"Did you discuss the merger at all?"

"No. Not at all. We never talked about anything that had to do with work. Just family, ourselves. As friends, nothing more." I feel like I child, lying through the skin of my teeth. While what I'm telling him is true, I know about my feelings, and that alone negates everything I'm saying.

"Okay. Do you have any proof that he reached out to you first?"

"Warren! Here we go again! I know for a fact that it's no one's business whom I make friends with when I'm outside of work." God, please let this be a true statement. "Lucas and I worked many long hours together. It was inevitable that we would become friends." I can't look directly at him, so I stare at the top of his head instead.

"Jade, I'm going to manage through this and respond to all the speculation out there, but I need you to promise not to have any contact with him going forward, at least until this deal is complete." His looks at me with gentle, understanding eyes. "I should have known better than to place you in this situation. You're an extremely attractive woman. The men in this office know this and are very protective of you. I probably shouldn't have exposed you to someone like that, given the emotional state that you're in."

"Someone like what?" I ask, puzzled and utterly irritated.

"A predator. That's what he is. I heard the rumblings around the office by the women who were falling all over him. He's the love 'em and leave 'em type; there are newspaper articles going on about him and various women."

"His personal life is none of our business."

"It is when it affects one of our own. Listen, Jade, will you promise not to communicate with him going forward?"

I've sunk to the lowest level I possibly can. "I promise."

"Jade," Warren leans in towards me and reaches out for my hands, his face masked in apprehension, "I trust you implicitly. I will always have your back. I'm sure that this is all a misunderstanding. You've always acted with integrity, putting our company first in everything you've ever done. This trust hasn't wavered because of what I've heard, so please don't let this be something else for you to worry about. As far as I'm concerned, this conversation is done. Let me smooth things over. Leave it to me. You take care of you. Recover, recoup. We're here for you."

"Thank you, Warren." I don't want to prolong this conversation any further, so I stand up to leave. I grip the phone in my hand, determined to delete the last three months of my life, deeply embedded in hundreds of text messages. I do it as soon as I'm out of his office. I erase his entire contact information from my phone.

There. It dies its own death.

SIXTEEN

The Non Christmas Season

CHRISTMAS IN CHICAGO is like any other cosmopolitan city in the world. You can count on snow. You can count on incredible shopping deals. You can count on the crowds. And you can count on the office being a ghost town when everyone takes what's left of their vacation days before the end of the year. But not for me. I worked every single day between Christmas and New Year's, save for the long weekend I spent in San Francisco with my parents. I will never forget this holiday season, simply because it was the worst one I had ever experienced in my life. Given what happened more than one year ago, my heart can never be broken more than it has been in the year that has passed. Lucas tries to call and text but I don't answer. Shutting him off from my phone was easy. Shutting him out of my heart is not. Not a day goes by that I don't think of him. Who did he spend Christmas with? Who was lucky enough to receive his first kiss of the New Year?

At the same time, I remember the new low that I had sunk to in recent months. The desperate craving that I had for anything he could throw my way. I feel conflicted. My mind still runs away with crazy thoughts of him. I have sex with someone else and think of him. I call his name out in the dark. I don't love him. I can't love him. I channel my anger at him for telling someone about us. This marks the end of our screwed up story.

There are numerous text messages from him and Skype notes asking me where I am. I'm too afraid to respond, knowing that all eyes are on us. And those stupid work phones. I knew I had lost it when I think of all the messages that we sent each other on our work phones.

I have no pictures. There are days when I try to remember the details of his face, the ones I so meticulously memorized when he was here the first time. In the time of Instagram and Facebook and in the midst of the selfie boom, this just highlights the sinister nature of our relationship.

The office comes back to life on January 6. It seems that everyone is desperately trying to catch up on all the year-end deadlines. Early that morning, I find myself back in Leya's office reviewing a checklist with the team to ensure that we have everything we need before reporting our annual results.

The room is full of people, staff members and peers who cheer when I walk in. "Here she is! The woman of the hour!" Nick, the Head of Strategy exclaims. "Jade, you'll get a kick out of this. The client wants us to front another two million dollars for factory material on net ten day terms."

"Tell them to suck shit," I say matter-of-factly.

"There you go, the goddess has spoken." Nick leans back in smug affirmation. "There's no gray with this woman. She's black and white. I love it."

The meeting continues for another thirty minutes. I catch Leya staring at me. I nod my head at my friend and smile weakly as I adjust my eyeglasses to shield myself from her glare. She knows that the glasses are there for a reason. I never wear them except when there's an on screen presentation. Or when I'm trying to hide my eyes as a way of protecting my secrets from the world. As the meeting comes to an end, she lifts her right hand to stop me from getting up. "Stay a few minutes, Jade. I need to run something by you."

Everyone nods and leaves the room. Leya gets up to shut the door.

"Jesus. Why can't people make these decisions on their own? He's a VP, for heaven's sake, and he has to wait for me to tell him what to do?" I twirl around in the chair, trying to deflect her serious demeanor.

"He's not the only one who can't make a decision. Jade, you've got to stop doing this to yourself."

I blink my eyes under the false pretense of confusion about what she had just said. "What?"

"You look like crap." *This woman. She doesn't quit.*

I glare at her and roll my eyes, still without saying a word.

"Well, okay. You're still sickeningly gorgeous, but your eyes… they look like marshmallows."

Still no reaction, not a single acknowledgment from me.

"Oh, Leya. I've never felt like this before. At my age, who would have known that I would feel like I did again with…" I stop myself. *That was a lifetime ago. A time and a place long forgotten.*

"When you told me that it was going to be fine in a month, what did I tell you? When you swore it was going to be just a fling, what did I say?"

106

"That it's not that straightforward," I admit, my voice breaking in a choked whisper.

"Why are you fighting it?"

"Because he can't want someone like me."

"And what exactly is someone like you?"

"A lifeless shell of nothing. My heart can't take it, Ley. I just can't do this anymore."

"Do you know that people actually die of a broken heart? Have you seen yourself in the mirror lately? Your pants are falling off; you've lost more weight."

"I'm working out. I'm doing the half marathon in March."

"Bullshit." She bends down to fish into her purse and hands me a small black phone. I shake my head and squint my eyes impatiently, confused about her latest gesture. "It's an unmarked phone registered to my daughter. Use it. Call him. Tell him what's going on. Put some context behind this. You can't just cut it off without speaking to him about all this shit."

Her words release all my anxieties of the past few months. I start to cry. She rushes over to hold me. I don't try to speak, I just let my tears flow because I know that she understands. She has been here for all this. She knows.

Once she loosens her hold on me, I pull a Kleenex from her filing cabinet, wipe my tears, and press the phone close to my heart. "Thank you," I whisper as I turn on my heels and head back to my office.

I PACE BACK and forth before huddling in my favorite spot in the office, on the floor by the corner window, staring out at the cloudy winter sky. My hands are shaking as I manually dial his number into Leya's phone.

"Martinez," he huffs hurriedly after the third ring.

"Luke! It's me."

"Oh my God, Jade! Where are you? Whose phone is this?"

"Luke, can you talk? I just wanted to explain what happened before the holidays." I hear voices in the background.

"I'm at a party right now but I can leave and call you right back. Give me fifteen minutes."

He's at a party.

"No, let me call you again. How about tomorrow? Just text this number to let me know when you have time to talk."

"Please, Jade. I want to talk to you. Can you not give me an hour to just get situated and then we can talk?"

I know he's with someone because there's a woman's voice in the background. I think she's asking him who it is. "No, let's talk tomorrow. Just text me."

I hang up and immediately call Leya to ask her if I can keep the phone overnight.

"Of course," she says. "Keep it for as long as you need to. Just don't prolong having that conversation with him."

ON THE TRAIN on my way in to work the next day, he texts me.

Unknown Number: *Hi. Can you call me?*

Jade: *When?*

Unknown Number: *Now.*

Jade: *On the train, give me an hour?*

Unknown Number: *Okay.*

Forty-five minutes later, I lock the door of my office and quickly dial his number.

"Jade! What's going on?"

"Hi. The day that I arrived from vacation, Warren called me into his office to tell me that you told someone about us. Whom did you speak to about this, Lucas? Why would you do that?"

"I swear, I didn't say anything! I mentioned to a friend of mine that I saw you again briefly while I was in Chicago. This friend has nothing to do with work at all. Fuck!"

"Well, whatever. It got to Warren and the rest of the executives. Listen, you have to delete all of our texts. I'm really worried about them, especially the pictures, Luke."

"You didn't send me anything inappropriate."

"No, but I think pictures of me shopping will show that we have more than a casual friendship."

"Shit! I'm just so pissed right now. No one has a right to tell us who we can be friends with."

"You yourself said that this could ruin everything. I really just wanted to explain to you why I haven't been taking any of your calls. Once we end this one, I'm going to give this phone back to my friend. I won't be contacting you anymore, so I wanted to let you know why."

"I'm sending you a fucking phone tomorrow. This has gone too far. To hell with the merger. It's my money, my choice."

"Lucas, you don't know what you're saying. Let's just keep it quiet for a few more weeks," I plead with him.

His tone changes, his mood suddenly lightens up. "How have you been, Jade? God, I missed your voice."

"I've been well, can't complain. And you?"

"I just got back from two weeks in Mexico."

"Oh, for work?"

"Well, yes and no. One week for work and the other sort of a mini vacation."

"Who'd you go with? Was it fun?"

"I went with a friend."

"Hmm. A woman friend?" I knew what he was going to say next. And yet, I wanted to hear it. I prayed he would finish me off. It's the only way for me to truly stay away. *Stop the bleeding. Just bludgeon me with one swift blow and get it over with.*

"Yes. Do you remember Cristina? I think I mentioned her to you once."

"The one you were engaged to?"

"Yes." Awkward silence. "She had a modeling assignment close to where I was going, so we decided to travel together. What about you, Jade? What's going on with you? Are you dating? Are you at least trying to take some time outside of work?"

"Oh, yes. I actually met someone. It's new, but I'm enjoying his company a lot," I lie. I refuse to be the only one with no life to speak of.

"That's great, Jade! Keep me posted, okay?"

"I will. And hey, since we're both trying to start up our personal lives, no need to send me that phone. We'll just catch up whenever, okay? Take care of you yourself, Lucas. And I hope we see each other again sometime."

"Jade—"

I hang up as I hear him say my name. I bury my face in my hands and cry.

What is this? What's happening to me? Get a grip, Jade. I roughly wipe my tears with the back of my hands. *Round and round I go in this endless loop of fighting and giving in. Why do I even take his calls? He's there, I'm here. What is the point of all this?*

SEVENTEEN

The Friend Zone

THE WINTER THAT lasted forever is finally over, and I'm enjoying the crisp spring air while I make my way into the office on a Saturday morning. I figure I'll get a few hours in for a project that's due on Tuesday of the next week. The executive floor is empty save for a cleaning lady who is making the rounds and cleaning up after the happy hour that apparently occurred last night. I'm wearing jeans and Converse sneakers, my hair is in a bun, and not a trace of makeup is on my face. I quickly rush down the hall, rummaging inside my bag, as usual, to retrieve my keys. I literally walk into someone. Only that someone is someone I didn't want to see.

"Jade!" he exclaims as my forehead smacks right into his chest.

"Lucas? What are you doing here?" I ask, smoothing my fingers over my hair and suddenly conscious of the holes in my jeans. His hair has grown out, dark curls above his eyebrows and over his ears.

I can't see the side of his face—it's covered in a neatly groomed beard.

"I was about to ask you the same thing. Thank God you're in town." He grins from ear to ear. "I'm here to sign the merger papers. My flight was delayed yesterday and I just arrived an hour ago. Warren was supposed—"

We hear the sound of the sliding doors as Warren shuffles in. "There you both are. Sorry I'm a few minutes late. Why don't we all step into my office?"

"Warren, I'm here to finish work on the Almeda project. I don't have to be present for the signing. As long as you're comfortable with obtaining all the signatures, we should be good."

"No, Jade, I'm glad you're here. Let's get Martinez the signing pen so he can put this baby to rest." His expression makes me feel like he knows more than he's letting on. His kind heart has always looked out for my best interests and I wonder whether he's doing the same now.

We both walk into Warren's office and stand awkwardly to the side, waiting for him to unpack his briefcase and furnish Lucas with the pile of papers to sign. Lucas watches me as I stare out the window. I don't turn my head in his direction. I can feel the heat of his glare on my cheeks.

"Ah, here they are. Lucas, sign three copies, all pages, and date the last one."

Lucas follows his instructions. No one says a word. I watch the smooth glide of his fingers as he signs the documents. I think about that one day six months ago when this all started. How it took weeks for the proposal to be drafted and approved but months to negotiate the terms of the merger.

Once he's done, he hands the pen over to me. It's the same kind of pen... My mind takes me elsewhere and I forcefully will it to come back.

"Now your turn," he dares me, deliberately stroking the pen with his fingers. As I lean down to cosign the same pages, I catch him discretely typing a message on his phone.

007: *It's killing me, standing this close to you without being able to touch you.*

My phone buzzes softly as soon as I lay the pen on the table. For a transaction that took months to accomplish, the conclusion turns out to be pretty uneventful. Not much unlike the end for Lucas and me.

"That's it, folks. The deed of sale is done. Lucas, we'll send you three executed originals in the next day or so. Both of you are, well, free to go." Warren emphasizes the word *free* as he swats his hand in the air to dismiss us.

I don't move. Lucas doesn't either. He's waiting for me to leave Warren's office so he can follow me out. He looks at me with obvious disdain, wondering why I remain standing there.

"It was nice to see you again, Lucas." I extend my hand out to shake his. "I need to catch Warren for a few more minutes with questions about my project. Have a safe trip home."

Warren swings his head from side to side, glancing at him and then at me. Lucas reacts initially with a slight shaking of his head and a bewildered look on his face, but once again, his business side takes over and he plays along so glibly.

"Thank you for everything, Jade. Good luck with all of your future endeavors."

My heart breaks at the finality of his words. He walks out the door without a sound and I'm left trying to find the perfect excuse to remain in Warren's office.

But not before he takes the pen with him.

"What was that about?" Warren asks, his face enveloped in worry.

"What? The pen?" I spit out distractedly.

"What pen? No! I want to know if you're okay," he restates.

I shrug my shoulders casually, trying to expel the concern on his face. "Yeah, I didn't want to prolong the poor guy's stress. At least it's over now and he can stop having to travel here for these day trips." I laugh in my attempt to lighten up the conversation. "Thanks so much for managing through the earlier fiasco, Warren. I truly appreciate it."

"Anytime, Jade. You did a wonderful job with the proposal. This is just another successful project under your belt. You should be proud of yourself. Now, about Martinez. I would still suggest that you stay away from him. I don't trust the guy. I think his letting people know about your friendship was an underhanded move on his part. There are users in this world, and I think he's definitely one of them."

I don't say a word. I feel dishonest and hypocritical. I had played just as large a role in our deception and it's never going to be the same after this. The image of honesty and integrity that I had built over the years was all a farce. Everything catches up with you eventually; the truth always wins out. And when it does, I'm going to have to own it. Every little fractured piece of it.

MP: *I wasn't able to tease you about your hair.*

I RUN DOWN the building steps to catch a cab four hours after I see him in Warren's office. As I stand on the corner with my hand up in the air, I'm caught unaware when he wraps his arms around me from behind. In his right hand is a bag of Cheetos and his left hand holds two bottles of Coke by their necks.

"Come sit with me," he whispers into my shoulder as he kisses it, "for old times' sake."

I can't help but smile and nod my head. He leads me down the street away from the building and across the bridge. We find some steps to park ourselves for a few minutes. The March air is still chilly but tolerable.

"I'm sorry about what happened this morning," I say, gently rubbing his arm with my fingers.

"I understand what you're doing. I don't blame you. I've been a total shit."

We tear open the bag of chips and devour what's inside it for a few minutes. I laugh at his words. His Spanish accent makes it sound like "sheet." He digs his fingers into his hair and I gently reach out to smooth the unruly strands that have just been mussed up.

"Long, no? I haven't had a haircut in two months."

"It looks good," I assure him tenderly. "When do you leave?"

"I'm taking the midnight flight out. I have to be in Seoul by tomorrow."

"Ah. Ever the jetsetter." I absentmindedly take a swig of my Coke.

"Did you really mean what you said in there, Jade? Is it over between us?"

"What does that even mean, Luke? What do we have?"

"Well, now that the merger is complete, can we take time to figure that out?"

"How?" I react emphatically. "You're only here for a few hours at a time."

He doesn't answer. I know that he agrees with me. "There's just so much going on."

I give him an out. I know that he needs this. Surprisingly I feel stronger, more resolved. "I know. And I completely understand. Listen, I really value our friendship. I don't want to lose you as a friend. Can we keep it this way for now until things settle down? I can't give you anything more at this point. Not this way."

He doesn't protest. Instead, he lets out a deep sigh. "I just don't want to lose our connection. If you promise me that we'll still talk as often as we can, I'm going to try to be okay with that."

"I promise," I nudge him warmly, savoring the closeness of that instant in secret. "You're my forever Skype buddy."

He pulls me tightly in a warm embrace. My chest is pressed against his and my head settles in the crook of his neck. And although my eyes are closed, I hear every word he whispers. "That will have to be good enough for me." He bends his head down and kisses my forehead. "For now."

EIGHTEEN

Picture Book

"CAUTION, THE DOORS are about to close."

The automated announcement as the train stops at every station rings in my ear. I say it in my sleep, I could hear it in my head. All day. Every day. Sunlight beams through the train windows as I silently stare out, deep in prayer. For the past two years, this has become my daily routine. Get on the train, check work email, pray the rosary. A few minutes of meditation to ask for forgiveness, to pray for my family and for my life. Fifteen minutes later and the best part of my morning will begin. Granted, it lasts for a mere thirty minutes, but that brief catnap with my eyes closed and my thoughts clear makes the 75 minute commute so well worth it. How funny is it that I wake up in the morning only to look forward to going back to sleep on the train?

Closing Doors. Is that what my life has been about? Is that why I am now doing the complete opposite? Opening them. Rebelling against life's best laid plans? Living with the need to break free? But what is it that I'm running away from? What am I searching for?

I glance around the train at the people sitting close to me. Like me, they are all business people, familiar faces, commuting with me day in and day out. From experience, I could clearly gauge the amount of success they've had in their careers. By their purses. The lady with the fake leather bag, falling apart, ripping at the seams, loose threads hanging from end to end—secretary, perhaps? Is her salary even worth this commute? The lady with the latest Coach purse, no rips, no torn seams, but old and weathered shoes. Mid-level management for sure. Struggling, but smart and ambitious. She might get there when she becomes my age. And then there are only a handful of women just like me. Impeccably dressed from head to toe with a matching high end luxury brand computer bag and handbag. Burberry coat, rings on their fingers. Executive level women who don't take advantage of the parking perk at work. Women who love the commute because it gives them the time to read, to write, to think. To escape. Sitting among a group of strangers makes me feel inconspicuous. Everyone has their sins too, I bet. Were mine worse than theirs? Did they live their life in full color? How can I get in on that life?

Who am I to judge these women? Look at me. Every other day, I alternate between a black outfit and a brown outfit. This is so reflective of my monochromatic life. I guess that's how I've managed to keep the distinct separation between my work life and my home life. Black at work, strong, professional and always on top of everything. White at home, bleached, waxen and faded. Except that the black and white is now gray. The fear of living, the hesitation towards anything out of the mundane and ordinary has been blown out of the water. I've crossed the line this time, and there's no way I can ever turn back. The sudden weight of a body on the seat next to me transports me back to the present.

"Hi."

I glance over to find a man dressed in jeans and a leather jacket looking right into my eyes. "Hi," I whisper back, turning my head away to stare out the window.

"Nice spring day, huh?" He smiles, his eyes never moving from mine.

"Yes." I nod, my look expressionless as I slide away from him, squeezing myself closer to the window and avoiding the light brush of his jacket against my arm.

The rest of the train ride continues in silence. I close my eyes and force myself to clear my head. Restart and regroup. That's what I need to do. Instead, my thoughts run away from me so fast that I find myself lost in a tunnel of memories.

Inside my head is a picture book of the people I have loved. And lost. And when the truth finally surfaces, who will be left to love me? When the damage is revealed, will it explain the reasons for my actions? Will it justify the way I reacted towards him? Will it clarify the reasons why I was willing to risk everything for one single moment of color in my life? Why did I choose him? Or did he choose me?

PART II: BREAKING

The Past

"Rushing and racing, and running in circles
Moving so fast, I'm forgetting my purpose
Blur of the traffic is sending me spinning, getting nowhere
My head and my heart are colliding, chaotic
Pace of the world, I just wish I could stop it
Try to appear like I've got it together, I'm falling apart
Save me, somebody take my hand and lead me
Slow me down, don't let love pass me by
Just show me how 'cause I'm ready to fall
Slow me down, don't let me live a lie
Before my life flies by
I need you to slow me down."

"Slow Me Down" by Emmy Rossum

NINETEEN

First Love
Twenty Years Ago

DID I JUST hear a rooster crow? I turned my head from side to side, afraid that I had ended up somewhere else between last night and this morning. A smile crept up my face when I saw him sleeping next to me. I was where I always wanted to be. Where I always knew I belonged. Just as I turned around to try to go back to sleep, he pressed himself against me, hugging his arms tighter around my chest.

"Morning," he mumbled as he kissed the back of my head.

"Did you by any chance hear a rooster crow?" I asked, reaching my hand back to outline his face.

"Yes! Ugh. I forgot to tell you. My neighbors now have chickens living in their apartment."

"Oh no! That's it. You know you have to move, right? I won't be able to come over anymore," I teased him, ruffling the top of his head.

"I know, right? Seriously. Chickens. In an apartment."

"Hmm. Interesting," I said, turning around to face him. "Only in California?"

"No, only in my neighborhood," he reminded me. "Your dad would freak if he knew where you were spending your nights."

"He would freak if he knew what was in me every night. Not necessarily where I *am* every night."

His smile always lit up my mornings. In a way, he was right. Chris lived in a warehouse turned makeshift apartment in what they call the Tenderloin District in downtown San Francisco. We had both just graduated from U.C. Berkeley and he was living on what little was left of his college scholarship while deciding what he wanted to do with his life. I was set and ready to attend Business School at Stanford in the fall. I was an only child living in a loving and stable home, brought up by the most devoted parents. I never really felt the need to fit in. While girls my age were desperately looking for attention from the opposite sex, I was busy traveling the world with my parents or hanging out at the stables caring for my horses. Sure, there were always boys who paid attention to me, but I was never interested in anyone until Chris came along.

We met three years ago at a frat party where he followed me home after I left early to study for my midterm exams. I'd been in love with him ever since.

Chris and I were a contradiction in every sense of the word. While I was extremely organized and maddeningly serious, Chris was laid back, spontaneous and funny. He tempered my incessant need to have a plan, to foresee the future. Chris just winged it no matter what the situation was whenever any decision needed to be made.

"Have I told you before how the highlight of my day is waking up to those dazzling emerald eyes of yours?" he teased as he slid close enough to fold his legs over mine.

"Yes, you have. Numerous times. I'm beginning to think you don't mean it anymore."

"Oh, Jae, what did I do to deserve someone like you? Look at you, and then look at me." He gazed at me searchingly, as if asking for assurance. Obviously, he didn't see what I saw. Lying next to me was a fine looking man with shorn blond hair, sheer blue eyes, and a perfectly chiseled nose. The blueness of his eyes was transparent, soul-bearing and clear like blown glass. They reminded me of the deep dark sea, sparkling and playful. They were perfect. They were him.

Our conversation was interrupted by the shrill ring of his phone. He jumped out of bed to grab it from the rickety old table he used as a desk. The sight of his naked body made me feel warm all over, impressive in a forsaken apartment with nothing but a small space heater. His back was ridged and his arms and legs were well defined. A real athlete's body. A soon to be pro-basketball player's body.

"Hey, man." *Joshua*, Chris mouthed to me. "No, that's fine. I'll still be there. I just have to leave on time to meet Jade at her parents' for the fundraiser that they're hosting at their place. Oh? Great! I'll see you there then."

Chris flung the phone on the floor and jumped back onto the bed, lifting me on top of him as I tugged at the blanket and threw it over us both. He slid his hands under my shirt as I leaned towards his head and kissed him on the lips.

"What did he want?" I asked with my eyes closed as he sensually rubbed himself against my open legs, pulling my panties to the side so we're skin to skin.

"We have practice tomorrow from one to six and he says he's attending your parents' party too." This wasn't the first time that

Chris' tone helped me predict what he was going to say next.

"Don't say it, baby. It's not true."

"I hate that his parents are friends with yours and that you grew up together," he spat out despite my plea. "In Pacific Heights, no less."

"I don't live there anymore, and who cares?" I felt like we'd been here so many times, but I didn't show it. I ground against him, hoping to divert his attention from the same old conversation.

"More often than not, I think he has a crush on you. I'm just a bit irritated that he's at every fucking social event with your parents."

This was the first time that he had actually voiced his thoughts out loud. I did my best to bring him back and get him focused on wanting me, because I was interested in everything but talking.

"Babe, he's your best friend. Of course he's always around. You guys grew up together. And his parents are like your adoptive parents. They love you."

It started to work. The flustered look on his face began to fade away.

"I guess," he agreed pensively. "All my life, I've lived under his shadow. The poor orphan friend. And with you, I still feel like I've undeservingly won the lottery." His touch turned urgent as his hands lightly tickled the small of my back. I placed my weight on him and moved slowly back and forth.

"Well, lottery winner, why don't you stop talking and start claiming your prize?" I reached back and took his hands, bringing them to my face and slowly kissing his fingers. "Besides," I hushed, "he's not really my type."

"Yeah?" He smiled as he lifted his head up to kiss me. "What exactly is your type, Ms. Albin?"

"Let's see…" I gently traced my finger down the bridge of his nose. "Blond." I kissed his forehead. "Sexy blue eyes." I kissed his eyelids. "Full, sensuous lips." I kissed him passionately.

"Hmmm," he murmured, reciprocating the meeting of our tongues with a soft bite of my top lip. "You're the best kisser, ever."

"I had a good teacher." He was my first in every sense of the word. "Besides, more often than not, you've been proven wrong. About many things," I whispered, removing my top at the same time and bending down so that my chest was pressed against his. I kissed him gently, but he returned it by playfully flipping me onto my back.

"Am I wrong about how much you want me?" he hissed in my ear, trailing his lips across my cheeks and resting on my mouth.

I arched my back up in response, guiding him inside at the same time. "No. Never."

"I love you, Jae. I love you more than anything in the world," he said, and the look on his face filled my heart.

"I love you too, Chris. I will never love anyone else but you."

TWENTY

The Boy with My Heart
Twenty Years Ago

"HI! YOU'RE HERE!" I ran down the steps of the grand stairway to greet him. "Mom and Dad are in the great room with some of their friends." I let him know this mainly because I wanted him to take me in his arms and kiss me without worrying about my parents. He did. I remained standing on the second to the last step, buried in his embrace, absorbed in the warmth of his love. This was us. Always touching, always kissing. Always in our own little world.

"You look out of this world gorgeous, Jae." He rubbed his nose against mine.

We held each other for a few minutes until he took my hand and led me down the rest of the steps. He held my hand tightly as we trudged down the long hallway towards a small group of people convened by the indoor water fountain in the middle of the foyer. Our house looked more like a museum than a home. Everything perfect, everything always in its respective place. Antiques and portraits and collectors' paintings lined the walls leading to the main reception area. Despite its grand, exhibition-type appearance, it was always a warm and happy home.

"Hey. It'll be okay," I whispered, stopping in the middle of the crowd to stand on my toes and brush my lips against his neck. "We've done this so many times before."

His tension increased visibly and his entire body stiffened up as we approached my parents. Joshua was standing by my mother's side, deep in conversation with her.

"Mama, Dad, Chris is here," I announced, ignoring Joshua completely and proudly watching Chris as he shook my father's hand.

"Christopher. Welcome, son. How is the recruiting process going? Any new bites?"

My mother rolled her eyes as my father asked his usual questions. I stepped closer to her and tried to catch her attention with my eyes, silently appealing for her to soften up.

"Not yet, sir, although I'm still hopeful it will happen," he responded calmly, respectfully. He then turned to Joshua with a drastic change in his tone. "Hey, man. No wonder you left so quickly after practice." Terse, pointed, accusatory.

"Just wanted to make sure I wouldn't be late," Joshua quipped indifferently. "Did you need a ride? Sorry, man, I didn't think that the bus schedule would be bad at this time of day."

I wanted to slap him right there and then. Never had Joshua been as openly insulting to Chris as he had been lately.

"Mrs. Albin, let me help you greet the other guests," he continued, turning to grasp my mother by the elbow and lead her away from us. I looked at my father, infuriated.

"Dad—" I started, incensed by the attention they had paid to his friend.

He leaned over to kiss my cheek while his right arm tapped Chris' shoulder at the same time. "Don't sweat it, darling. This boy is the one that has your heart."

As soon as he walked away, I pulled Chris out of the fray and into the safety of my bedroom. Ordinarily, my mother would have had a fit, but she was too busy entertaining her guests to worry about where I was off to.

"Let's hang out here for a while until dinner," I suggested, leaping into his arms as soon as we closed the doors. Though it was redesigned every so often as I was growing up, my bedroom still had remnants of my life as a little girl. There were pictures all over, including a portrait of my family, and two original Andy Warhol silk screen paintings. My mom was a Studio 54 girl whose group of friends consisted of the high profile New York personalities of her time. He was one of them. My shelves still held the Madame Alexander dolls that my mother owned when she was a young girl. Enmeshed between them were various stuffed animals that Chris had given me over the years. His jerseys from previous seasons also littered my walls, held up with push pins that used to drive my mother crazy.

"Mmm. God, Jae, I know what I'd rather be doing right now." His voice was muffled in my hair as he stepped effortlessly towards the canopy bed and gently set me down. He sat next to me while I placed my head on his lap and lay on my stomach. His hands snaked up my dress and rested on the back of my thighs. "Your dress is too short." He smiled impishly, lifting his head up and turning his attention to the wall next to the windows. "Wait, I've been looking for that one!" he teased as he pointed to the blue and gold jersey neatly posted on the wooden board. "You've had it all this time?"

"What can I say? I stole it. I needed to stink up my room so it smelled like you when I missed you," I taunted back.

"I still can't get over the fact that this bedroom is twice the size of my apartment." His eyes roamed the room for a few seconds until they rested on a pile of shopping bags on the floor by the walk in closet. "When did you go shopping?"

"The other day when you were out job hunting. Wanna see what I bought?" I pushed myself up off the bed and crawled on the floor towards the bags. "This." I held up a pink halter top blouse with a bow on the front.

"Sexy. And your favorite color."

"Yup. And this." I held up a printed black and white checkered pair of slim pants.

"Sexier. When are you going to wear that?"

"Maybe when we go to the Smashing Pumpkins concert?" I fished another item from a different bag. "What about this?" I held up a pair of red lace underwear.

"Sexiest!" he affirmed, laughing lightly. "Why don't you model it for me now?"

"Because we're in my mother's house and Concha has cameras all over the place," I joked.

"True," he agreed. "But we're leaving here right after dinner!"

As if she really *did* have cameras everywhere, the annoying beep of the intercom system penetrated the room and Concha's stern voice rang through the speakers. "Jade! The guests are gathering for supper. Come downstairs now!"

Two hours later, we found ourselves sitting at the incredibly long dining room table having dessert while everyone was immersed in their own side dialogues. The coral-colored solid jade dining room table continued to be a central topic of everyone's conversation. It was custom-made and shipped here from Hong Kong, lifted by a crane and installed by forty carpenters, etc., etc., etc. This expectedly blossomed into a conversation about the hand-carved crown molding and the original Picasso mural that was installed on all four walls.

It made me happy to see my mother being complimented on her exemplary taste. My father was a self-made businessman who needed my mother's support and confidence to help steer him in the right direction as a young immigrant from another country. Sometimes I wished I was more like her. She said that she married him because she recognized his potential, but I know she married him because she fell deeply in love. She was his partner, his lover, and his wife. My parents still held hands whenever they strolled together, still whispered secrets into each other's ears, and still shared their own private jokes, oblivious to whatever else was going on around them.

Chris and I were seated across from each other, with Joshua next to me on my right, Someone else's daughter, named Millie, was busy chatting Chris up with stories about herself. He stared straight at me, making sure that I noticed how his eyes never left my face. I smiled warmly at him and licked my lips, sending him our very own code that we would have our time together afterwards. Soon. From the corner of my eye, I saw my father stand up to begin thanking everyone for their company this evening. He lifted up his glass in a few toasts to his business partners and friends, the same speeches he always gave. I managed to catch the last one only because everyone turned their heads to look at me.

"And last but not least, to our daughter, Jade. The light of my life, who never fails to make me a proud man. Jade has been accepted at the Stanford School of Business and her mother and I are filled with pride at how this young woman has just blossomed on her own. To you, Jade. Congratulations!"

"Cheers!" everyone responded, clinking their glasses together.

It happened in slow motion. Everything else faded out and I sat frozen in place as Joshua leaned over to give me a kiss on the cheek. He moved in way too quickly for me to react. "Congratulations, Jade," he murmured. Panic overtook me as I turned my head over to Chris, who was no longer in his chair but standing right behind mine.

I pushed my seat back and stood up slowly, calmly. "Excuse us, please, everyone. Thank you all for your well wishes."

TWENTY-ONE

Crazy Talk
Twenty Years Ago

"WILL YOU SLOW down, please?" I yelped, yanking Chris' arm back to stop him from pulling me across the garden. "Let me take my shoes off first. The heels are digging into the grass and I'm going to leave my ankles behind if you pull me any harder!"

He finally stopped without letting go of my hand. "Sorry. I'm so fucking upset right now, I'm going to explode!"

This time, I took the lead. With my shoes in my left hand, we slowly walked down the stone path on the way to the wooded area behind the swimming pool. My childhood playhouse came into view and immediately, I felt both relieved and relaxed. Chris pushed the old wooden door open and I stepped in first, trying to deflect his mood by pasting a sly smile on my face. He followed me inside, watching as I lifted my skirt up to allow my legs the freedom to climb the ladder to the second level where a built-in bed was nestled directly under an elevated roof with a skylight. Chris was so tall that he had to crouch down and remain seated in order to fit into this little loft. His legs dangled down as he sat at the edge of the bed next to me.

"Okay. Talk," I ordered, taking his hand in mine.

"Who the fuck made those seating arrangements? Was it your mother?"

"No, her secretary does all that. I'm sure she got instructions from my mother to alternate us like they always do in all these events."

"I swear, Jae, he's posed to take you away from me. I watched him all evening. He wouldn't stop looking at you."

"He's your friend, Chris. Your close friend. Maybe he thinks he's doing it for you."

"Doing what for me? Angling for my girl?"

"No, no. Trying to make sure that he's around us all the time. Like watching over me when you're not there."

"That's bullshit. When you think about it, he has more of a future than I do. I bet everyone wishes you would end up with him."

"Stop that crazy talk." I scooted my backside further up the mattress and lay down on the bed, pulling him towards me at the same time. "Come here."

He complied obediently by moving himself upwards until his face was two inches away from mine. He propped himself up on his left elbow while his right hand caressed my face. "I think your mother is playing right into it," he breathed, right before planting tiny little kisses down my nose.

"I seriously think she's trying to challenge you. She's just looking out for me."

"No, she doesn't think I'm good enough for you. And she may be right. You were born into all this," he said, waving his free hand in the air, "and I have nothing but a semi-okay athletic ability that isn't even getting me anywhere at this point."

"You, Chris Wilmot, have a super duper athletic ability that recruiters are going to recognize anytime now. And your love," I said, running my fingers along the side of his face, "is the only thing that will ever be good enough for me. I would give up everything I have to be with you."

"I love you, Jae." His thumb lightly brushed over my eyelids as I closed them momentarily to savor his touch. "Please be patient with me. I want to be able to give you what you're used to. Once I've got my future all figured out, I want to marry you, start a family with you. Will you stay with me, Jae? Please don't leave me. You're my home."

"I'm not going anywhere."

Chris bent his head down to kiss me, slowly at first, nipping at my lips until I opened up my mouth to taste him. I enclosed him in my arms and pulled him close to me, running my fingers down his back. We spent a few minutes kissing until his lips left mine and started to inch down my neck towards my breasts.

"Baby, wait. Let's go back to your place. We have no protection here." I gasped, reproaching every single lapse of time without his skin on mine.

He responded by removing his shirt and gently pulling my straps down to expose me. No words, just his hands on my breasts, his lips trailing a path, alternating between the downward pull of the fabric and the scintillating touch of his tongue. We smiled at each other as we heard the plop of my dress hitting the floor below us. My eyes were lost in his as I eased myself slowly out of my panties. I gently took hold of his face and guided it back up towards me, wrapping my legs around him so that I could feel him through his jeans. He sat up for a few seconds, only to undress himself completely. He spread my legs with his knee and with one gentle push, he filled me.

"You're mine, Jae. Only mine. Say it," he commanded, and his thrusts became rougher, stronger, more intense.

I was at a loss for words. Not because I didn't mean it or because I wasn't sure of it. I was buried in my ecstasy, focused on his movements, his roughness, his severity.

"Jae, Jae, say it," he panted as he grabbed my breast and squeezed it sharply.

My thoughts snapped back to hear his voice as I was wracked by my own convulsion. "Yes! Yes! I'm yours!" I cried.

And just like that, he released all his doubts inside me, trusting me, giving me everything of himself, his heart, his soul. *His life*.

TWENTY-TWO

Take My Heart
Twenty Years Ago

SUMMER IN SAN FRANCISCO is one of the best in the whole world. The weather is warm, but not humid, and the cool breezes are a welcome relief from the rays of the hot sun. My days were spent preparing for the time when I would leave the city to go back to school. Chris had taken a summer job in construction for a company that owned a number of buildings in the downtown area. Surprisingly, not for my father, who still controlled most of the buildings in the vicinity. There were times when I didn't get to see him for days and tried not to go crazy missing him. My mother made it her main objective to keep me busy, first with apartment hunting in the Stanford area and next with shopping and furnishing what's going to be my home at least for the next few years while I'm in school.

I also took an internship at my father's company, doing the books for him three days a week. We spoke every day and stole quiet moments together either at his place when he wasn't on call or at my apartment when he had time to swing by while on the road. He still didn't own a car, but drove a company truck that broke down every so often. I had accepted the fact Chris wasn't going to be recruited to play professional basketball anytime soon. He had two or three offers to play pro ball outside of the country, but his disappointment at the opportunities hindered his ability to decide fast enough. Pretty soon, the offers dried up. This had made him resentful and angry, and all the more insecure about the differences between our financial situations. I tried to assure him that I didn't care, and that he could move in with me in the meantime, but he didn't want to commit. He rarely talked about the future with me; his emphatic blue eyes were often distant and empty. But he told me that we would figure it all out and that he loved me. I believed him. I didn't know anything else in my life except for the love of my family and the love of Chris.

On the afternoon of our fourth anniversary, I let myself into his apartment and tidied up, knowing that he would be off from work in a few hours. He still lived in the same place, with one old bed in the middle of the room and a lamp on a makeshift desk. Nothing had changed, but that's why I loved him so much. He stayed true to himself. If only he would stop trying too hard to prove himself to me. The apartment was warmed considerably by the open window that allowed the bright sun in. The first thing I noticed was his unmade bed, but I thought nothing of the two pillows that lay side by side, hinting at the unthinkable, the impossible. I hustled about the place, making the bed, straightening up and organizing some ingredients on the kitchen counter. I was going to make his favorite spaghetti, complete with garlic bread and a salad and a bottle of his favorite Cabernet, straight from my father's wine cellar. With two more hours to kill, I decided to go for a quick run.

One more mile, I thought as I walked briskly towards the corner of Bush and Taylor, resolved to do the uphill climb that awaited me just around the bend. My heart fluttered with excitement as I saw Chris step out into the street. Just as I was about to run towards him, I noticed a woman directly behind him. I watched numbly as she wrenched his shoulders and caused him to turn around to face her. She looked just like him—sun-kissed blonde hair, short and bobbed, her faded jean shorts matching the color of his eyes. She lovingly reached out to him as he gave her a quick peck on the lips and walked away. I turned around and ran as fast as I could in the opposite direction, thinking about the various scenarios to justify what I just saw. Surely, this was all explainable. At least, that's what I told myself as I made my way back to the apartment.

I sat in silence on the bed and waited for him to arrive. I was too stunned to cook, too shocked to cry. Up until this point in my life, I had never been abandoned; everyone I loved had loved me back. I just didn't know how to react. Chris didn't return until two hours later. By this time, the sun had decided to take a rest for the evening. The room was dark; I sat motionless for more than an hour, staring outside the window at the pigeons and seagulls that paraded the dirty landing in front of me.

He opened the door and smiled warmly when he saw me. Was that relief that I saw in his face?

"Did the lights blow out or something? Why are you in the dark?" he asked cordially as he walked towards the bed to greet me. His mouth gaped open in shock as soon as he saw my tear-streaked face. "Jae, baby, what—"

"I saw you," I whispered, pronouncing every word succinctly. "Chris. I saw you."

"You saw me? Where?"

"A few hours ago. Leaving Connie's Pizza."

He didn't say a word, but took a seat next to me on the bed.

"Who is she?" I asked, and my voice trembled, my ears shutting down at knowing what I was about to find out. I wasn't sure I wanted to hear the answer.

"No one. A friend."

"What kind of a friend touches you the way that she did?"

He sighed and took my hands in his. I will never forget the look in his eyes. They were absent, he wasn't there. "Listen, Jade, it wasn't going to work between us anyway. We can never have a future together." His voice was calm and subdued, like he had been thinking this through for a while.

"Don't. Don't you dare put this on that again!" I yelled. I pushed his hands away and quickly stood up to leave. "I have never, ever, made you feel like you weren't good enough for me. Nothing ever mattered to me, Chris, only you! Why would you decide this for us?" I jumped up and rushed towards the table to retrieve my purse. My insides were broken; I couldn't see anything through my tears. I had no hesitation about holding back my emotions. I loved him so much, he needed to know that.

He watched me for a few seconds until I saw the sudden look of realization on his face. Somehow, he looked frightened. He knew that I was leaving him for good, that this wasn't a game.

"No! No!" He screamed as he took two steps toward me, wrapping himself around me tightly, barely giving me any room to breathe and effectively stopping me from moving any further. "No, Jade, please. Please don't leave. I'm so sorry! I was trying to replace you, to keep myself from falling apart, knowing that I would have to give you up!"

With all the strength left in me, I shoved him away with my arms. "Why in the world would you have to give me up?" I sobbed.

"Because I'm not good enough for you. All my life, I thought I would be able to play basketball. I never had a backup plan; no real prospects. Look at me! I'm not even good enough for them. And you. You deserve more than me."

"So you sleep with someone else to prove that to me?" I choked the words out. I wanted him to say the right thing, to deny that anything ever happened. I would have forgiven him. *My life meant nothing without him.*

"Yes."

"The two pillows…" It all made sense then. The lack of time. The vacant eyes. Guilt. That's what I had been too blind to see for the past few weeks. "The pillows," I said again, my heart constricting each time I heard my own words.

"Jade. Please. Please forgive me. I won't ever see her again. I'll move away. I'll live with you while you're in school. I'll get over this, accept things as they are. Please."

"This is what you wanted, Chris. Congratulations. You sabotaged this yourself and now you've successfully pushed me away." As I said the words, I knew that no other goodbye would ever be as painful as this. *An unplanned loss is somewhat easier than a conscious decision to walk away.*

"Jade, please, I'm begging you." He dropped to his knees in a praying position, tears dripping down from his face onto the blemished wooden floor. *You never notice the ground until you're forced to look down upon it.*

"I'm leaving my heart with you, Chris. From this day on, I will no longer have any use for it. I will never love anyone as much as I loved you."

TWENTY-THREE

My Felicia
Eighteen Months Ago

IT WAS ONE of those days I decided to take off from work to get caught up on life at home. It wasn't unusual for me to take a break immediately after a trip away from the family. As I sat by the kitchen counter checking my work emails, her sweet voice roused me from my thoughts.

"Hey, Mommy-o!" She bounded down the back staircase that led to the kitchen wearing a white polo shirt tucked into a plaid red and blue kilt that somehow seemed way too short for a school uniform. Her endlessly long legs were straight and perfect, her thick, lustrous hair neatly swept up in a ponytail.

"Good morning, my darling daughter. Aren't you running late for class?" I slid off the counter stool and got busy making her breakfast.

She walked over to me to wrap her arms around my shoulders.

"Scrambled eggs and toast?" I asked as I kissed her on the forehead.

"Yes, please." She turned around to make herself a cup of coffee. "It's Open House Week. Seniors get to come in late today and we're a half day, remember?"

"Oh, yes, I forgot. Is today the day we're meeting for lunch?" I poured some half and half in her cup.

She took a seat on the barstool next to me. "Yup! I'll meet you at 1:00 at Ciao Bella. The one right by Pyott Road."

"Sounds good," I respond. "How was your week?"

"It was great. We didn't have any homework. Daddy gave me a ride to Paul's house for a study group last Wednesday night." She winked at me in jest. "I think Dad should attend my school functions going forward."

"What? Why?"

"Because every time you show up at school, someone calls you a MILF. Josh Roberts and Steve Graus are the latest ones. They saw you last week when you went to the office to drop off my tuition payment."

I rolled my eyes at her. "Not funny, Ci."

"I'm serious, Mom! Paul was there and he asked me if I wanted him to beat those guys up. I just laughed about it. Fact of life. Hot mother."

Time to change the subject. "How are things with the two of you?"

Her face lights up immediately, the warmth of her tone reminding me of the innocence of first love. "Great! He's so busy with his practices and games but we're doing okay."

"Cia, he knows you're going to Barnard in the fall, right?" I asked cautiously.

"Yes, Mom, he does," she answered defensively, rolling her eyes at the same time.

"And?"

"He's hoping to play for Cornell so he says we'll worry about it when we get there. He's in on conditional status—he's missing a grade from History class." She sounded confident, like this was a sure thing.

"Ah." I bobbed my head up and down in understanding. She trusts him completely. She believes in everything he says. I've been there before; I know.

I watched her closely that morning. I don't know why, but I noticed everything about her that day. The way she added three more cubes of sugar when she thought I wasn't looking. The squeezing sound of the bottle as she lathered her eggs in catsup. Her perfectly shaped eyebrows. Her unlined eyes. Not a trace of makeup. My natural beauty. So confident, so secure.

"How was your trip, Mom?"

"Same old. I had to meet with three different clients while I was there, that's why I stayed all week."

Her facial expression changed suddenly and I could tell that her thoughts were focused on something else. "He played for Berkeley, right?"

"Who?"

"My real dad. Didn't you say he played basketball for your school?" She pushed her chair closer to me.

"He did."

"Yeah. I told Paul about him. He thinks it's so cool that he has the same interest as my father."

She'd always been inquisitive and insightful, so it was no surprise that she was asking me these probing questions. We spoke about him often. I wanted to dispel any doubts that she may have had about him, so I figured it was as good a time as any to press on.

"Baby girl?"

"Mmmm?" she let out as she chewed on a piece of toast.

"Why the sudden barrage of questions about Chris? Are you okay? I know it has something to do with you turning eighteen—are you planning to do anything?"

"No," she answered quickly, meeting my eyes. "I've just been thinking about him more. Like the similarities between Paul and him. And to be honest with you, I've been thinking of you, Mom."

"Me? How? Why?" I asked.

"I want you to be free. I see it more and more. The way you have that blank look on your face, the way you are with Dad. I want you to be happy too. I'm old enough now to see things as they are. I think being in love myself, I just know and appreciate those feelings more." There it was again. That look filled with so much contentment.

"Oh, Cia. I'm all right. I made a commitment to your dad and I'm sticking to it. Look around you. We are blessed with so many things. I have you. You're all I need."

"I'm going away this fall, Mom," her tone was tough and admonishing, "and these blessings—a walk in closet full of purses and shoes—they've been your cover for so long. Those things can't fill your heart up."

"Oh, I know. But I have my work. And a nice car to drive long distances to see my daughter," I teased lightheartedly.

"He adores you, you know. I know he has a temper, but he's under so much pressure with the Chief position at the hospital and all."

"I know, baby. I love him too. I do. Whatever it is you think you're seeing, cast it aside. It's all for the best and I couldn't ask for anything more. We have a happy life. Now let's continue this at lunch. You're going to be late!" I kissed her goodbye and she bolted out the front door, leaving her wallet and purse behind. I ran right after her. "Cia! Your bag!"

"Oh geez, Mom! Thank you!" she exclaimed breathlessly as she ran out of the car to meet me halfway. I remember thinking at that very instant how much she had of her father in her. His long graceful limbs. His breeziness. Always fleeting in and out.

"I love you, sweetie. Have a good day. See you at one."

"Love you too, Mommy. Later!" she squeaked as she stuck her arm out the window to wave happily at me while backing out of the driveway.

I WAITED FOR her to meet me but she never arrived. While at the restaurant, my phone rang off the hook but I didn't answer when the numbers came up unrecognized.

Four coffees.

A basket of bread. Two butters.

Tip, tap. Tip, tap. My fingernails on the table, playing a tune, drumming to a rhythm so discordant, Cia would surely disown me.

Thumping my feet. Admiring my new shoes.

Checking emails. Making phone calls. Noelle. The insurance guy. Leya.

Looking up Cia's Facebook status for any hint of where she's at.

Exactly two hours later, Joshua came flying through the doors, his hair disheveled, his face red from crying, his voice hoarse and gruff.

"Jade!" he barked hysterically as he pushed his way through the waiting crowd to reach our table. "Please, we have to leave now. It's Cia."

"What about her? Where is she? I've been waiting for hours for that girl."

He turned his head to look away from me. My heart stopped beating. There wasn't enough air in the world to fill my lungs. His eyes told me all I wanted to know.

"Accident. There's been an accident."

"NO! No. Josh, tell me she's okay! Where is she?"

He flinched as all heads turned towards my high pitched scream.

"She was flown to Northwestern. We have to get there now. Please, Jade. Come with me."

I stayed in my seat, my legs suddenly feeling like they were buried in cement. I couldn't move. My eyes blinked uncontrollably. I was shaking violently. *The last day of life. My last day of color. My last bright and sunny day. This is the day my life was brutally snatched away from me. Why was I still standing there, living, breathing?*

"Josh, No!" I cried and collapsed on the seat while he slid in between the booths to try to catch me.

Two police officers approached the table. One of them started to speak.

"Mrs. Richmond. We are so very sorry."

"No. No. Please, I'll pay anything to get her to the right hospital. My parents! Please call my parents. My father will have a helicopter fly me there now. My husband is a neurosurgeon. He has friends who can help. Wait a minute, please. Let me call them." I grabbed my phone and attempted to still my trembling hands enough to start dialing.

"Jade, your parents are on their way." Joshua tried to reach for me but I blanched at the mere thought of his touch. I wedged myself into the far end of the corner and huddled in a fetal position.

"Mrs. Richmond. Your daughter died on impact. We're here to take you to her."

Died. Did he say died? Who died? "Don't touch me!" I shouted as the air in my chest expanded the contents of my stomach, causing me to vomit forcefully all over myself and the table. "Get away from me, all of you!" I heaved, bending over on the ground and seizing my heart, desperate to hold on to it before it disappeared forever. "Please leave me alone!"

HOURS LATER, I sat in a dark, cold room, my back against the wall, my feet flat on the floor. A rancid stench lingered in the hall, but my senses were too numb to really care. I focused my eyes on the cement slab that separated me from her. All her life, I was never far away. It wasn't going to start then. I lived for her. I loved for her. There was never any other purpose in my life; I thought that I was born to be her mother.

As I waited for daylight to come, for the time when she would be taken away from me forever, the events of the day kept rambling through my head. In the blink of an eye, I lost my identity. Who I was and what I stood for lay lifeless on the steel bed before me.

Slowly, I stood up and walked towards my baby's body, without fear or repulsion. I was filled with undying devotion as I stroked her hair and kissed her lips. She was still so angelic, like a porcelain doll with golden hair and immaculate skin. How many times had I looked into this face and imagined the life that could have been? How many times had this face fulfilled my dreams, my hopes, my need to be loved?

She never went through an awkward stage. I was always amazed at the way that she went from perfect child to perfect woman. Always an angel.

She remained warm to the touch but nothing about her felt real. There were bruises on her arms, but not a single cut on her face. Where were the wounds? Internal bleeding, they said. Something about the probability of her losing her focus, which caused her to slam right into a parked garbage truck. Her Mini Cooper was wrapped around a lamppost as a result of the force. She was gone by the time they found her.

"I no longer have anything to live for, Cia," I whispered as I climbed into the bed beside her. "Please take me with you. My life is nothing without you."

TWENTY-FOUR

Guardian Angel
Eighteen Months Ago

OUR DAUGHTER WAS born and bred in Chicago, but San Francisco was where her heart always belonged. For the past eighteen years, our summers were spent there. Cia loved spending months at a time with her grandparents. My parents' neighbors and friends looked forward to her visits every year. With my father on the Board of the local golf club, she spent her summers working as a caddy on the greens. He loved to golf and so he found the perfect excuse to have her there with him whenever she was in town. It was only fitting to give in to my parents when they requested that she be interred in San Francisco. We had no family in Chicago and often spoke about relocating back home once Joshua's contract with Northwestern Hospital had expired.

When I was twelve years old, I obsessed endlessly about death. For some reason I realized one day that once you are born, there is no other way out of this world than to die. I was so afraid to die that

151

I stressed out about being alive. For months, I lay awake at night fearing death, horrified at the prospect of dying. I imagined what it would feel like to close my eyes and never wake up. Do you just black out in total obscurity and cease to exist? Why invest in life then, if you become nothing when you die? I began to search for answers, for the truth about the soul, and immersed myself in the church's teachings about heaven and hell and the afterlife. I forced myself to believe, assured myself that there's got to be more to this than waiting for my turn to die.

Years later, there I was, living in the irony of all my apprehensions, swept up in the maelstrom of my greatest fear.

She looked so tiny at the very end of the long aisle of St. Dominic's Church. It was a grandiose structure with arched walkways and gothic architecture. A large red carpet covered the original Italian marble floor and a glorious light shining through the French stained glass windows illuminated her casket. The church was full of people; close friends, acquaintances, and strangers. Parents of children who grew up with my daughter, guilt ridden and bereft over the loss that could easily have been theirs. There were flowers everywhere; the aisles looked like a blooming garden of colors. There was no room to move. It felt suffocating and confining. People and flowers blocked my view when all I wanted to see was her.

I sat at the front with Joshua, his mother, and my parents. For days I had been heavily medicated, waking up only to change and to eat despite the fact that I was also fed intravenously for fear of malnutrition. My husband was my rock throughout the entire ordeal. He picked up right where my life left off. I will always be thankful to him for that.

We decided on a closed casket at her wake despite the fact that Cia's face and body looked untouched. I didn't want people to remember her as anything other than the girl who was so full of life.

"Hija, I think your boss is here. I can see him approaching the altar," my mother notified me, rubbing my arm.

Joshua held me by the elbows to help me to stand up. The medications and lack of sustenance still had me feeling extremely weak. Slowly, we made our way towards Warren and Skip, who took me in their arms as soon as I reached them. I made no qualms about dissolving into tears; everyone who knew my daughter knew how close we were. Cia used to help do my filing for me on weekends. She was also the little girl who ran around the office spilling juice on the white carpet and writing on the walls with her crayons. We exchanged a few pleasantries before they left me to kneel in front of the casket.

I was about to sit down upon making my way back to our pew when I noticed a man walking hesitantly in my direction. I stopped in my tracks, supporting myself by leaning on the arm rest at the end of the wooden bench. He looked exactly the same as when I last saw him, his hair was a little longer but still bright and golden, his eyes were as blue as ever.

It was like seeing Cia come back to me in the form of an angel.

Or an archangel.

The fallen one. The one who started this all.

He continued to trudge slowly towards me, his gaze fixed on mine, never blinking his eyes until we stood two feet away from each other. I wanted more than anything in the world to touch his face. *Was he real?*

"Jae—" He cleared his throat. "Jade."

I tried to open my mouth to speak, but my vision turned hazy and it felt as if my eardrums had exploded. I attempted my best to force my eyes open, not wanting to lose sight of him ever again. But no matter how hard I strained to remain conscious, the darkness snatched him away from me and I was left with nothing.

"WHAT HAPPENED?" I croaked when I woke up to find myself lying on the couch of what looked like the church rectory.

Joshua was crouched down on the floor holding a bottle of smelling salts. *Did he take this from the church's old medicine cabinet? Smelling salts. Really?* "You fainted. How are you feeling?" he asked worriedly.

"I'm okay. I don't know what came over me. I just blacked out." *I saw him. That's what came over me.*

"Yeah. The exhaustion is getting to you. I think I should take you home as soon as you're able to get up," he said gently as he stroked my forehead with his fingers.

"Was that him? Was he here?" I asked, knowing full well that he would know who I was referring to. A tiny flickering light caught the corner of my eye. I turned my head from side to side, wondering what it was that had suddenly disturbed my attention enough to distract me from the conversation.

Josh didn't notice anything. "He still is. He refuses to leave until I tell him that you're okay."

"Can I see him?"

It was a moth. A tiny, colorless moth with powdery wings that flapped around me in a circle. It finally rested on top of the unlit lamp on the table beside me.

"What for? He walked out of your life nineteen years ago. No, you can't see him." He positioned himself directly in front of me and I responded by moving to the end of the couch.

"I walked out of his, Josh. Please… let me see him for a few minutes." My high-pitched tone seemed to get his attention. He knew better than to upset my fragile emotional state any further. After all, it was a miniscule request in the grand scheme of things. "I'm okay. Please help me straighten up."

He grumbled to himself but offered me his hand so I could pull on it as I sat upright. I swung my legs over the couch and leaned against its back with my feet tucked under my legs. Joshua left abruptly, only to be followed in immediately by the man I left my heart with years ago.

They used to look like night and day, but twenty years later, the boy I left behind looks just as accomplished and well put together as the man I married.

"Jade!" He rushed over to me and took me in his arms. "I'm terribly sorry for your loss."

Surprisingly, I didn't shed any tears. "Thank you, Chris. How did you know?" I pushed him away only because I wanted to look at him. *Cia. I see Cia.*

"It was weird… you'll never believe it. Something in me told me that you were in town and that I had to see you. I can't explain it, but I called your parents' house and Concha told me what happened." He held my face in his hands. "You haven't changed at all. You still look the same."

"You too. You look great."

"Oh Jade, I can't imagine what you must be going through. I am so sorry about your daughter. I've stayed away for too long. Please know that I'm here now, for you, as your friend. I know you need to get back to the church, so I won't keep you, but may I call you soon to catch up?" He removed his phone from his back pocket. "Could you program your phone number in here for me?"

I punched in my number and handed the phone back to him. He held my hand for a few seconds before releasing it.

"I'm so sorry again, Jade. Please know that you and your family are in my prayers. I'll call you tomorrow to see how you're doing."

And as I watched him walk out the door, I turned to the moth on the lamp and whispered, "Thank you, Cia, for watching over me."

TWENTY-FIVE

Used

Nine Months Ago

LIKE CLOCKWORK, MY car pulled into the driveway at 9:26 pm. And as in many nights past, I sat in the dark for minutes after the garage door had closed to prepare myself for the long night ahead. I leaned my head back and allowed myself to reflect on the feelings that I'd been holding back. My entire perspective on life changed when I lost my daughter. At first, I spent those days trying to put the blame on someone else. No one else was with her on the day of the accident, so it wasn't like I could fault someone else for her death. Even the driver of the garbage truck suffered the wrath of my anger. He had simply parked the truck during his lunch break to enjoy his sandwich. Then there was no one else to focus my anger on except for my husband. I blamed him for buying her a little car—I told him that he should have known better. Did he check the safety ratings before giving in to her request? Did he speak to the paramedics and should we sue them because they gave up on reviving her too easily?

What use was he to me? A world class neurosurgeon and he couldn't save our daughter. But then, as days went by, I realized that it was my feelings for Joshua that had changed. Undoubtedly, the loss of Cia had brought on the demise of my marriage. I loved her enough to sacrifice my heart for someone who gave us a stable home. After she died, I couldn't bear to be near him any longer. My heart was as lifeless as the body that I spent the night with at the morgue.

With a deep breath, I opened the car door and stepped out, acknowledging the fact that he was home that night.

We lived in a gorgeous home in a gated neighborhood, custom built with a flowing floor plan and more bedrooms and bathrooms than our little family could have ever filled. It had been professionally decorated by one of the city's top interior designers, whose personal touches included walnut floors, stone tiles, coffered ceilings, crown molding, and a gourmet kitchen with state of the art appliances and granite countertops.

The lights in the kitchen were bright and blinding. He was standing by the immense stove, stirring a pot of stew.

"I'm making your favorite. Vietnamese beef," he said, smiling as I untied my scarf in an attempt to ease the choked up feeling I'd been having every time I had to face him.

"Hey." I held my coat in my arms as I made my way towards the closet.

"How was your day?"

"It was good. And yours?"

"Same old. Surgery went well today. I got it done in four hours."

With a contrived movement, I ambled towards the cupboards and pulled out two plates to lay them on the table. The muted feeling of distress was deafening, so much so that I banged the plates together as I placed them on the mats just to break the ice between us. This had been my life for the past year. Rehearsed and hushed. I continued on for a few seconds until his voice broke into my thoughts.

"I loved her too, you know," he said sadly.

"I know you did."

"Jade, how long are you going to shut me out?"

"I don't know, Josh. I'm trying."

"I've begged you to see a marriage counselor with me. I love you. We need to save what we have."

What do we have?

"I can't talk about it right now." The room was filled with pregnant silence. Silence that might give birth to words. Words that can't be taken back. Words that can't be ignored.

"Did you ever love me, Jade?"

"I don't know, Josh. Please. Not tonight."

How should I have answered his question? Our lifeline was gone. She helped me hold it all together. That night, like all the other nights, I no longer wanted to try. It happened on the day that she died. My heart threw it all up like a cancer that had slowly ravaged my body over a span of nineteen years, leaving me with nothing but shame and hatred for the life that I had. I was desperate to feel love, to revive myself. I wasn't going to keep it together for the sake of anyone anymore.

I caught a glimpse of a large vase full of flowers in the middle of the counter.

"Whose flowers are those? Who put them here?" I demanded, my tone full of venom and spite. "Sylvia knows better than that. I've told her time and again, no flowers in this house. Ever."

He stepped away from the stove and slowly walked towards the table. Calmly, he lifted the vase up and left the room, carrying it in his arms. As my eyes followed in his direction, I noticed an empty bottle of scotch next to the sink by the bar. He returned in a few seconds and his tone was forceful and challenging. "She was trying to fucking help. It's not her fault."

"Well, she knows better than to do that. Next time she tries to help, I'm going to fire her. It's not like we can't find another housekeeper." I wanted to stop but I couldn't. "I'm going to go upstairs to change before dinner."

He grabbed my arm as soon as I tried to walk away. "Sit," he commanded. "You're going to talk to me whether you like it or not. I deserve more than this, Jade. You've been distant for so long. I'm so tired of second guessing what you're thinking. It's been nine months since we lost her. How long are you going to make me pay for your pain?"

I saw the hurt in his eyes as he uttered those words. He was right. He needed to know the truth. That there was no more need to pretend.

"What can I do to make it right between us?" he asked, stroking his hand up and down my arm.

"Nothing. I just need time. Please." I found myself cringing from his touch.

"Time for what? Look around you. I've given you a good life, everything you ever wanted. I took your bastard daughter and made her my own. I loved her and raised her and now that she's gone, you're making it seem like it's been such a hard life for you." He spoke through gritted teeth. "What in God's name do you want me to do?"

"All I'm asking for is some time. Please understand. I'm nothing without her. I'm trying so hard to cope with everything. My job. My travels. My parents. They're what's holding me together."

"All of them and not me."

"Josh, it isn't like you didn't know this before. I tried to tell you, even when she was still here. I tried to tell you that things haven't been working between us. But you never listened." There was no more room for niceties—it was time to try to break free.

"My life was perfect with you."

"It wasn't!" I countered. "Please try to remember. Felicia was the glue that held us together. Our love for her—we translated it into our love for each other. We deserve to find happiness. You're a wonderful person; you're just not for me."

There was something oddly off about him. He seemed agitated and jumpy. He wasn't slurring his words, but he had a glassy look in his eyes that I would never forget. I coaxed myself not to fall into his trap because I was afraid to say more than I already had. But he kept on going. He continued his charge to egg me on.

"It's him, isn't it, Jade? You never gave me a chance. Why would you love someone like that? He's a nobody."

"Joshua, please. I'm warning you—"

"Warning me about what? All these years, did you think of him while we were together? I saw how you reacted to him when he came to the service. Did you think of him when I fucked you that night?"

Sex. I repaid him for his love with sex. What does that make me? "Stop it!" I yelled, struggling to get away from him. As soon as he released my arm, I gathered up my things and did anything I could to keep my hands busy. I lifted my purse. I put it down. I moved around the kitchen. I took a kitchen towel and started wiping down the counters. Anything. He wasn't going to let me leave the kitchen, so I tried to move around him instead of standing still.

"Please, Jade. I'm begging you. Try. Try to love me again."

"That's it," I said. "I don't know if I ever did. You were so good to me, so kind to take me in and raise my daughter as if she were your own. I will always be grateful to you for that. But it's over. I don't want to be with you. I'm drowning. I need to get out." I gagged as the words escaped from my mouth.

"You're going back to that lowlife, aren't you?"

"Joshua. I warned you. Please stop, now!"

"He's a good for nothing carpenter. How is he going to give you the life that you're used to living?"

"This has nothing to do with him. I'm just asking for time to figure myself out." My defense mechanism has always been to keep busy, to distract myself by focusing on the tasks in front of me. That night, my task was to get dinner on the table. I busied myself around him, taking a serving bowl and spooning some of the stew in it. I opened the refrigerator and retrieved the leftover rice from the other night. The shrill ring of my phone broke the silence. The problem was that it was lying on the table next to where he stood.

"Oh look, speaking of the motherfucker. It's the enigma that is Chris Wilmot."

"Josh, please just let it go to voicemail." The beeping sound of the microwave faded into the background.

"How often does he call you? Why is he calling?"

"I don't know. I really don't." The one honest thing that I said all night, and he didn't believe me.

He banged his fists on the table. The silverware lifted neatly into the air before crashing down onto the floor. "I'm going to ask you again. This time, not so nicely. How often does he call you?"

"He doesn't. I'm not sure why he's calling now."

"Bullshit."

The phone rang again. This time he answered it. He was visibly shaking and his hold on the phone was so pronounced, I feared that it was going to crumble in his hands.

"Wilmot. Stay the fuck away from her. Don't ever call my wife again."

I cowered back in fear as I heard the shattering of the phone against the brick wall.

He looked at me, his face grimaced in pain. It was like a scene from a horror movie where the villain's facial features mutated from a human being into a deformed monster. I knew what was going to happen next. I could see the venom in his eyes.

I tried to run past him, but he blocked me.

"Where are you going, whore?" he spat out as he pressed against me, bumping me with his chest. He moved forward, I moved backward. "You're not going anywhere," he screamed in my ear as he lifted me up by my arms and pushed me against the wall.

"Please, Josh. Let's talk. Please let me down!" I cried, trying to push him away.

He started to cry. An excruciatingly painful howl emerged from his chest. "Don't you understand, Jade? I've loved you for so many years. I've taken care of you. I've given you my life. I can't stand the thought of another man touching you, of another man seeing this immaculate body of yours." He squeezed my breast and brought his face down to kiss it. "Look at you, my beauty. You look just as young as when I first met you. You were his then. You came to me because there was no one else. I should have known that the empty look in your eyes was because he still had you. Well, guess what? No one deserves you but me. I took you in when you were a used rag pregnant with a child. That should count for something, shouldn't it?" His wicked laugh was revolting. Bile rose to my throat.

"Josh, please, please, you're hurting me. I'm going to be sick."

"Sick? I'm sick. I'm sick with love for you. "No more talking. I love you, Jade. No one is ever going to touch you but me."

Roughly, he slid me down the wall and yanked my feet away until my head hit the floor with a thud. I tried to reach my arms up to hold his face, but he was shaking so violently that I ended up scratching him on the cheek.

"You bitch!" he yelled as he lifted his hand and hit me on the face.

I felt the warm sensation of blood trickling down my lips. Was it from my nose? My cheeks? Was that horrible gurgling sound coming from me?

"This is mine," he growled as he rolled me over on my stomach and roughly hiked my skirt up to my waist. I heard him unbuckling his belt and pulling down his pants. My head was turned sideways, my left cheek on the marble floor. I couldn't move; he had me pinned down by his full bodyweight. My hands were twisted behind my back, my shoulders felt like they were being pulled out of their sockets. He entered me furiously, rotating his hips, his movements intended to tear my insides apart.

"I'm sorry, Jade. If I can't have you, no one will," he whispered gruffly in my ear.

I felt his weight lift off me as he continued his thrusts, only to be replaced by the full weight of two hands on my neck. *Take me home, Cia. I miss you so much.*

The pain in my chest was indescribable. It felt like all my insides had burst and blood was spurting out of my lungs; I could feel the heat spreading from my chest to my shoulders. Everything happened in slow motion. Before I knew it, my vision was slowly, slowly dwindling in and out. The scratches on the marble floor, vivid and marked before he put his hands on my neck, were fading. For the second time in my life, I noticed the ground underneath me. It hurt to cough. It hurt to blink my eyes. Images of my life started to play out in front of me. All I could see was a young, broken girl at 23, holding her baby in her arms, and an ardent young man who wanted nothing in his life but to love her. I owed him so much. He did take me in. He took care of our daughter. He made us a family.

"Jesus Christ! What am I doing? Oh my God! Jade!"

Let me go, Josh, it's okay. I'm craving sleep. I'm just so exhausted.

TWENTY-SIX

Damage
Nine Months Ago

I WOKE UP feeling like I had just been run over by a truck. I floated in and out of consciousness, but my eyes felt so heavy that it took a great effort for me to lift up my eyelids. I kept them closed despite hearing voices all around me. My nose was uncomfortably itchy and when I weakly reached my hand over to touch it, I found that it had been casted. My other hand was held by someone else sitting close by my bed. I couldn't remember where I was or how I got there. There was a burning pain between my legs that seemed to dissipate as long as I held them close together. As time went by, the voices around me, although somewhat muffled, became clearer.

"Mr. Albin, the police report is complete except for a statement from your daughter as soon as she regains consciousness."

"I don't want anyone speaking to her until she is well enough to do so," my father said sternly. "Her physical injuries will speak for themselves. I want that bastard put away forever!" His voice was filled with so much pain. I knew that he was crying. "It kills me to think about what could have happened if Mr. Wilmot hadn't rushed over to check on her."

"What did the medical report say?" the voice continued.

"Multiple lacerations on the face and neck. Tissue injury of the neck, broken shoulder blade, broken nose. Rape."

My mother let out a shrill cry and I heard my father's heavy footsteps move to the side of the room where I assumed she sat. As they spoke around me, the hand that held mine squeezed tighter.

Slowly, I mustered all my strength to open my eyes. He was looking right at me, the man who held my hand.

"Jade? Frank, I think she's awake!"

I glanced around to see my mother and father rush to my bedside.

"Jade! Thank God! My baby girl!" my mother cried. "Don't move, don't."

I pointed weakly to the remote control and motioned for them to adjust it so my head was slightly elevated.

"I'm okay," I whispered softly. My throat was on fire. I spoke in a breathy whisper. No voice. "Where is he?" Flashes of what had transpired ran through my mind, the pain in my chest becoming more pronounced as I tried to process everything.

"Don't talk, honey. It's okay. It will all be okay. We're here," my father assured me.

Everything went black before I could do anything else. By the time I reopened by eyes, Chris was the only one sitting next to me. I heard the soft, heavy breathing that told me he was asleep. I crept my hand over to where he rested his head and stroked his hair. He lifted his forehead but kept his chin resting on the mattress.

"You still have a lot of hair," I whispered. He chuckled lightly and closed his eyes as if savoring the memory. I always loved touching his hair.

"Hi." He smiled. "I'm so glad you're back."

"Now that my parents are gone, will you tell me what happened?"

"Okay. Where do you want me to start?"

"How—" I covered my throat. It hurt so much to talk. "How did you get to me?"

"I called to let you know that I had just arrived in Chicago. I had a meeting with another construction company the next day and wanted to check to see how you were doing. I feel horrible, Jade. I know it was my phone call that set him off."

"No, it wasn't, really. I was trying to explain how I had been feeling that night. He was already angry by the time he picked up your call."

"I rushed over right after he hung up the phone. By the time I reached your house, the ambulance was on the way. He was kneeling right next to you, freaking out about what he had just done. He didn't contest anything. He told the police exactly what happened."

"Where is he now?"

"Undergoing psychiatric evaluation at St. Alexis. Your father seems to think that he's going to be committed. The stress of what happened to your daughter plus the alienation of your marriage could have caused him to have a nervous breakdown."

"I'm not pressing charges. A large part of it was my fault."

"No, Jade. He's the only one who's responsible for what he did. He nearly killed you."

"I wanted to die. To be with Felicia."

"No. You'll get through this. I'm here now. I'm not going anywhere. I'll see you through every step of your recovery. She left you here for a reason. It's time to start living for yourself. I promise you, you'll be happy again someday."

I didn't register what he said, still vacant and unaffected. "I'm so tired, Chris. I just want to sleep."

"Rest, my love. I'll be right here when you wake up."

I closed my eyes, still holding onto his hand. Where did my heart go? I had lost two people in my life and all I wanted to do was close my eyes and vanish.

"Pajama, pajama, pajama," I can hear my mother chant. "That's what you would say, Jade, when you were five. You thought closing your eyes made you invisible. You would repeat those words over and over again whenever you were upset about something."

"Pajama, pajama, pajama."

CHRIS REMAINED WITH me for another week as I recovered in the hospital. It took an argument between us for him to finally agree to head back to San Francisco to tend to his business. My body was taking longer to recover from the damage of the assault than anticipated. I sustained multiple bodily injuries including abrasions and bruises on my neck. I was told that it may take years for them to disappear due to the broken blood vessels caused by the pressure that was exerted when he choked me. The mark of his fingers almost resembled a ligature mark, something I was told was common to the trauma of strangulation. My neck was swollen due to internal hemorrhaging. My vocal cords were almost ruptured. My left shoulder and my nose were in casts. I underwent physical and psychiatric counseling and attended a rape support group while I was at the hospital.

I held no hatred for Joshua. Only pity. He loved me so much, and he did what he could to make me love him back for almost twenty years.

As the weeks went by, I felt strong enough to begin the process of healing. Until a few days ago, I hadn't been able to return to our home. My father had purchased a two bedroom condo on Lakeshore Drive to ensure that I had a place to stay after being released from the hospital. I wasn't well enough to fly to San Francisco, although my mother tried to move mountains to get me to yield to her desperate pleas. I was in contact with Joshua's mother, as I held no ill will against him (or her, for that matter). I just wanted to put this behind me and move on with my life.

I went in through the garage like I always did and slowly made my way around the house, an overwhelming feeling of being loved surrounding me. This was the home where we raised the most amazing little girl. I will always want this house to remain as a testament to the love we had as a family. I will never forget what Josh had done for us. He was her father, he was my husband, and he was my friend.

One hour later, I found myself sitting in the middle of her room surrounded by everything she had accumulated in her very short life. The ringing of my phone quickly postponed the tears that had just begun to form in my eyes. I broke out in a smile as soon as I heard his voice.

"Hey. Are you at your house? Is everything okay?"

"Yes. Concha is here with me. My mother sent her to Chicago to care for me for a few weeks. We're going through Felicia's stuff. I think she was a closet hoarder." I held the phone away from me for a quick second, intent on hiding the sound of my sniffles.

"Oh God. Really?" He snickered. "Why does that sound so familiar?"

I blush as the memory assails me. "I thought I'd do a little at a time. I'm going to leave most of her things as is, but wanted to just pack up a few of her pictures to take with me to the condo. Paul had also asked for a couple of her things."

"Sounds like a good idea. Aside from that, how are you doing? Are you okay?"

"As okay as I can be, I guess. I miss her so much." I paused to lighten up my tone. "I've started running on the treadmill. Really slow for now and only one mile, but it felt great!"

"Baby steps, Jade, okay? Promise me you won't go overboard."

"I promise," I said as I weaved through the piles of Cia's clothing on the floor.

"Good girl. I'm going to try to take a few days off to see you next week. Will that be okay?"

"You don't have to, Chris. I know how busy you are. I'm really doing fine. Concha is fattening me up with her adobos and empanadas," I argue.

"I want to. I'll call you once my schedule is more certain."

"Okay. Thank you for checking on me."

"Take care, Jae. I'll call again tomorrow."

PART III: COLLIDING

The Present

"You're the only truth, that I ever knew,
Like the stars we burn forever.
So listen when I say to you,
'I'll be there, you're not alone.'
When the sun turns into shadows,
When you call and no one's there.
When the lights go out inside you,
I'll be there, you're not alone."

"When the World Breaks Your Heart" by The Goo Goo Dolls

TWENTY-SEVEN

Truth

THE LOSS OF my reverie is marked by the conductor's gentle nudge on my shoulder. "End of the line, Miss. Boy, I wish I could sleep as deeply as that!" he chides as he watches me rub my eyes and glance at the empty seats around me.

"Sorry, I must have really been tired from working late last night," I make the excuse as I gather up my things. The guy sitting next to me must have thought I was a basketcase - crying, laughing, constantly moving in my seat. I stand up, embarrassed and resolved to find another car to sit in tomorrow. I take a taxicab to the marina for my planned morning run, pulling out my phone from my purse as the driver careens through the dizzying lines of traffic and pedestrians on Wacker Drive. I see a few missed calls from Lucas and finally a text message:

Lucas: *It has been a while without hearing from you. What is going on? Please answer your phone.*

I'm about to relapse from all this. Same old routine. He texts, I don't answer. I miss him so I give in and text back days later. Every time this happens, the counter is reset to zero and I start the cycle of breaking this addiction all over again. I've prayed for so long for the strength to move on from this and yet, here I am staring at my phone and interpreting every single word he has written to me. I delete his texts, I delete his number. And then it pops back up on my phone and I reset him up as a contact. It's a habit I can't seem to give up. Yet.

I run my normal loop towards the Shedd Aquarium, enjoying the crisp spring air. My head is finally clearing up from this morning's daydream. The past is the past, and I must face the future ahead of me. It's a future alone, without a specific purpose, but a future all the same. I make good enough time this morning to take a leisurely detour to enjoy the newly renovated river walk. There are boats on the water, gliding across its ripple-less surface as if sliding on smooth, solid ice. I stop to watch some university students calling out instructions as they guide their scull around the larger boats.

"Jade." I hear that familiar voice and immediately know who it is. I turn around to find his gentle eyes fixed on me.

"Chris? What are you doing here?" I am genuinely surprised. It's been a while since I last saw him. I pulled away from my old life in the nine months after being hurled into the eye of the never ceasing storm.

"I figured you'd be out for your morning run. I stayed after my two day convention to try to find you." He steps in to embrace me and I let him. "How have you been, Jade?"

"I'm good, thank you. I'm sorry I disappeared for a while. I figured I needed some time on my own to try to get better."

He gives me his knowing look as he steps back from me. "A lot has happened to you since we last saw each other, huh?"

I nod my head, not really knowing what else to say.

Quietly, he takes my hand and leads me down the path while we walk in silence. "You look great."

"Yeah, right." I remove my running cap and attempt to smooth my hair down. "Sweaty and all, huh?" I chuckle. The truth is that he's the one who looks amazing. The women walking past us do a double take as their eyes catch a glimpse of his good looks and rugged appearance.

"Jae, I just have to ask you. It's been eating me up for the past year after I saw you again at the service. I've been wanting to tell you how I feel. I want you to know. I never stopped, Jae. I never stopped thinking about you. Do you ever wonder why I never married?" He retreats abruptly and turns to face me, zooming straight into my eyes. *As if they held all the answers. He's right. They're all buried in there. And if I close them long enough, I can still disappear.*

"It's been so long, Chris. I don't question anything anymore. Things are the way they are and I think I'm managing to stay afloat for now," I answer bitterly.

He leads me by my elbow to a park bench directly facing the lake. We sit and watch the other runners pass us by. I freeze when a bird comes too close to us. Chris shoos it away and laughs. "I haven't forgotten. How did we survive San Francisco?"

"We never went back to the Wharf after that seagull stole my churro."

I'll never forget that day. The bird was no less than mammoth-sized, and its giant, orange webbed feet covered my entire face as its long, sharp beak snatched the food directly from my mouth. Chris found me on the wooden bridge, shocked and in tears, knocked down by the force of the seagull's wings. I haven't been able to share my space with a bird since.

We both laugh. I don't know why, but the old feelings come back and I'm not too pleased with him again. I'm resentful. But not at him. At myself. For never moving forward. I know that now as we sit on this old bench holding hands. I still love him. Not the way I did when I was younger, but this love never left me. It never gave Joshua a chance.

"Why are you here, Chris?"

"Because I want a second chance, Jae. I may not have amounted to much, but I never stopped loving you. But before anything else, I want to ask you something. Call me crazy. Tell me I'm wrong." His blue eyes look darker than normal. He shifts his body sideways to face me, and pulls me closer to him. "Felicia."

The mere mention of her name still rattles me. I lean back away from him for fear that the truth will be revealed by the look on my face. "Chris, please. It still hurts to talk about her."

"Jae. Pictures of her at the funeral. Throughout the years we were apart. She has my eyes. She has my hair. I remember years ago, when she was 12 or 13, I saw you two walking out of your parents' home and the way she looked, her movements—I remember thinking that I was looking into a mirror, that I was looking at myself." His voice cracks as if it pains him to say it. And his eyes. They want to hurt me, slash me, punish me.

Ear infection. Water in my ears. That's how I feel at this very juncture. Flashes of him and her bombard my thoughts and then they merge together as if they're one. I can't hear a word he's saying. My heart beats so loudly that his voice starts to muffle; the only sound I can discern is the booming thump in my chest. I stand up to leave. "I can't do this right now." Quickly, I turn on my heels and run.

"Jade!"

I don't even know why I attempt to do that. He catches up with me in three steps and roughly yanks my arm, twisting me around to face him. He grips me by the shoulders and gently touches my face with one hand. "Tell me."

Anger takes over my guilt. He left me. He cheated on me. Why would he deserve her? I smack my hands on his chest. This time, he loses his footing.

"No! Chris! She's mine, no one else's. Don't take her away from me. She was all I ever had and I'm not giving her up to anyone else!" I screech, loud enough for people walking along the path to look our way. I break away again and run. I run as fast as I can, knowing that I'm going to be at a dead end soon. He runs right behind me, knowing this too. It's a route I know too well. It ends at the stone structure protecting the walls of the city aquarium.

It all concludes here. Now.

I halt when I literally hit the wall. I don't turn around because I know he's right behind me. I feel his breath on my neck; we're both panting and gasping for air. Maybe it's time for me to share this secret. He deserves to know. I spin around slowly to face him. Gradually and deliberately, I say the words out loud: "Yes. She was yours too. She was our daughter."

Any devastation wreaks havoc in its wake. There is pain and sorrow and a loss that can never be replaced. I left my heart with him and in its place I took his child. We have nothing to show for it now. In its place is a gash so deep that neither of us can ever hope to forget. Nothing in this lifetime will bring comfort to this affliction. Nothing in this world will make it disappear.

The wail that bursts from his lips as he drops down to his knees and sobs uncontrollably is a sound I will never forget. He bows his head down and covers it with his hands. Impulsively, I kneel down to touch him, but he recoils when I try to enclose him in my arms.

The waves never cease crashing against the breakwall, marking the ebb and flow of the tide. It reminds me that life doesn't stop despite the blows, the pain, or the setbacks. You can allow the pain to wash you away or you can hold on for dear life and pick up the pieces of the broken shards left lying on the ground after the storm subsides. A work of art, though horribly disfigured, is still a thing of beauty. Such is the task that's been placed right in front of us.

Live or exist. The choice has always been mine.

TWENTY-EIGHT

Who Will It Be?

TWO DAYS PASS after my meeting with Chris. I don't take calls from anybody. Not him, not Lucas. Contrary to the past few months, I no longer sit and watch my phone. I fill my days with work, making sure that I schedule back to back meetings and immerse myself in the millions of projects I've started. I read books like there was no tomorrow. I force myself not to get lost in my thoughts. I live here and now. I don't think of the past, I don't hope for the future. For some reason, I feel relieved. I no longer feel as alone I have for the past twenty years. Sharing this secret with Chris makes me feel lighter, less burdened.

This afternoon, I'm lost in silent reflection while I sit in the front pew of my church, waiting to speak to someone I've been avoiding for a few months. He approaches me slowly, a warm smile on his face. The silver in his hair and the speed of his gait are a direct contradiction to his booming voice and magnetic personality. He has been my friend for as long as I can remember.

"Good morning, Jade," he says lightheartedly. "How have you been?" He genuflects slowly before rising up to take a seat right next to me.

"Hi, Father Mike. How are you? Sorry I haven't called in a while. Busy with work and all."

"I understand. I've been thinking and praying for you. How are things? You still look a little gaunt and tired." He takes my hand and squeezes it gently.

I nod my head, accepting the fact that I'm still a work in progress. "Father, I thought I'd stop by to make sure that everything is set for Felicia's mass. I know that you moved your schedule around to accommodate it and wanted to thank you personally for that."

"Jade, you know I wouldn't have had it any other way. Everything is set. I saw the mass schedule and the ladies at the church will touch base with Noelle for some pictures and whatever it is you want to place at the altar."

"Thank you. I'll let her know to expect the call."

He casts his eyes on the ground before squinting up at me. "She was like a daughter to me. I've been wanting to talk to you about her. Is today a good day for that?"

It's been two years since she left me. I think it's time to hear what he has to say. "Today's as good as any. What's wrong?" I take a deep breath. This doesn't sound good, but I need to be ready.

"She always knew, Jade. She would talk to me about it. She would always ask me about her father. And as she got older, she would tell me how much she appreciated your honesty about Joshua and Chris." There's no one in the church but us. He doesn't need to whisper. His tone is sure and articulate, inflecting at some points together with a squeeze of my hand.

"It was important for me that she knew where she came from. I wanted her to know that she was a product of pure love."

"Because she knew that you had none of that for Joshua." Somehow we've never really said this out loud. He doesn't look sad or uncomfortable. It's like pointing out a fact of life that's no surprise at all.

"Yes. The day that she—" I stop to swallow my tears. "The day she died, she told me how she felt about it."

He takes hold of my other hand before he continues. Protectively, he holds them steady, as if preserving me from a fall. "She told me that it hurt her to see you try so hard. Those eyes of yours couldn't fool anyone, not even your daughter. She asked me to pray that you find your happiness one day. She loved you so much."

"I loved her more than my life." I choke on my words and start to cry. I cry because I feel her love enveloping my heart and I can't reciprocate it now that she's gone.

"She knew that. She left us with so much love and security in her heart. She lived a happy, protected, and stable life, Jade. She used to tell me how lucky she felt when compared to all her other friends, how loved she was. How you and Joshua had given up your realities to focus on raising her properly."

"Sounds so much like Cia. I don't know where all that insight came from. She was always so intuitive, so mature."

"I wonder whom she took after?" he teases, the lines in his venerable eyes lightening up, making him look as young as ever to me.

"Thank you for letting me know, Father," I say, feeling safe and secure in his presence. He keeps his hold on my hands, shaking it back and forth as he stresses a point.

"You did a good job with her, Jade. She was a light to many lives."

We spend the next few minutes sitting silently. No words, just memories. I retrace my steps in my head and unwittingly play with my hands.

He consciously pulls me out of my trance, letting go of my hands and leaning back in relaxation. "What else is going on? Have you heard from the Tribunal yet?"

"I received an update letter telling me that it should be final by the end of September this year."

"Yes, that's more or less how long it should take. How are you feeling about it?"

"You were right. Getting an annulment is the first step. I don't know what the next one should be, but I really want Joshua to have his chance at finding real love," I say, waving my hand in the air emphatically.

"And you? What about your chance?" he asks.

"I told him, Father. About Felicia."

"You told who what about Felicia?"

"Chris. He confronted me a few days ago. Said he knew from the moment he saw her pictures at the funeral service."

"A father will always know, Jade," he replies, his voice soft but matter of fact. "I'm not surprised. How did he take it?"

"It broke him. At first, seeing him suffer in front of me made me feel vindicated. But then I realized that that's not what I want for him. I want him to make peace with it."

"And you have to help him get that peace. I'm sorry to have to tell you this, but you need to reach out to him and help him with his pain. Healing him will heal you too."

"I know, Father. You're right."

"What about Lucas? What's going on with him? Did you tell him about Felicia?"

"No. Not yet." I laugh wickedly at the statement. "He's only 14 years older than her. Closer to her age than mine."

"Jade." He shakes his head at me. He doesn't find me funny, this friend of mine.

"Sorry."

"Are you in love with him?"

"I thought I was. Yes. Until Chris two days ago."

"You saved Joshua with what you thought was your love. Don't do this again with Chris. You can't fix everyone. You need to be selfish enough to want to fix yourself. If Lucas is your heart, give in to it. You don't have to force Chris' love on you, or your love on him, just because you want to help him to know your daughter."

I take his hand in mine and move close enough for him to drape his arm around my shoulder. I lean on his chest, feeling the soft cloth of his robes on my cheeks.

"I love you, Father Mike."

"I love you too, Jade. God loves you more than you will ever know. Accept his love. Know that His peace will come to you soon. You are a remarkable woman and you deserve to be loved."

TWENTY-NINE

Crescent Park

"HI, CONCHA! IS Mama here?" I hug her tightly as I walk into my parents' home. Danilo the chauffer has taken my bags from the car and handed them to her. I don't really wait to hear her answer, I proceed towards my parents' bedroom to find my mother in the dressing room.

"Hi, Mama!"

"Jade!" She turns around to enfold me in her arms. "I'm so happy to see you! Daddy will be home in a couple of hours. Are you here to meet with him? He's out golfing with the Mercers."

I don't answer her question, but walk around the living area connected to their bedroom, familiarizing myself with the new renovations that were done a few months ago. A warm feeling of contentment takes me by surprise as I fix my eyes on a life-sized painting of Felicia on the hallway wall leading to the other bedrooms. My mother's dressing table is filled with pictures of her; suddenly, I am filled with deep love and admiration for the way that she weathered through our loss in a manner more dignified than mine. I know it wasn't easier for her, but someone had to stay strong. She did it for me.

I feel ashamed and selfish to have these thoughts at all. Everywhere I turn there are freshly cut flowers in vases and in pots, in and around her bedroom. I feel claustrophobic, suffocated; the feelings of that day still surface so easily. Another panic attack washes over me, only to be soothed by the sound of her voice.

"Hija? Come sit down with me for a while. Have you had lunch? Let me ask Concha to bring us some cold cuts." Slowly, she goes from table to table, removing the flower vases and placing them on the floor outside of her bedroom door. She clears the room in minutes.

"Remove the traces of her trauma and give her time to accept them again," the therapist advised my parents.

"Thank you for doing that," I say as I lean over to kiss her on the cheek.

We sit next to each other on the couch, face to face, my hand in hers. She knows why I'm here.

"Chris came to see me last week," she starts out.

"What? He did? Why?"

"He wanted to know about Cia."

"It was time to tell him, Mama."

"I know, Jadey. I know. And I'm so sorry for the way I acted towards him before." She starts to cry. "He would have been such a good father to her."

"Don't cry, Mama. Twenty years is too long for this ruse to continue. I want Chris to regain his spirit. I want Joshua to find his happiness. I want to clean up this tangled mess so we can all live what's left of our lives in peace."

"It's time to add some color into your life. The brightness of your eyes doesn't match the sadness in your soul. When you were born, I wanted to name you Jade because all I could see were those big green eyes from where I was on the hospital bed as they took you away to clean you up. And your dad. Do you know why he agreed with your name? Because he said that Jade also means tranquility. Years later, he told me that your presence in his life gave him the serenity he longed for at the end of every struggle he went through, moving to this country, trying to make a name for himself..." She daintily dabs her eyes with a tissue. "You are our peace."

"Oh, Mama."

She straightens up and looks at me pointedly. "What does this mean for you and Chris?"

"I don't know yet. These past few months... this self-destructive behavior... no one can stop the cycle but me. I alienated my husband and hurt him, I risked my job and career, I disregarded my health and well-being." I laugh half-heartedly. "Cia wouldn't be very happy about this right now."

"She would tell you off and cuss you out," my mother agrees.

"I'm so sorry I disappointed you, Mama!" I cry, seeking penitence for the past twenty years. "Not just for what has happened in the last two years, after Cia, but for luring you into believing that everything was fine with my life."

"Oh, Jade. I only wish that I knew how you were feeling. I would have been there for you. You're my daughter, and I love you. You have never ever done anything to let us down. You have always made being your parents such a privilege for us."

"Thank you." I shake my head slightly, knowing that nothing more needs to be said. I need to accomplish what I came here to do. I allow her to cuddle me for a few minutes before kissing her forehead and getting ready to leave.

"Go," she encourages me. "Take whatever car you want. I'll let your father know that you'll be out for the evening."

THE GPS ON my mother's car leads me to a newer neighborhood called Crescent Park in Palo Alto. I drive cautiously, looking from side to side to find the house number that's scribbled on a Post-it note. I find myself parking in front of a simple yellow brick home. Its rather new exterior boasts bay windows and a wrap-around balcony on the second floor. As I make my way up the brick-paved driveway, I admonish myself for showing up at his house unannounced. The neatly manicured front yard and the tidily planted flowers immediately give me the indication that he's not living here alone. *It's spring, after all, people do that with their yards.*

I stop in my tracks for a few seconds, deciding what to do. And as I turn around to run back to my car, he opens the door. He looks the same as the day I left him. Shirtless. Jeans. No shoes. In my mind and in reality, he will always be the only boy I ever loved.

"Jae?"

I turn back towards him, feeling displaced and unsure of myself. "Chris, I—"

He flings the door open and runs towards me, scooping me up in his arms and lifting me up from the bottom. I wrap my arms around him and allow him to carry me inside. He doesn't hesitate as he kicks the door shut and carries me upstairs. I'm still wrapped in his arms as he settles me at the edge of his bed and kneels in front of me, holding my face in his hands. He kisses me slowly, cautiously, waiting for me to respond. "Jade." He starts to unbutton my dress, but his impatience has him ripping it open with his bare hands. I don't say a word as he cups my breasts and pulls my bra upwards so his mouth can touch my skin.

"Jade." He says my name again as he lifts me up to pull the dress over my head. He pushes me down on the bed and in a few seconds, I am naked underneath him.

I can feel his love through his lips. Right then, I make a conscious decision to allow myself to be swept up with the tide, with the waves; I finally jump into the ocean. The anxiety that I had all these months over my work, my life, Joshua, Lucas—I let it all go with Chris. My Chris.

I smooth my fingers over his back and shoulders, looking for that familiarity I've been searching for over the past twenty years. It's still there. The sound he makes as he enters me. The feel of him, the fit of him; he feels good and ever-so-safe. I spread my legs wider, making sure to take him all in, wanting to show him through actions, not words, how much this means to me.

"Jade, say my name, please," he groans, pausing only to look into my eyes. "I want to hear you say my name."

"Chris," I whisper, "It's me. Oh, Chris."

"Oh, God, Jade!" he exclaims as we try to forget the tragedy that led us to rediscover each other. "Take your heart back, Jade!" he cries. "I still have it with me. I've kept it for you all these years."

THIRTY

The Passing of Time

A FEW MINUTES later, we're snuggled together on his bed, face to face, whispering in the dim light of the setting sun. I've covered myself with his t-shirt while he's wearing nothing but the sheet on top of him. Next to his bed are three ostentatious picture frames with images of our daughter. Cia as a baby, Cia at twelve, and Cia at seventeen. Not only do they look out of place, I know whose home they came from.

"Did Mama pick those pictures for you?" I ask, playing with the fingers that are clasped around mine.

"She did. She ran after me as I was walking down your driveway." He chuckles, lovingly pulling my hand to his face.

"Which one is your favorite? I can tell you all about the picture, if you'd like."

"Tell me about all three," he requests. I notice that his eyes are bright blue again, the darkness temporarily cast away.

"Okay. Let's see." I point to the oldest photo. I pick it up in my hands and lightly touch her face with my finger. "This one is one of my favorites. She was obsessed with that basketball. She was two and could hardly keep her balance, but with that thing, she was able to roll it in front of her while riding her body on top of it. I remember Daddy telling me that she was really your daughter. I kept that close to me all these years. She was rambunctious as a baby. Always finding herself in little fixes. I caught her trying to climb into the dryer once. The other time, she fell down the stairs trying to make it to the kitchen on her own. She managed to climb over of the baby gates on the stairway."

"This one." I pick up the second picture frame. He moves his head close to mine as I hold it up in front of us. My heart stops when I hear her squeal of delight in my head. "She's twelve. Do you see that purse she has on her? She was posing with her first ever Prada bag. Joshua finally caved in and bought her one. I thought she was too young to have something like that, but the look on her face when she got it was priceless. She kept that bag for years and years. In fact, she was—" I pause without warning to compose myself. "She was using that six-year-old bag on the day of her accident. Your daughter was very practical. She never asked for anything outrageous, never cared about name brands."

Chris stops me for a moment and repositions our bodies so that my head is on his chest and both of his arms are around me. I lose myself in his scent. It feels like nothing has changed at all.

"Ah. This last one. You need to know the story behind this one. This was during our mother-daughter trip to New York. It was Fashion Week and we were there to see the new spring collections. Mama has the rest of the pictures, but this one was taken right when she was freaking out but trying to stay cool because her favorite guy from One Direction was speaking to her. She was that enthralling.

Everywhere she went, people paid attention to her."

"She's a perfect combination of me and you," he commented quietly, a smile touching the corners of his mouth.

"Felicity means happiness. I named her Felicia because that's what she was to me. She defined my life, my joyous moments." I reach for my phone and show him the last picture I have of her, in the midst of one of the feather-related pranks she used to play on me. "Look, she even has that wide-mouth laugh just like you!"

This elicits a heavy-hearted smile from him and he turns to look directly at me, meeting my gaze. "Jae?"

"Uh-huh," I answer, sinking into deep relaxation as I lay in his arms.

"Can I go and get you something to drink? I'd like to speak to you about what happened after you left. I need to tell you everything."

I scoot myself up against the headboard and turn my head towards him. "I'm ready. No drink needed."

He sighs and follows suit, folding his hands calmly in his lap.

I push my knees up towards my face and wrap my arms around my legs. "I'm here, Chris. I'm listening."

He starts to speak. I feel every word he says, just like I'd never been gone.

"The night you left my apartment, my world just crumbled all around me. I realized that I had lost you right there and then because I knew how much I had hurt you. I didn't leave the apartment for days. I broke it off with her and was determined to win you back."

I can't help myself. I find the need to interrupt. "What was her name?"

My question throws him off. He takes a deep breath and looks away. "Katie."

"Katie with the blue shorts." I wink at him before reaching over to touch him with my hand. "Sorry, please go on."

He starts up again, eager to move on from that moment. "You stopped answering my calls and I often wondered how you managed to do that, after everything we were to each other. Could you imagine my surprise when I came across the newspaper article about your engagement to Joshua? I was angry and confused, I felt deceived. Did you love him all along? Were you attracted to him after all? Why did you marry him one month after you left me? I was too young and selfish to put the pieces together at that time. I went to see Joshua shortly afterwards. We had some words and I worked him over quite a bit right before threatening to kill him. He took out a restraining order on me, which affected my prospects of finding a decent job. After your engagement, I packed up my things and moved away. I drifted from one job to the other until I saved enough money to start my own construction company. That's how I ended up in Las Vegas for a few years. I came in just when the housing market exploded, right before the recession. I'm not going to pretend that my years were not filled with many women. There was one in particular… her name was Emily. I thought that loving her meant that I was in love with her too. We wanted to get married and planned to start a family together. We were together for ten years. And then I woke one day feeling like my entire life was one big joke."

"God, I know how that feels," I interject.

He nods his head and continues to speak. I don't change my position. I'm still wrapped around my legs, staring straight out in front of me.

"When I saw you the day of the funeral, I decided that I could no longer live this kind of a life. I had to admit to myself that I had never stopped loving you. And so I moved back here, replanted my roots, started applying for coaching jobs in the area, and accepted the assistant coach position for the Wildcats. So far, it's been great. One part of my life feels complete. The other, well, the other is sitting right in front of me now."

"Oh, Chris. So many years have passed between us," I say apologetically. "Joshua reached out to me the very next day after the last time I saw you. I confided in him and told him about my situation. He didn't care that I still loved you. He wanted to take care of me and the baby. I still went to Stanford in the fall, right after our wedding, and he helped me finish school despite having a little one to care for at home. His medical career was just starting and soon enough, we got caught up in the everyday life of working and raising a child. He was good to her. He treated her as if she was his own."

"I will always be thankful to him for that," Chris admits. "But I still hate him for snatching you up so quickly."

"It's my fault. I played the game for so many years. I thought I could do it. Cia's death severed the very fine thread that held us together. He did nothing wrong."

I start to cry because I know I've robbed him of the privilege of knowing his daughter. After all the years of guilt and pain and denial, here I was, face to face with the only person I have ever loved. The one who hurt me, the one who deserves to hear of my suffering. "I'm so terribly sorry for keeping her away from you. You didn't deserve that. No matter what, you are her father. Y-you deserved to know her just as much as I did." I pause for a moment, finding it hard to speak through my brokenhearted sobs. "I can't turn back the time to undo the past. How can you ever forgive me?"

"To be honest with you, I think I'm going to be angry about it for a while. I'm going to seek help so that I can talk through it with someone." He remains calm and focused, brushing away my tears with his fingers.

"I am so sorry, Chris," I murmur through the tears that won't stop. "I've always been sorry."

"I know you are. And I'm sorry that you lived through this with Joshua. I'm sorry that he wasn't able to give you what you needed."

"I have something else to tell you," I say softly, clinging to this as a small light of redemption. "She knew about you," I blurt out. "Felicia. Cia. Your daughter. She was aware that she wasn't his. After she turned 10, I told her all about you. I told her that she was made with so much love, that I loved her father so much, but it just wasn't the right time and place for us. She saw pictures of you. She knew she looked just like you and she was proud of it. Out of respect for Joshua, she didn't want to open up the past until after she turned 21, but she knew where she came from." I look down at our hands, still clamped together with no sign of letting go. "She asked all kinds of questions about you, Chris—about your personality, about your skills. *She knew.*"

If there were different types of tears for every occasion, these were tears of comfort. He covers his face with his hands and leans towards me so I can hold his head close to my heart. This time, he allows me the privilege of consoling him.

"The other day at the park, you kept on saying that you weren't good enough for me, when the truth is that it's me who doesn't deserve you," I say sorrowfully. "The lie I lived, the people I've hurt… I'm not worth your love and I don't know to prove to you how much I regret what I did. But when I told you that nobody else would have my heart, I meant it."

No matter what happens, he needs to know the role that he played in my life.

"Show me, Jae," he hushes as he aligns his lips with mine and kisses me. "Show me that you never left me."

THIRTY-ONE

Just You and Me

I DRIVE BACK home the next day, after leaving Chris and with a promise to call him as soon as I arrive back in Chicago. We spent the rest of the night reminiscing about our past. I overloaded him with memories of Cia; we laughed and cried together. In the end, we both agreed that he would have to work through his anger at not having been a part of her life, and I accepted full responsibility for whatever feelings may emerge out of this new revelation for him. I'm going to be there for him, and as I process all these feelings, I'll figure out what that means. Whether as a friend or more than a friend, I realize that we have a lot of work to do.

We're both grieving for the loss of our child. I don't think it matters whether I had her in my life for eighteen years or whether he's only known about her for two weeks. It's a mourning for a life that was cut short, for a bright light that suddenly burned out, for the waste of a precious heart and soul. She could have changed the world, made it a much better place to live in.

I'm exhausted by the time I pull into the circular driveway of my parents' home, fully aware that I have a flight to catch in four hours. I lean over to the passenger seat to retrieve my purse when I notice a black Mercedes E350 parked on the sidewalk from my rearview mirror. As I approach the car, I realize that it's Lucas. He's wearing sunglasses and is leaned back on the driver's seat, fast asleep. I tap lightly on the window before opening the door and slipping into the passenger seat. He is casually dressed in jeans, his trademark button down shirt, and Converse sneakers. His chair is almost fully reclined and his legs are stretched out on top of the steering wheel. I lightly caress his arm with the very tips of my fingers. "Luke?"

"Jesus, Jade! You scared me!" he says, bolting upright and adjusting the seat back while removing his sunglasses and furiously rubbing his eyes.

"Sorry. When did you get here? Why did you sleep in your car?" I ask, my voice tinted with humor. "Are these leather seats all they're made out to be?"

"Very funny. What does it look like? Yes, I slept here—I'm on a stakeout. I knocked on the door and your parents told me you weren't home. And the leather seats? I don't know, I haven't been able to test them yet," he bounces back quickly. That's Lucas for you.

"Secret agents don't fall asleep during stakeouts," I joke. I see him suppress a smile. "When did you arrive in Chicago?" I ask, keeping a light hold on his arm.

"Yesterday morning."

"You're kidding. And you flew here shortly after that?"

"Yes. I asked Taylor to call Noelle and pretend that we had to set up a meeting with you."

"More covert operations. You're getting so good at it." I smirk. But truth be told, I missed him terribly. My heart is doing somersaults at the fact that he's here to see me.

"It's not funny anymore. I'm done with it," he snaps, his eyes penetrating mine, squinting, reprimanding. "We're going to talk about this today. Now."

"Okay. But let's talk in Chicago. I have a flight to ca—"

"Cancel it. We're spending more time in San Francisco. Just you and me. Lucas and Jade. Not Ms. Richmond or Mr. Martinez. Not MT Media or Warner Consulting."

I pause for a moment to take it all in. "Okay. But let's go in to have some breakfast first. My mom and dad are going to be wondering what happened to me." I laugh. "Look at me, still having to check in with them at my old age."

My mother opens the door with a wary smile.

"Mama, this is my friend, Lucas Martinez." I lead him inside by the hand and he immediately lets go of me to give my mother a kiss on both cheeks.

"Very pleased to see you again, Mrs. Albin."

"Jade? Is that you?" My father bursts in from the dining room with outstretched arms, a cup of coffee in one hand and his glasses in the other. "So, I see you've found her," he comments somewhat sarcastically.

"Dad, this is Lucas. Lucas, this is my father, Francis Albin." I walk right into his arms.

"Yes, we met him last night." My father glances at my mother, who shakes her head.

The men engage in small talk while my mother pulls me aside. She doesn't say a word, just gently takes my face in her hands; I silently close my eyes as she rubs her forehead against mine. It's her trademark gesture to pull me out of my shell, my pajama moments.

"Come back to me, Jade," I imagine her saying.

I take the silent pause in conversation as a sign that we need to keep moving on. "Is there any breakfast left? We're starving."

THIRTY-TWO

Secret Agent

ONE HOUR LATER we're in his car driving along the coast towards Half Moon Bay.

"I've made a reservation at the Ritz Carlton, if that's okay with you. We can even get separate rooms if you prefer," he says impassively, keeping his eyes straight ahead on the road.

"Okay," I answer, waiting for a reaction from him. There is none. "I said okay. No separate rooms."

His face breaks into a wide smile. He reaches his right hand over and rests it on my thigh. I cover it with mine and we continue the drive in silence.

The hotel is nestled on a cliff overlooking the expansive Pacific Ocean. The check in process is quick, especially since there's a special concierge that caters to guests staying in the luxury suite. He gathers me into his arms as soon as we enter the room. It feels like forever since I've stood this close to him. The smell of his cologne, the feel of his skin—these are things I will never again take for granted. My friend, my confidante. My almost lover.

"Double O, I've missed you," I mumble into his chest.

"And I you, MP. But we need to talk, okay?" he says as he releases me.

"Okay. Let me freshen up and then we can go for a walk." I loiter around the suite, looking for the bathroom so that I can do just that.

The room is absolutely magnificent, decorated in beige and gray, with a large leather-lined sleigh bed in the middle of the master bedroom. There's a living and dining area as well as an outdoor fire pit on the balcony off the bedroom. I feel my anxiety taking over as I spy a large vase with fresh orchids in it. Lucas senses my reaction and immediately takes the vase outside, placing it on one of the wooden chairs by the open ledge.

I close the bathroom door but leave it unlocked out of habit, brushing my teeth and taking a minute to observe myself in the mirror. I don't have any makeup on. My skin is paler than normal and I look tired. I reach into my makeup bag to touch up my eyebrows, laughing to myself when I remember that I'm in a hotel suite alone with a man almost ten years my junior. Accentuating my eyebrows is the least of my worries.

Silently, the door opens and I don't say a word when he wraps his arms around me from behind.

"I think we're going to have to postpone that walk for a few minutes," he murmurs, pulling me backwards so I'm leaning on his chest. "I can't stand this any longer. I have to have you, Jade. Whatever happens after we talk, I need this moment with you." He tries to take my hand. "Come into the bedroom with me."

"No," I say sternly, pulling him to me. "I need you here and now. Take me here."

I watch his face in the mirror, my gaze fixed on his. I close my eyes as his hands move slowly upwards to touch me, gently unbuttoning the front of my blouse while fastidiously caressing every inch of my skin with his lips. He slips the fabric off my shoulders and unclasps my bra. I am now naked from the waist up.

"Luke," I say shyly, conscious of the fact that he's staring at me in the mirror.

"You are the most exquisite work of art I have ever seen," he professes as he turns me around to face him and sets me up so that I'm sitting on the edge of the bathroom sink.

I try to break the tension by cracking a joke. "Wow. That's a loaded statement, considering the millions of women you've seen."

"Uh-huh," he grunts, lightly outlining my lips with his finger before kissing me and inching his way down from my neck to my shoulders. "Way to ruin a perfectly romantic moment."

I sigh when he brings his mouth to my breasts and kisses them gently. His right hand finds its way under my skirt while he uses his left to hold up my legs, which are now wrapped around him. I gasp as he pushes his fingers inside me.

"Tell me you want me just as much, Jade."

"I do. I've never wanted anything more in my life," I say, giving him permission to pull my skirt down and undress me completely. I do the same for him, drawing his shirt upwards and pulling it off his shoulders. I unbuckle his belt, unbutton his pants, and push them down around his knees. "Wait," I say as I hop off the sink and turn back around to face the mirror. "This way, Luke. I want you this way. I want to see you. To see us. I'm not made of glass, I won't break. Wake me up from this daze, fill me up completely."

He groans when I touch him and I don't let go as I pull him closer to me, guiding him, encouraging him to take me, to fulfill six months of wishing, wanting, yearning. He gently obliges my request, allowing me to take the lead as I press harder and harder against him. Once he is all the way inside me, I start to move.

"Baby, wait. I might not last that long. It's been months since I've done this."

Months? I smile from ear to ear before teasing myself with my hands, encouraging his intense movements as he watches me in the mirror. I lean my body back, supporting my weight with both hands flat against the sink. He starts to move in and out, faster and faster, bending down to keep his mouth on mine. I can feel him expanding; I can feel everything about him. His hands grab my breasts roughly, squeezing them with every push.

"Take me, Jade. I'm yours!" he sputters.

I reach my arms backward and pull him close to me just as he explodes, his heart beating wildly, his insides pulsing, his body shuddering. I crane my head sideways and kiss his face, his nose, his neck and finally his lips. We kiss for a while. Sweet, loving gentle tugs with our teeth and our tongues.

For all our hellos and our goodbyes and everything else in between.

"My angel," I hear him whisper in between deep, rapid breaths.

I'm sated for a moment, overcome with the high of his touch, but just as quickly I am filled with so much sadness when I suddenly realize that nothing that's happened in the past has ever made me feel as much as I do now. With him.

THIRTY-THREE

Stuck in the Sand

THE SYMMETRY OF the clouds surrounding the setting sun and the riveting beauty of the shoreline makes me think of Cia. Is she watching me from where she is? If what Father Mike told me is true, is she happy to see me with him? Does she know? Can she feel my heart coming back to life?

Lucas and I sit side by side on the sand, close enough for our knees to touch but distant enough to focus on what we're here to follow through. The sun is no longer sharing its warmth with us and still I'm inflamed despite the cool, comfortable breeze.

"The water looks so inviting. Maybe we should go for a swim tonight." He turns to me with his arresting eyes and smiles. I try not to stare but I can't help it.

"No thanks. Me and the ocean don't really go together. I'll be perfectly fine watching you from here, though." I wink at him.

"Another one of your fears?"

"Even as a child, I was always intimidated by the ocean. I can't touch the ocean floor. I don't like stepping into things I can't see. You know, me. Black and white."

He nods his head but I can tell that his mind is on something else. "Jade, where were you last night?"

"With an old friend who needed me. I flew here to wrap up some open wounds that I caused twenty years ago."

We both remain firmly rooted in stoicism. He makes no attempt to move closer to me. "Will you tell me about them? The men in your life? The people who mean a lot to you?"

"Yes. I want to," I say, and I start by telling him about Chris. "He was the boy I fell in love with while I was in school. He was funny and simple, so unlike me. He played basketball for our school and wanted so much to be recruited professionally. I loved him so much, but it just wasn't the right time for us, I guess. Chris spent most of our time together worrying that he wasn't enough for me. That the paths we'd chosen were too divergent. In the end, his fear of losing me tore us apart. He cheated on me because he thought that it was only a matter of time before I left him. Joshua was his best friend. Our families grew up in the same social circle—he was at every party, every event, and company function. When I left Chris, I was six weeks pregnant with Felicia. I married Joshua one month after that in an effort to give my child a stable home, a loving father. Joshua truly believed that I would fall in love with him one day. And as we fell into the vicious circle of our careers and raising a child, I honestly thought that eventually, he would have my heart. But it never happened. I focused on bringing Cia up and taking care of her. For eighteen years, Cia filled the void in my heart. She made all the pain and emptiness go away. She was my reason for living; she allowed me to be content and complacent. Chris came back into my life almost one year ago." I pause for a moment as his face scrunches up in puzzlement. I know he wants to ask a question, but he latches his jaw as it slackens up to say something, so I prattle on.

"As a father, I guess he knew immediately that Cia was his after he saw her pictures," I hear myself say. "I couldn't handle keeping this secret from him for much longer. He deserved to know. And what happened between Joshua and me… honestly, the breakup was a long time coming. I don't hold any hatred for what he did to me. I just want him to move on and be happy."

I surprise myself immensely when I realize that I'm not shedding any tears. I feel guilty for a moment but then I think of Cia and how proud she must be of me for not dwelling on her death and endeavoring to live instead.

It takes me almost an hour to tell my story. He doesn't say a single thing all throughout my monologue. He lets me go through my emotions, laughing, tearing, and digging at the sand. I even tell him about my hatred for flowers, how I've seen enough flowers in the past year to last me a lifetime. That they're a waste of space in this world, how it's a joke to believe that flowers are all one needs to provide a sense of comfort for desolation and sadness. *How can those pretty little petals ever soothe a pain so deep?* He listens until my story is over and he knows it's over because I maintain an extended silence before turning my head to face him.

"This is it. This is me, James."

He doesn't make a move to pull me towards him. In fact, he moves away slightly so no part of us is touching. "Did you sleep with Chris last night?" His tone is nervous and his voice is shaky.

I avert his question completely. I've had too much truth for the past few days and I know that nothing I say will change our situation.

He lets out a heavy sigh and shakes his head, anger clouding his eyes and immediately taking over. "What in fuck's name does that mean for us?" He raises his voice, still staring straight into the ocean.

I don't say anything because I don't have the answer for him. After what happened with Chris, I know I can't be in two places at the same time. He waits for me to explain, his agitation increasing with my reticence.

"Goddamn it!" he yells, slamming his fists into the sand. "What are we to each other? Are we friends? Are we colleagues? One fuck doesn't even classify us as lovers! What are we?"

I shake my head furiously, incredulous at his outburst. That's what it was to him?

"Just a fuck?" My voice is barely a whisper.

"Defend what happened last night to me. Say something. Anything."

I finally turn to my head to look at him. "Chris just found out that he had a daughter a few days ago. He had come to Chicago to see whether we could have a second chance together. How am I going to leave him alone now, when I robbed him of his right to get to know his child? Besides, I don't think it's fair for me to defend anything when we don't even know what we are to each other. Up until a few hours ago, I had no idea that you'd be here. You still haven't told me why you came looking for me!" I exclaim. Whether he's here or on the phone, he's still as exasperating as ever.

"Really, Jade. Give me some credit here. I don't fly halfway around the globe for someone who's 'just a fuck' to me." He enunciates the last few words sarcastically.

"What exactly do you want from me, Luke?" This time I turn my head to glare at him.

"I want you to tell me that Chris means nothing to you. That I'm the one. That you're mine. This shit has been going on for too long." He stares back, showing me that he's not backing down.

"Ha!" I laugh out loud. "Well, maybe one day when you have kids of your own, you can tell them about the time when this one older woman was so crazy about you, she couldn't think straight."

"Was? As in past tense. What does that mean?"

"I can't deal with this right now. I'm going to work it out with Chris. At least I know where I stand with him." I can't accept another minute of taking the blame for the six months of love and pain and anxiety that he caused me. I struggle to maintain my balance on the uneven sand so I can stand up and walk away. I manage to prop myself up, but he catches hold of my foot to prevent me from taking a step forward.

"No, Jade. We're going to finish this here!" He yells. "Make up your fucking mind!"

His forcefulness startles me. I can't help myself. I start to cry. "What? Finish what? Decide what? Do you realize what you've put me through for the past six months? You waltz into my life just as it's imploding. You make me fall for you and then you disappear for weeks. You call me, you play with my mind, you mess with my head. I tell you time and again that I have nothing to offer you, and yet, you insist. You insist on getting to me. You make me feel things for the first time in twenty years. You make me guess, you make me wonder, you make me fall in love with you. And then you have the gall to demand that I define what we have when you've ruined me! I was willing to jeopardize my job, my reputation, my career for you!"

"You told me that you didn't want anything from me," he argues.

"I begged for every call. Every text message. I valued myself according to the attention that you paid to me. What a fool I've been! And now that I can finally see beyond today, you decide to show up and expect me to give up what I finally have a chance to amend for whatever it is you think we have?"

"Tell me then, Jade," he explodes angrily, "what the fuck just happened two hours ago?"

I have an epiphany. Right there and then. "Closure, Lucas. It was closure."

"Jade, please sit down. I didn't mean—" His tone changes to quiet, somber, almost repentant. He makes a motion as if to stand up. "What if... what if it were our kids who would be listening to the story of us?"

Those words cut through me like a knife. Is this a cruel joke? "No! Don't move! Don't you dare come near me! Listen to me. Hear me now—I'm going to tell you this once and for all. I don't want to love you! I don't want you! I want you to leave me alone! Leave me and my pitiful life alone. Leave me the fuck alone! It's over. I can't do this to myself anymore! Whatever bullshit we've had or didn't have or don't want to have—it's over!"

I kick the sand furiously until he lets go of my foot. And then I run. I run for my life. I run away from this life. I don't look back even as I get inside a taxicab that takes me directly to the airport for a flight to Chicago. No more mind games. Peace at last. I finally let him go.

THIRTY-FOUR

Transition

"THANKS SO MUCH for taking the time to meet with me, gentlemen," I address the other members of the Executive Team as we sit around the long conference table first thing the following Monday morning.

"How was your trip home, Jade?" Skip asks as he passes a pot of coffee around.

Everyone gets busy pouring themselves a cup and reaching out for the tray of creamer and sweetener in the middle of the table.

"It was good, thanks. It was nice to see my parents for a few days." *And Chris. And Lucas.* "Anyway, I don't want to keep you for too long. I just wanted to make an announcement as well as clarify something that has been weighing heavily on my mind lately. I'm putting this issue to bed once and for all. You know how I have loved this firm as if it were my own, and I have never done anything to jeopardize either your professional reputation or the reputation of this organization. Lucas—" I hesitate briefly before opening up this part of my life to them. "Lucas Martinez is not who you've accused him to be. He is a kind and generous man, and extremely ethical especially when it came to his dealings with this company. He never did anything to detriment the merger while it was in progress. He was professional at all times; we never spoke about work or business when we were together."

"You were together?" Dave asks, surprised.

"We were together, yes."

"How long has this been going on?" Mark interjects. No one seems upset. Everyone looks thoughtful and sad. I think they know what's coming.

"We became close through all those nights we worked together. As friends, mostly. But there was a point when I can say I think I was in love with him, however warped that love seems to have been." I pause a moment and gather myself. "We're no longer together. There are new developments in my life that have taken precedence and I must deal with them above everything else."

Tim's eyes look disappointed. "Jade, what's the point of this, if you're no longer with Martinez?"

"I still think that this poses a conflict of interest, past or present. And this is why I am hereby resigning from the company effective today. I sincerely apologize for my behavior and will accept the consequences of my embarrassing and degrading actions. Please know that I am so thankful for all the faith and confidence you have placed in me. Especially you, Warren. The way that you supported me through all this. I will never forget that. It's time for me to take a break and be with my parents for a while, enjoy life a little bit more, make amends with those I have hurt in the past. I've missed so much of myself lately. I gave up so much when I lost Cia. The thing is, I know now that I have to keep on living. For her sake."

Watching tears stream down the faces of five grown men is the most awkward experience in the world. Warren is the first one to stand up and hug me. He tells me that there's no need to resign, that we're all human and that things like this do happen. He then admits that he met his wife while she was an intern at the same company. We all laugh and call him a cradle snatcher. When the seriousness returns, however, I make it clear that my decision has been made.

"I'm going to take some time off to recover myself and maybe I'll finally join my dad so he can retire from his businesses soon."

The meeting ends when we agree to a three-week transition period. I call Noelle in and watch her cry openly as I tell her about my plans.

The following weeks seem endless. I'm in wrap up mode, making sure that all my studies and projects are passed on to the appropriate people. Chris and Lucas take turns calling. Like a comedy of errors, their calls intersect, one after the other. I take Chris' calls. I don't answer the ones from Lucas. I've never been duplicitous. My heart can only handle one thing at a time. For now, it chooses to focus on Chris.

Lucas: *I don't need anything from you but your friendship. I miss my friend.*

Chris: *I love you. I've realized how much I still love you.*

Lucas: *I'll wait, Jade. Get your shit together. I miss my Skype buddy.*

Chris: *I'm arriving today. Let me help you pack and then let's talk about trying again.*

Lucas: *MP, James misses you. These secret missions don't mean anything without you.*

"So ANYWAY," I start off as I munch heavily on a bite of my sandwich, "I really think I'm better. I'm getting over this craziness. I don't think about him everyday anymore."

"Cut the crap," Leya responds, sticking another fry in her mouth.

"Okay. Once a day. And it's only because he won't stop texting and calling. I'm with Chris now, remember?"

"What does that mean, you're with Chris? You mean 'with' with, or trying to be with?"

"I haven't told him yet, but I'm going to move in with him when I get to San Francisco."

"Oh."

"Yup! And I'm excited!"

Leya shakes her head at me before attempting to wrangle out the truth by looking directly into my eyes.

I put down my sandwich and respond with a glower. "What?"

"What does that solve? You haven't really looked into why you acted crazy for Lucas like that in the first place. Now you're moving on to Chris? Do you love him?"

"Who?"

"Chris. Do you love him?"

"Of course I do. He's the father of my child and we have a lot of memories together."

"You had nineteen years of memories with Joshua and you don't love him."

"Leya, please. I get your point. I'm trying here."

"What I don't understand is why you have to try. You love Lucas. I know you do. Why are you trying your darndest to run away from him?"

"Because he's thirty fucking three years old and he doesn't know what he wants. I'm too old for his bullshit." I stiffly crumple my sandwich paper and throw it into the bag.

"Okay, Granny Feisty. I get it." The sound of our laughter rings throughout the cafeteria.

"I'm going to miss you, Ley," I say sadly. "You've done so much for me. You helped me survive the past few months. What will I do without you?"

"I'll make sure you won't find out. San Francisco will be my new favorite vacation spot!"

THIRTY-FIVE

Domestication

"I THINK THIS is it, the last of the boxes." Chris exhales as he slowly lowers a large brown carton on the floor in the middle of the foyer.

"Thanks!" I say, lifting the lid to peek inside its contents.

He towers over me as he watches me unload the picture frames and pile them neatly on the floor. My eyes gaze upon something inside the box, but I suppress my reaction so that Chris doesn't notice anything.

"Your mother says she's sending lunch over in a few minutes." I nod my head as I continue with my chore. I've moved into the pool house on my parents' property. Chris has been helping me to settle in for the past few days. It feels good to be home, although I'm still feeling a little bit displaced by my new situation. The house is big enough for me, two bedrooms with an open floor plan, teak stained wood floors and pure white interior. Massive french doors lead out to the swimming pool, complete with a diving board and cabanas lining the opposite end of the garden.

"Take a break and sit with me for a while." Chris reaches out to take my hand as I slide myself off the floor to stand up. We bask in the warmth of the summer breeze blowing softly through the open windows and doors. The limitless sunshine ushers in a new frame of mind, one filled with hope for a new beginning with Chris.

We walk towards the couch and take a seat. He swings my legs over so that my feet are resting on his lap. He lovingly runs his hands up and down my calves.

"Ah, that feels good," I say with my eyes closed. "What time do you have to leave tomorrow?"

"My flight leaves early. 7:00 am. I want to be there before the builders show up." He has a trip to Vegas in the morning to check on a construction project. "Will you miss me?" He leans his body over so that he's lying on top of me, his face covering mine.

"Of course I will," I answer as I caress the top of his head. His hair feels so much like Cia's. Thick and unruly, yet soft and velvety to the touch. Subconsciously, I pull his hair back to stare into his face. *He's my Cia on earth. My last link to her. I don't know how I can ever let him go.*

He drags his lips down my neck to my chest, lifting my shirt up so he can plant tiny pecks on my stomach. "I can't get enough of you, Jae. You just get so much hotter as time passes. How can that happen?"

"Aren't we too old for this? We just did it two hours ago!"

I shriek as his touches turn into tickles down the side of my ribs. "Chris! Stop! Please!" I bring my knees up to protect myself and accidentally hit him in the face. "Oh, God! I'm so sorry, Chris, baby! Are you okay? So sorry!" I repent, kissing him all over his face.

He winks at me, all sly and sexy and inviting. "That's not what hurts, this does." He pushes himself up against me so that I'm flush against him.

"Well, I guess I need to fix that, don't I?" I unzip his pants and touch him. The phone on the table starts to play "Skyfall" from the latest James Bond movie. *Shit! I need to change that ring tone!* I reach my arm backwards and press the decline button with my free hand. My other hand is resting on his shoulder for support. It rings again. And again. And dings with a text.

"Someone's trying to get a hold of you," Chris says curtly. "You'd better get it."

"No, wait, hold it right there. Let me just see…" I bring the screen to my face.

Lucas: *You moved away from Chicago and didn't tell me? Who are you with?*

Chris senses who it is by my barefaced reaction. "Have you told him about us?"

"He's just a friend. I didn't think I had to report back to him with everything."

"It doesn't look over, Jae." He gently lifts me off him and deposits me back on the seat next to him.

Just like Lucas to invade my intimate moments. Again. He needs to get out of my head. Now.

"I'll tell him. Don't worry, I will." I pull him down on the couch until his full weight is on top of me and my legs are wrapped around his waist. "Tomorrow."

THOSE DARN BIRDS and their chirping in the wee hours of the morning. By the time I open my eyes, Chris has left for Vegas. I stamp my hand around the night table until my fingers come across my phone. I press the dial button and smile as I hear his voice through the receiver.

"Hi," I croak, "Good morning."

"Hey, Jae."

"Just making sure you got there safe. I miss you already."

"I miss you too, baby. I've been here for an hour. I'm hoping to get done tonight but not counting on it. I'll fly back first thing in the morning."

"Okay. Do what you have to do. Don't worry about me."

"Jae, call him today. Do it while I'm away so I don't get jealous," he teases. His tone is light, which is a great relief to me.

"I will. I'm sorry about last night. I'll turn my phone off next time."

"There'll be no next time once you tell him."

"Good point," I say, going along. "I love you, Chris. See you tomorrow."

"Love you, Jae."

As soon as I hang up the phone, I get up to start my day. Concha has left coffee on the patio by the pool. The fresh air seeping in through the open doors feels good. I delay the inevitable, choosing instead to delve back into the boxes to gradually unpack my things. My mind goes back to the item I found in the yesterday's pile so I decide to fish it out before sitting down for some coffee. I hold it up and then I hold myself up from the rush of emotions that overcome me. It's a picture of us, taken by the Buckingham fountain at Grant Park. I'm sitting on his lap with my legs up in the air, laughing ridiculously at the fact that I was trying to avoid a group of pigeons by my feet. I could have sworn that he secretly threw them some bread crumbs on purpose. As I lay the picture on the table, Concha sneaks up from behind to pour me a cup of coffee.

"That's him, the man who was here a few weeks ago. Whatever happened to him?"

"Nothing, really. We were just friends."

"That's not what it looked like to me." She snickers. "Jadey. How long have I known you?"

"Concha! Why should we remind ourselves about our age?"

Her hearty laugh has always lifted me out of my dark moods. "That's the thing. You were acting just like you were in high school when you were with that man. I haven't seen you like that since... well, since you were in high school!" We both giggle at her last statement before I decide to rein this conversation in.

"That's the past, Concha. Feelings like that only happen once. I had it with Chris. And I'm so lucky that he's back in my life. Things will be fine from here on."

"I hope so, Jade. I hope so." She clears the empty plate of fruit from the table and traipses away.

THIRTY-SIX

This Isn't Love

I CAN'T DELAY it any longer. I have to return Lucas' call. It's only fair to both him and Chris for me to lay out the future terms of our friendship. I'm nervous and uneasy. In honor of him, I rush to the gas station and buy a pack of cigarettes. I pop open a bottle of red wine and gulp down a glass before sitting outside by the pool to call him. The nicotine rush feels unfamiliar; I stub out the cigarette even before I dial his number.

"Jade?"

"Hi, Lucas."

"Oh, Jade. It's really you. Where are you calling from?"

"I moved into my parents' pool house temporarily."

"Who's with you? Let me call you back now on Skype. I need to see you."

"Lucas, there's no need to—"

"Turn fucking Skype on, Jade! Now!" he yells. "I need to see you."

I hang up the phone and rush back into the house to log on to my computer. The green icon rings even before I'm able to pull a seat up to the table. His face comes up on the screen. He looks tired and sad. His eyes are staring right into the monitor as he lets out a sigh. "You look well, Jade. Still as bewitching as ever. God. I've missed you," he says in a feeble voice.

"We need to talk," I start. "Do you have time now? Where are you?"

"At the office. I know everything. I finally know all about you. Of course, I wished you would have told me yourself, but now I understand what all that mystery was about. You're still married, Jade. Why did you think I wouldn't find out eventually?"

"I never thought that. We never got a chance to talk about these things."

"This is a fucking joke. What the hell is going on?"

"Nothing, I—"

"Explain to me why you never told me you were married. And your daughter—" He reaches out as someone hands him a folder and he waves his hands to dismiss whoever it is who walked into his office. He frantically leafs through the pages of the stack of papers. "I just had them run a file on you. Do you want me read through this or are you going to tell me what's really going on with you?" His face suddenly fills with horror as he focuses on a page in front of him. "Oh my God. Oh my God, Jade. I am so sorry."

"What are you looking at?"

"A-A police report," he stammers out in shock. His face registers a look of dismay. "Your daughter. Your hospital stay. Your injuries. Oh my God, Jade." Tears fill his eyes as he looks directly into the screen. "Baby." He hurriedly shuts the folder and pushes it away from him. *He acts like he can't bear to read any more of it; he's lucky he didn't have to live it.*

I say nothing. I force a weak smile as I wait for him to digest everything. "Now you know."

"This just happened. In the past two years. Oh, baby. I'm so sorry."

I shrug my shoulders, at a loss for words. "I'm not your baby," I fume under my breath.

He ignores my comment. "I'm here," he whispers. "Why didn't you tell me?"

"I didn't want you to feel sorry for me. I'm in the process of getting an annulment. I never lead you to believe anything other than the truth."

"I feel everything for you but sorry. This doesn't make me love you more—I don't think I can feel any more for you than the way I've always felt."

"Love? Who said anything about love?" I jeer sarcastically.

"Jade, I love you. I always have. I'm sorry it took so long for me to tell you."

"It's too late for that now, Luke. I'm with Chris."

He shakes his head dubiously. "You're with Chris? What does that mean? Do you let him inside you, Jade? Is that what you're getting at?"

"Oh, Luke, why are you doing this to yourself?"

"This doesn't change a thing between us. Leave him. For me."

"There you go again," I accuse, irked by his spunk but entranced by his troubled eyes.

"There I what?" he snaps.

Now it's my turn to look at him disbelievingly. "There you go again telling me what to do. How dare you make any demands of me? You have no right."

He takes a deep breath to calm himself down. "I'm sorry, baby. I didn't mean it that way. I just want another chance, Jade. Please, will you give me another chance?"

"Stop calling me baby. It's too late for that. I'm happy with the way my life is now. I'm sorry about what happened between us. I've just now gotten my dignity back; please don't make me fall into that again."

"Into what? What are you talking about?"

I throw my head back incensed by his astonishment. "Don't pretend to be so dense. I had sunk to such a low level, I was waiting for every piece of scrap you threw my way. I lived for those texts, and I would have died for them too. How ridiculous was that? And then I figured it out. It was timing. You arrived right when my world was turning upside down. When my heart was just blown open and rendered empty. You filled it. In your own assholey way and in my need to be loved, you quenched my thirst. For the worst reasons; for the wrong reasons. I'm not going through that again, Lucas. Those days are over." My eyes start to fill with tears. Tears of shame, of humiliation, of loss.

"Assholey? Is that even a word?" He ought to win an award for his ability to turn from remorseful to snide in the blink of an eye.

"Yes, coined just for you. You're an ass. The way that you fully expect me to drop everything for you." I let him have it. I'm angry and upset because it's too late for us. "It's a real asshole move."

"Please, Jade. I have so much to explain to you, if you let me, I can tell you—"

"No, Lucas. It's over between us. I can't do this anymore. I have Chris now. He's good to me. He's the father of my daughter and I love him. Please understand."

"Your daughter is gone," he says sadly.

His words squeeze the life out of me.

"Fuck you."

"Jade, no, please I didn't mean this in a bad way. What I'm trying to say is… Oh, fuck. This language barrier is going to kill us. Listen, what I meant to say was that you don't have to stay with Chris for anything."

"I want to be with Chris. Chris," I chant repeatedly.

"That's it, then? It's over between us?"

"It never began, Luke. It was all in my head."

"Then it was in mine too," he says, finally yielding to the truth about the past seven months.

"This is goodbye, Lucas. Please respect me enough to grasp what I'm telling you. I'm saying goodbye. For good." I turn my head away so that he doesn't see me cry. For a few seconds, he's stuck looking at the back of my head.

"I can't. I can't say goodbye. There's so much for me to tell you. I'll fly over there so we can talk. Can I do that? Can we at least see each other one last time?"

"No. Please move on with your life. Marry Cristina. Have a family with her. Live your life and always remember what's important. Immerse yourself in the love of those around you instead of trying too hard to gain it from those that aren't. Thank you for everything, Lucas. I will always remember you and I hope that we can be friends one day when this is all in the distant past."

I force out a smile before taking a deep breath and moving my cursor over to log out of this phase of my life. Permanently.

THIRTY-SEVEN

Special Delivery

"WELL, THAT WORKED out, huh? Are you glad you made that trip out to Vegas?" I ask as I pass Chris a salad plate at dinner the following night.

"Yeah. We signed the deal right there and then. My biggest one yet." He puts the plate down, takes my hand, and brings it up to his lips. "Now we can move out of here and into our own house—Pacific Heights, Telegraph Hill—you name it, baby. Anywhere you want to live."

I smile warmly at him but don't say a word, afraid that he'll be able to read into my vocal expression. I'm choked up. The conversation with Lucas hasn't left me for a single second. *The last time I felt like this was when I walked out on you twenty years ago, I want to say to him.* Most people don't go through two heartbreaks in a lifetime. And here I am with fragments of my heart splintered further into tiny little pieces.

"Jae? Are you okay?" He tugs at my hand to get my attention.

"Oh, yes. Sorry, babe. I didn't hear you."

"Did you speak to him?"

"I did."

"How'd it go?"

"Uneventful. He said he understood. It was a three minute conversation," I assure him.

He nods his head in acknowledgment and continues on with telling me about his business deal. I try to listen intently, but I don't hear a word he says. We go to bed early, each exhausted from our respective eventful days. I move around the bed restlessly, praying for sleep to take over, to sweep me up into a state of apathy. While Chris lies fast asleep, I get out of bed and walk out through the French doors, desperately searching for relief out in the open air.

"Always look for signs, Cia," I used to tell her. "Be intuitive. Signs are God's way of speaking to you. If you keep an open heart, you will see them."

Slowly, I lift my head up and try to find anything to tell me that things will be okay. "Give me a sign, Lord," I pray, searching for a single light in the absolute darkness. "If I find a star, I'll know what I need to do."

My heart takes a leap when I see a tiny light streaking across the clouds, only to realize it's an airplane. And as in the past two years of my life, once again I find myself lost and alone, blanketed only by the forlorn, empty sky.

"GOOD MORNING!" I greet my parents as I waltz into their dining room dressed in jeans and a t-shirt, ready to continue a day of unpacking more boxes. I braved an early morning jaunt across the garden to my parents' house to join them for breakfast since Chris had to leave early for work.

"Good morning to you, darling," my mother answers, motioning for Concha to add another place setting right next to her. "How's the unpacking going? Are you making any progress?" she asks as my father continues to pore over the newspaper.

I walk around the table to give each of them a kiss on the cheek. "It's going," I say as I take a seat and reach out for a cup of coffee. "I thought I'd stop by to ask if you wanted to drive out to Nordstrom's this afternoon? I thought I'd check out their spring sale and could use the company."

"Sure, I would love that." My mother eyes me suspiciously. "But what are you looking for? It's not like you're going to need work outfits in the next few weeks at least. I thought you were going to take a break, sweetie?"

"I am. I just want to get out of the house."

"Is everything okay?" My father's attention is now focused on me as he folds the newspaper up and places it on the table in front of him. He leans over, intent on hearing what I have to say.

"I'm fine, don't worry! I'm just a little stressed about moving in and all."

"Everything okay with you and Chris?"

"Yes, why would you ask that?" I'm flustered by her uncanny intuition.

"Oh, I don't know. Lucas Martinez called a few times and I told him that you still had the same cell phone number and to call you on your phone. I could tell that you weren't taking his calls."

"It's all good. I forgot to tell him I was moving."

"Forgot?" My mother laughs acrimoniously.

"Mama. I forgot. Let's leave it at that."

"Oh well. He's a charming young man. Very determined."

"Young is the word." I smile at my father, who winks back at me.

The atmosphere turns silent as we casually turn our attention to finishing breakfast. We talk about my father's business and the investments he has instructed his banker to transact for him in the past week. He always runs these things by me and I'm always happy to help and advise him about any new stock that I hear about. This week, I don't have any suggestions for him. I've been out of the work force for one week and already I'm feeling out of touch.

The doorbell rings just as we're finishing up our meal. Danilo reluctantly enters the room with a FedEx box and lays it on the empty spot adjacent to me on the table.

"Ms. Jade, this package came for you."

"Hmm. Who is it from?" I ask as I pull the parcel towards me to examine it.

"Not sure, ma'am. It says MT Media."

My parents turn to look at me and watch as I tear on the tab that opens the box. "Thank you, Dani. I'll take it from here."

Inside it is an envelope with a letter addressed to me. Attached to the letter is a white composition notebook, like the ones we used for school, except that the cover is pure white. Emblazoned across the front of the notebook are the words, "TOP SECRET AGENT NOTES." Tears spring to my eyes as I remember the hidden meaning behind those words. The notebook contains only two tabs. One of them is "BEFORE JADE" and the other is "AFTER JADE." The pages behind the first tab have been removed. In its place is a blank piece of loose leaf paper with "TO BE TOLD IN PERSON" written across the lines. I stand up from the table slowly, cradling the box in my arms, and bid goodbye to my parents. I walk back across to settle myself in one of the cabanas by the pool, and with shaking hands, I tear open the letter.

Dearest Jade,

I just couldn't leave things as they were without explaining myself. For all it's worth, I hope it helps you understand what happened in the last few months that prevented me from seeing you as often as I wanted to. While it's true that my hectic travel schedule was mostly to blame for our lack of time together, I was also under extreme time constraints to complete the program that I entered into the weeks before I met you in Chicago last year. I had checked myself into an outpatient rehabilitation program, Jade. After Isabel Riley left me to go back to her husband, I found myself spiraling out of control. I finally made a decision to check into a rehab facility to allow me to recover from my drug addiction. The terms of the outpatient program required me to check in each week. Chicago was an exception—I was given a two week dispensation due to the importance of completing the merger. Since then, I have never missed a session or appointment. I graduated out of the program two weeks ago and I believe that joining the program was the best thing I've ever done for myself.

While in therapy, my doctor suggested that I keep a journal. I haven't told you everything about myself yet, but therapy helped me to understand that there were certain events in my life that I needed to deal with out in the open. Writing my thoughts on paper helped me understand the feelings and emotions that I had not only about what happened to me, but that I was currently going through as well.

So now, dear Jade, here it is. My Secret Agent thoughts about my Secret Agent life. I've always wanted my life to be an open book with you. Here are the final missing pieces of the puzzle. In giving you my words, I am giving you my heart.

Read my words, Jade. Know that I have felt the same way about you from the first day that we met.

I've taken a one month leave of absence from work and am staying in San Francisco, hoping that you will be willing to see me sometime in the near future. You will know where I am. I hope that you come and find me soon.

With much love,

Lucas

THIRTY-EIGHT

Forgiveness

I'M OUTSIDE THE doorway of an imposing high rise condominium called Lake Point Towers situated right on the shores of Lake Michigan. It is one of the first investment properties he purchased years ago when his medical career was just taking off. Today, he calls it his home. The doorman greets me with a warm smile as he nods his head in the direction of the elevator. I calmly press the button for the 30th floor and am slightly disappointed at the speed at which it takes me closer to my destination. The long hallway leading to his place is tastefully bare, modernized and redecorated since the last time I was here.

She opens the door immediately after the musical chiming of the first bell. "Jade?" The look on her face isn't surprising.

"Hi, Cara. Is he in?" I ask delicately. The waft of homemade cooking permeates the air.

"Jade, you're not supposed to be here. The restraining order is still in effect, is it not?" She holds on to the door, allowing me only a small glimpse of the inside. Just as I'm about to respond, I hear his voice in the background. He stands right behind her with the same look of concern.

"Jade? What are you doing here?"

"Joshua. I was wondering if we could talk for a few minutes?"

He nods his head as Cara steps back to allow me to move in closer. "Sure. Cara, it's okay. Let her in."

He opens the door and I follow his lead, the sound of our footsteps dominating the silence between the three of us. The panoramic view of the pier is breathtaking. It doesn't look at all like the place we furnished when we first put it up for rent. It's homey now, warm and inviting. The sparsely decorated place has been updated with rich hues of brown and gold and red. There are no pictures of our family, no pictures of me. But every corner is decorated with colorful pictures of Cia. *She looked nothing like him and yet they shared a special bond that only fathers and daughters do.* We stop at the living room, where he motions for me to take a seat. I sit down on a brown leather couch directly facing a wall-to-wall bar complete with a sink and built-in wine coolers embedded underneath the immense granite shelves.

"Red wine?" He moves about the bar, searching for the right bottle of wine, reaching into the drawers to find a corkscrew. I watch him as he works his way back and forth. He looks good. There are lines around his eyes that make him look dignified, but not weathered. His hair has turned gray somewhat, more salt than pepper, thinner but not much different from what I remember. He hands me a glass of wine and takes a seat on the ottoman right across from me.

"You look great, Jade. You haven't changed at all. What is it that I can do for you?"

"I thought I'd stop by to see how you are. I know you also received a final copy of the annulment last week." I play with my hands, looking at his face for a reaction. He has none.

"I did. It's just a piece of paper. We've been over for years. I get that now."

I desperately try to change the mood of our conversation. "You look well, Josh. How've you been?"

"I'm well, thank you. Teaching at the university has really been a blessing to me. It was the best decision I've ever made."

"I'm so happy to hear that," I say.

"How are they? Your parents?" he asks with genuine interest, and we fall into more comfortable small talk.

"Dad's supposed to be retired, but you know him. He still works out of the office a few days a week. Mom is busy with all her charity work. They're in good health except for the usual ailments that come with age. Dad golfs a lot and mom walks on the treadmill a few days a week." I laugh. "How about your family?"

"They're all doing great. I see them every weekend for dinner. Mom is slowing down a bit too, and we think she has early stages of glaucoma, so we're managing through that."

"That will be us soon," I say lightly, trying to elicit a smile from him.

He shakes his head good naturedly, but I can tell that his mind is somewhere else. "Listen, I've been thinking about you lately, wondering how you are. Are you still working at the same company? I heard you've been dividing your time between here and Frisco."

"I actually moved into Mom and Dad's place until I figure out what to do next. How are you and Cara? I'm happy to see that she's moved in."

"Yes, she's still working at the hospital, but she sold her place to move in with me."

I'm lost in thought as I look out the window towards the pier. The Ferris wheel, the Children's Museum… these places leave us with so many memories of her. "I can never get enough of this unobstructed view."

"I think of her every day. These places—they help me to remember." He leans in towards me as he says this, his hands clasped together and resting on his knees.

I nod my head in agreement. "Josh, I guess I just wanted to see you, to make sure that you were okay."

His eyes travel across the room and I twitch uncomfortably when I see that he's looking at my neck. "Is it still there? The scar?"

"It's better," I reply, mindlessly toying with the scarf on my neck. "Lighter and less noticeable."

"I am so sorry for everything that's happened between us, Jade."

"I know, Josh."

"I've learned so much in therapy. At first, it was remorse over what I had done to you. And then it was anger at losing you and her in the span of one year. And now, it's mostly just regret."

"There's nothing to regret. We had a good life, you and I. We did the best we could. And you helped me raise a wonderful human being. I'm filled only with gratitude for everything you did for me. I guess that's what I wanted to come and say to you. I want to thank you for spending all those years of your life with me. And I'm sorry that it ended the way it did. It was so selfish of me to think that I was the only one who suffered a loss. You took care of us for nineteen years, and during the happiest times of my life with her, you were there too."

"I appreciate your kind words," he says sadly. "Jade, I can never take back what I did. I will live with that forever. But I now know what happened to me that night. Can we talk about it?"

"Yes, I think we need to," I agree wholeheartedly. "I should have told you how I was feeling outright instead of keeping it all inside. But please understand, I tried to work it out. I tried to cast my feelings aside. I knew that you needed me as much as I needed you. I can't explain it, but everything just shut down after we lost her."

"No, Jade. You were never there. I never had you. Even when Cia was younger, I knew it in my heart. Your eyes give away so much more than you know. So it wasn't just you that felt that way. I felt it too. I tried to deny it for as long as I could. In a way, it was bound to happen. You were going to leave me."

I don't say a word. I'm at a loss for offering him any comfort. Anything I attempt will be a lie.

He gulps down a portion of his wine and proceeds. "I know now that I never had you. I think that subconsciously, I always knew that. I tried to fill that void in me with my career, and yours with material things. I loved buying you things because those were the only moments that made you smile. And the rest of our emptiness was filled by Felicia."

"You make me sound so shallow, so materialistic," I answer sadly.

He gradually scoots himself forward so that our knees are almost touching. "No, that's not what I mean at all. You took what you could, little snippets of happy moments, because that's all you could do. The only way I realized this was when I fell in love with Cara. Her eyes, they tell me every single second how much she feels for me. There was none of that with you. Ever. And so that night, I wanted to hurt you so badly to repay you for what you had done to me. But you had no heart. Your heart was empty. The only way I knew to get to you was to hurt you physically." He chokes up as he says that last word. To speak about the pain that you inflict on someone else is a valiant thing because it verbalizes the monstrosity of your actions.

"I didn't press charges because I knew that I had caused you so much pain."

His eyes dart around the room as if checking to see whether Cara is around. "No, Jade. What I did is no one's fault but mine. You didn't deserve that. I am truly sorry for everything."

"I forgive you, Josh. I do. I wanted to come over to tell you that personally. I'm so glad that you and I have been blessed enough with our respective second chances."

"Chris. Is he your second chance?" We're close enough to touch although we choose not to. I know it's because of the white elephant in the room. The restraining order.

"Yes," I answer softly. "I'd like to think so, at least. He was robbed of the opportunity to meet his daughter. I'm dealing with that guilt right now, but he doesn't seem to be lashing out about it yet."

"He will. You have to know that he will. Feelings can never be bottled up for too long. You and I have learned that. Just be there for him when that time comes. You'll make it through this, Jade. We both will."

"I hope so," I say as I place the empty wine glass on the side table and ready myself to leave. "I brought you a few things." I hand him a shopping bag laden with items from our old home.

"Thanks. What are they?" He reaches his hand in and starts to unload the contents of the bag. There are cards and little crafts made by Cia for the only father she ever knew. He centers his attention on a white cup that says "Stanley" on it. "My Stanley cup!" His eyes start to brim with tears. "Oh, and here's my Number One Dad trophy, too." Tears stream down our faces as we gaze down at his name, etched carefully on the trophy in a child's handwriting. "She ruined my Swiss Army knife to engrave this. I'm still surprised she didn't hurt herself."

"Well, that's because she hurt our dining room table instead," I comment, and our tears turn to laughter. I want to leave him with that sweet, ringing sound.

I straighten up my legs and stand up to leave. He hesitantly walks towards me and I hold my arms out to grant him permission to come closer. We hold each other tightly, my head on his chest and his big, strong arms wrapped around my waist. My protector, my savior.

"Thank you for saving me, Josh, for taking me in twenty years ago," I murmur into his chest. "Thank you for giving us a home and a happy life. You will always hold a special place in my heart."

"And you in mine, Jade. Always. Take care of yourself."

He doesn't move. He doesn't see me to the door. When I look back to catch a glimpse of him for one final time, I see him in the arms of the woman he deserves.

THIRTY-NINE

Skylight

"CHRIS! WHAT ARE we doing?" I squeak as he helps me up a few raised stoops after leading me by my shoulders down what I surmise is a cement path. I'm blindfolded and very dizzy at the moment—the car ride in darkness was brutal. "Honestly, I think I'm going to be sick!" I try my best not to retch.

"Few more steps, Jae. We're almost there." He gently pushes me along and I hear the creaking of a door. "Okay! Here we are!" he says excitedly, removing my blindfold with a flourish.

I'm standing in the middle of a huge foyer surrounded by floor to ceiling windows and offset by a large, winding staircase to the right. I look directly at him and scrunch my face as my mind rapidly tries to process what is happening. He fishes into his pocket and proceeds to get down on one knee.

"Marry me, Jade Albin. I am so in love with you. Whenever I look into those eyes, all I can think about is the inspiration, the healing, and the peace that they bring into my life. My home is wherever those eyes are. Let's build the life together that should have begun twenty years ago. Here, in our new home."

I bring my hand to my mouth and start to cry. I'm overwhelmed, but not with the kind of emotion that he would expect me to feel. Instead, I'm filled with sadness at my inability to elicit the reaction that he wants. Maybe I'm just too shocked. I can never give him up. He's my only link to her, I remind myself, as a visual of the Secret Agent notebook hits me smack in the middle of the brain.

"Oh, baby! It's incredible!" I squeal, holding my hand up and allowing him to slip the ring through my finger. Its brand new glimmer reflects tiny dots of light across the whitewashed walls. "Let's go see the rest of the house!" I turn on my heels and run up the stairs, with him following right behind me. We go from room to room, checking out all four of them on the second level, each the same size as the other.

"The master suite is on the third floor," he announces proudly.

"There's a third floor?" I let him take my hand and pull me to the end of the hallway where another set of stairs awaits. The master bedroom is an entire floor with two brick fireplaces, a sitting room, and two walk-in closets.

"Look up," he suggests.

"A skylight." I smile at him as he pulls me into his arms. "So much larger than the one we had, though. And you can stand underneath it."

"How about we relive our old memories right now?"

"What a great idea, Mr. Wilmot," I whisper as I stand on my toes and wrap my arms around his neck. "Oh, Chris. I've been waiting all my life for this." *So why do I feel like I'm on the outside looking in?*

"But?" He doesn't hide the concern on his face.

"But nothing. I love you," I declare out loud as I pull him down to the floor with me.

"ARE YOU COLD?" he asks as I lie in his arms, looking up at the glass ceiling, our clothes strewn across the floor.

The vast and endless sky invites me to soar up high, to leave the ground and break free. A skylight to showcase the boundless prospect of chances and possibilities.

"No, I'm good." I turn on my side to face him. "When did you close on this house?"

"Yesterday. I paid cash for it."

I lovingly trace the tip of his nose with my finger. "Don't you think this house is too big? What are we going to do with all those rooms?"

"Well, I was thinking that you could set up an office next to the baby room."

Did I just hear that correctly? "Baby room?"

"You want to have kids, don't you? Maybe we adopt one or two?"

"Chris. We're in our forties. I don't know that that's a good idea for either one of us."

The look on his face is one of bewilderment. "I want what you had, Jae. I want us to experience raising a child together." He sits up and moves away from me. "Please tell me that's what you want too."

I place my hand on his arm to calm him down. "Oh, babe. I didn't mean anything by it. I just want to make sure—"

"I want what you took away from me—is that too much to

ask?" The change in his tone is drastic. The temperature of the room turns cold. Icy. I could swear that there's a change in the color of his eyes. They're dark, vapid, and condescending. "Is it, Jade?"

"No, Chris, it isn't." My first reaction would have been to stand up and walk away. This time I won't do it. I'm going to see this through.

"I'm sorry, baby. I didn't mean that," he says remorsefully.

"Yes, you did. But I understand. It's okay." I lean over to give him a kiss on the cheek. "I think we'd better get going."

"Okay," he acquiesces and we get dressed in silence, neither one of us knowing what to say after this. This is the protrusive shadow of the past that will never leave us. It will always be a part of our life together and he will never ever recover from his loss.

We walk into the house thirty minutes later without having said a single word to each other. I do what I do best, stay busy to avoid thinking about the problems at hand. There are plates in the sink that need to be loaded into the dishwasher. I turn the faucet on and start to rinse them off. Chris comes up from behind and presses himself against me.

"I'm sorry, baby," he whispers as he kisses the back of my head. "I love you so much, Jade. You're all I need. Forget what I said earlier at the house. My home is where you are. We can live a happy life, just you and me. I'm okay with that."

I lean into his chest and turn my head, allowing his lips full access to mine. "I'm here no matter what, Chris. We'll get through this together."

FORTY

Please Don't Go

"WELCOME!" MY MOTHER greets the guests as they pile into my parents' home. It feels more like one of those awards ceremonies on TV rather than an outdoor barbecue, with cars pulling up the driveway to unload various groups of well-dressed attendees intent on showing off their latest fashionable wear. Despite the words *Casual Attire* in the invitations sent out by my mother, people are still dressed to the nines.

"Mama, please don't make me look like an idiot. I'm too old, for heaven's sake, and this is my second marriage!" I argued frantically when she started with the planning.

"Relax, Jade. It's just a simple get together. I'll even hold it outdoors. It's just nice to have something to celebrate after the past year that we've had."

The kind look in my father's eyes convinced me to give in. If my parents are so keen on advertising my eventual happiness to the world, so be it. My engagement to my childhood sweetheart—to them and to the rest of the city, it was an event worth celebrating, and now the house is filled with people, close friends as well as strangers.

My mother uses all of the experience she has with her own charities to plan this celebration. The garden is tastefully transformed to host this party. Tiki torches line the brick-paved walkway leading to the pool, where she's added brightly lit palm trees, a hardwood dance floor, a live band and a large open bar. The last I heard from my mother's assistant, there are 150 guests in attendance. Leya and the principals of Warner Consulting fly in to San Francisco to show their support for my newfound life. Everyone is genuinely happy that Chris and I have finally ended up together.

"This is so déjà vu," Chris says through his teeth as he holds my hand and leads me through the various groups communing in different parts of the house. He is no longer the insecure boy who attended a fundraiser at this same place twenty years ago. Gone is the nervous stance brought about by self doubt. In front of me is a smart and savvy businessman who has gained the respect of the city's financial community. "Jae, you look even more fetching tonight than you did then," he whispers in my ear.

"You got this," I say confidently as he takes hold of my hand. I lead him through the crowd to Leya and the rest of the team.

"Jade!" she exclaims excitedly as she puts down her drink on the bar so she can give me a big hug.

I return her embrace warmly. "Ley, this is Chris."

"Chris! So nice to finally meet you! Congratulations!"

"Thank you, Leya. I've heard so much about you. Thank you for taking care of my girl while she was in Chicago. She often speaks so fondly of you and the time you spent working together."

We stand together for a few minutes while Chris and Leya

continue chatting about Chicago, San Francisco, and the real estate market.

"Hey, guys, no business tonight. We're supposed to be celebrating!" I try to distract them, but they ignore me and continue their conversation.

I excuse myself to go to the washroom. Unfortunately, the one by the pool is currently occupied. I huff impatiently as I make my way back to the house, hoping that my bladder doesn't burst before I get there. The flurry in the house has thinned out, since most of the guests are outside lining up at the buffet table. I walk hurriedly down the hallway towards the guest bathroom on the ground floor, anxious to get back to Chris and Leya. The slight footsteps I hear behind me don't alarm me one bit. I assume that the servers are hustling back and forth between the kitchen and the outside buffet table. I turn the door handle of the guest bathroom with a sigh of relief. Great. It's unoccupied. As I hurriedly attempt to shut the door from the inside, two strong arms prevent me from doing so. I back away in surprise until we're both standing face to face. He turns around briefly to lock the door behind him.

"What are you doing here?" I gasp, intoxicated by the mere fact that I can almost touch his skin.

He doesn't say a word. Instead, he backs me up against the wall, takes my face in both hands, and kisses me. Tenderly at first, then turning brusque and angry; he takes out his fury on my lips. He breathes in my face, nestles his nose in my hair, and with barely a sound, he murmurs in my ear, "Why? Why did you get engaged?"

This time I have no words for him. Just action. And passion. And lust. And love.

We battle and fumble and tear at each other like our lives depend on it. He tugs at my hair and bites down on my lip. The sharp pain causes me to whip my head up sharply, but he sucks the blood off my mouth, tears open the front of my dress, and smears it across my breasts. I unzip his pants. He lifts me up and wraps my legs around him. In two seconds flat, he's inside me, stretching me, hurting me, marking every part of me with his hands. I feel so much that I soak his shirt in a flood of tears. He moans, I whimper. The faster he moves, the more I hold on to him. I hold on to him for dear life because I don't want to spend another day without him. For the first time, I can feel his emotions seeping through his touch. He is desperately trying to tell me something.

Being here with him gives me hope. For the first time in a long, long time, tomorrow doesn't seem so daunting.

When it's over, he pulls out abruptly and lowers me until my feet are back on the ground. I'm a sight to see—my dress is hiked up to my waist and its front is torn up, exposing my chest. More importantly, there is a searing sensation that has taken over my skin, my body, my insides and my heart. My heart is screaming out loud, "Don't go!" But the one I belong to is out there celebrating my love, waiting for me.

In a few seconds, the man who just penetrated my soul through his touch disappears like the fog. "Fix this mess up," he demands softly. "You know where to find me."

And then he is gone.

BY THE TIME I return to the party forty-five minutes later, Chris is making the social rounds with my father and Leya is sitting on a deck chair by the pool, chatting with one of his business associates. She scoots over sideways when she sees me approach them in an invitation for me to sit next to her. The couple excuses themselves and we're left alone, sitting side by side, nursing our respective drinks.

"Geez. I didn't know that there were going to be costume changes. I would have brought a few different outfits for myself."

I miss this. Her sarcasm. Her truth.

"I literally smashed into one of the servers carrying a tray of red wine on my way to the washroom. I had get out of those clothes and take a shower." I've been getting really good at lying lately. To others and to myself. I no longer feel the pang of guilt that normally accompanies the falsehood of these cursory words.

"I thought I saw Martinez lurking around the corner a while ago, but I figured it was just his doppelganger or something."

"Huh. I don't think he was invited." I sit on my hands to stop them from twitching.

"Well, Taylor said he took a leave of absence from work. Where do you think he could be?" She's playing with me now. There's a charade in her words, a pointed look in her eyes. I shrug my shoulders and look away. "Are you okay, Jade? You look a little flushed and your lips are swollen."

"Me? I'm fine. I'm great. Citrus will do that to me sometimes. I had an orange earlier." I nervously look away.

"And how's Olivia?" she asks. "I'm surprised she isn't here tonight." I'm sure it's because she's curious to know what my other best friend thinks about all this hoopla.

"She's been traveling all over for her showings. Her show opens in London tonight—that's why she couldn't make it. She called earlier and spoke to us on FaceTime," I say in Olivia's defense. My thoughts are all over the place. "Let's talk about you, Ley. How have you been? Are you still seeing Brent?" I try to immerse myself in the moment and concentrate on this conversation. I can't help but shift my legs together. I can still feel the rawness of having him inside of me. I want it again. I absentmindedly glance around the garden. *Is he still here?*

"Yes! It's getting more and more serious. He wants me to meet his parents next month," she enthuses, her voice pulling me back into the present.

"That's awesome! I'm so happy for you. How are you feeling about it?"

"I'm ready. I think it's him, Jade."

I move closer to her and put my arms around her shoulder. "This is great news, Ley. I can't wait to plan your wedding," I enthuse. "Or my mother can do it." I laugh at the afterthought.

Her eyes fix themselves on mine. I'm certain that she can see right through me. "Are you happy, Jade? Is this what you want?"

"What do you mean?"

"I don't know. Somehow I don't think your personalities complement each other. Chris is just so… well, so laid back."

"Well, maybe that's what I need in my life. He can curb in my OCD." I'm a bundle of emotion tonight. I need to keep this light and candid or else I'll break.

Apparently, she doesn't think I'm funny. "Have you seen Martinez at all? Spoken to him?"

"Not since the fiasco I told you about at the Ritz. He sent me a journal that he apparently used to write all his feelings about me." I roll my eyes like I don't care.

"Hmm. And?"

"It's too late. I'm not going to give Chris up. Giving him up means giving her up, and I can't do that. I will never do that."

FORTY-ONE

The Future

IT'S NOT HIM I need to find. I see him everywhere.

And I want to tell Chris. I really do. I want to tell him how sorry I am, how much I want to rid my head of all these lurid, maniacal thoughts. It's just my mind messing with me, planting different scenarios in my swirling subconscious. I'm not going to give in to him ever again. Chris is my future. Like a never ending mantra, I repeat it to myself over and over and over again.

Chris. I love Chris. I'm making love to Chris. It's Chris. It's Chris.

"Jae," he grunts, thrusting hard and fast. "I love you."

I love you, Chris. I do. I want to shout it out loud, I want to show you just how much I truly do.

But I can't.

It's been two weeks since I saw him at the party. I hide my sadness under the guise of the hectic life that we continue to lead. Chris and his business, my father and his. I've deleted all his messages. His calls come up under an unknown number again. I wonder whether he's still in town. It's funny how I don't even know him well enough to predict what the outcome of this will be.

Here's what I do know: Chris is my future. It's as clear as the day is long, as transparent as the open water when all you can see is the sun and the sky. Chris is my future.

But he's not my truth. My veracity rests solely in the hands of a man that I hardly know.

Living a lie can kill you. It erases the very essence of who you are. Pretending to feel, masking your thoughts, faking your words day in and day out—these actions leave you with an excruciating pain in your chest, a heaviness in your heart, a loathing for the person that you are. It's a slow and agonizing death. And I don't know how long I can fight to stay alive.

There are numerous attestations to the healing quality of time. I *want* Chris to be my reality. I *want* sunlit days without trepidation or concern. I *want* him to fulfill me. I *want* so much for us, and yet I *feel* like I have nothing. I drift away from myself in an out of body experience, watching this woman I can hardly recognize. *Look at him, how loving he is towards her. How much he adores her. How can she be so harsh? Why can't she love him back?*

"I wish I could get inside that head of yours so I can know what you're thinking," he says one night as he covers my body with his.

"What?" I ask innocently, compelling my eyes to convey something. Anything.

"Somehow, you look troubled. Like you're somewhere else."

"I'm sorry. I'm here. It's just work and everything else going on. I'm fine."

FOR NOW, I have to content myself with the sunny skies of Hawaii. When he asked if he could whisk me away to Oahu for a few days, I happily agreed.

"Hey, sexy. I'd move that Kindle out of your lap if I were you. I'm about to attack you and get you all wet," he teases as he swims towards me in our villa's private pool.

"Oh no! Anything but my Kindle!" I jibe back as I lay it on the deck chair next to me and hold my arms up to him.

He lifts himself out of the water and playfully splashes me before sidling up between my open legs. "Hmm. You feel so good," he murmurs as I scoot to the side so he can sit next to me while I continue to lie on my back.

"And you feel so cold," I counter.

He sits back to reach over to untie my bikini top, exposing me. He lightly brushes me with his fingers and I close my eyes to enjoy the feel of his rough skin against mine. Workers' hands, my mother used to call them. She said that they showed the true strength and character of a man.

"Chris?"

"Yes, ma'am," he whispers as he plants tiny kisses on my face.

"I stopped taking the pill a few days ago." *I'm going to make this up to him.*

He looks at me uncomprehendingly, scrunching his face to absorb the impact of what I just said.

"If living with a tired, old, and cranky pregnant woman isn't a big deal to you, I'm willing to try to have a baby."

"Oh, Jae." He leans forward to hold my face in his hands. "Really? You're okay with that?"

"I am. I want to give you what you've always wanted. If having a family means that much to you, I want it too."

He looks pensive, almost uncomfortable, but he quickly snaps out of it and kisses me lovingly, continuing his light touches all over my body. "Let's start working on that right now," he whispers as he lifts me up and carries me back to the room.

"SORRY, BABE. CAN we ask them to remove these orchids from here?" I whisper ever so quietly, afraid that the server will hear us. "I don't want any flowers on the table." We're sitting at an elegantly laden table on the beach, surrounded by white lantern torches and the faint sounds of Hawaiian folk music playing in the distance.

"Of course." He smiles as he raises his hand up slightly to catch the server's attention. He gives her the vase without saying a word. She takes it away without incident.

"Thank you." I lean forward to caress his arm across from me. Another server appears to be carefully rolling an ice bucket with a bottle of champagne in it through the soft, uneven sand. "Wow, what's this? A belated engagement celebration?" I ask, genuinely surprised.

"Well, that and… I have good news!" The look on his face is priceless. I think it's the happiest I've ever seen him. "Do you know why we had to fly here, Jae? I have a final interview with the Warriors tomorrow for the Head Coach position!"

"Oh my God! That's wonderful! Oh my!" I exclaim, springing up and running into his arms. I kiss him repeatedly. "Oh, Chris! It's your dream come true! Congratulations, baby!"

"I didn't want to say anything before things were more firmed up, you know. Remember the last time this happened." He laughs as we recall those precious memories from long, long ago. He peels the foil cover off the bottle, pops the cork, and fills both our glasses with Cristal.

"To you, Chris," I say excitedly, raising my glass. "You deserve this more than anyone I know. Congratulations! I am so proud of you, baby." We clink our glasses together and drink to his success.

"To the future, Jae." He toasts before pulling me close for a slow and tender kiss.

The events of the following day are a given. Chris secures the position as Head Coach of a highly ranked NCAA basketball team. I will always remember this day as the happiest day of his life. The look in his eyes is one of peace and contentment. He walks taller, prouder, like he's finally home.

That night, as I look up to the sky to thank God for his blessings on Chris, I finally find what I'm looking for. In the darkness of the night, I see it. Bright and twinkling high up above, the sign that I've asked for, the hope that I never had. I see a star. Many moons ago, it was a star that lead a group of travelers through the desert to find humankind's saving grace. This time, I feel empowered to do what I must.

It is time for everyone to delight in their own bliss. No matter what it takes, no matter how much pain it causes others. Everyone deserves their own shining redemption.

FORTY-TWO

Open Secrets

I'M HERE TO tie up loose ends once and for all, as I stand confidently in front of his rented apartment on Telegraph Hill. I hope I have the apartment number right. 608. I hold the white notebook tightly in my arms as I wait for him to answer the door. A striking young woman is standing in front of me, her eyes assessing me as she waits for me to begin my introduction. Her dark brown eyes are a stark contrast to her lighter features.

"I'm sorry. I think I have the wrong apartment," I say as I start to turn around to walk away.

"No, wait. It's you." She steps back, never removing her eyes from mine.

"Excuse me?"

"I'm assuming that you're here to see my brother? I'm Marissa, Lucas' sister. You're Jade."

"Yes." I instinctively hug the notebook closer to me with

one arm while I extend the other to shake her hand.

"Lucas isn't here, but would you like to come in for a few minutes? I just brewed a fresh pot of coffee."

"Sure," I answer, not quite certain whether or not this will be a friendly visit. She makes a sweeping motion with her arm, asking me to come inside. I am instantly taken aback at the sight of wall-to-wall glass overlooking the Golden Gate Bridge. "What an unbelievable view!" I exclaim as she leads me towards the couch facing an incredible outline of Alcatraz Island. "Wow. This is really terrific," I say, trying to augment the awkward silence between us.

She moves about the kitchen counter and walks back towards me with a tray filled with two cups of coffee and a plate of sugar cookies.

"Sorry, this is all I have. My brother cleaned out the fridge before he left."

My heart takes a plunge all the way down to my toes. *He left?* I feel another panic attack taking over. I try to focus on the pretty young woman sitting next to me.

"You look just like him."

"Twins often do," she says with a smile. "Did you know he had a twin sister?"

Of course not. I hardly know anything about him. Case in point. How do you fall in love with someone you know nothing about?

"No, I didn't." I pause for a moment and continue. "May I ask where he went? I just wanted to stop by and deliver this back to him." I bow my head in the direction of my lap to show her the notebook.

She ignores my question purposefully. "What does that mean, Jade? What does delivering that mean to both of you? Was it going to be accompanied by a goodbye? Either way, I'm afraid I'm not going to be able to take it from you."

"How did you know it was me?"

"Your eyes. He told me about your eyes."

"Marissa? How is he?" I take a sip of my coffee and try not to show my disappointment at his absence.

"How much do you know?"

"Only that he was in rehab for a while. It's funny, but meeting you here today, makes me realize just how little I know about him. Are you also from Southeast Asia? Is that where you live too?"

"No, I'm actually living in New York. I'm in the fashion business."

I'm more confused now. I always thought she lived close to her family. "You haven't told me how he's doing. Is he on the way back home?"

"Listen," she says shortly, "I thought that maybe we could talk for a few minutes about my brother. He's in a really fragile state at the moment, still dealing with the events that have happened in his life recently. Checking into rehab was a huge step for him. He's always been so stubborn and self-sufficient, so driven and arrogant. A hotshot, to put it directly. Life has just thrown him a couple of curveballs lately, and he's been trying to deal with everything on his own."

"Is your mother a good support system for him? I know she lives in the same area as he does."

"What exactly did he tell you?"

"That he moved home because your mother is from there."

"What's in that notebook, Jade?" she asks, still baffled by my ignorance about the facts of his life.

"I don't know. I didn't read it. I read his letter and didn't see the point of continuing on."

"Jade. Our mom passed away three years ago. We grew up in Spain with my father. My mother walked out on us when we were very young. Three years ago, Lucas found out that she was in hospice, dying from terminal brain cancer, penniless and alone. He moved there to take care of her until she died. None of us really knew her as much as he did. He got to spend six months with her, and he was really broken up after she was gone." She pauses, as if she's trying to decide what to tell me next, and how much to reveal. "After that, he threw himself into building his company. With his success came the excesses of living a fast life."

Our secrets are the same. Our losses. Our heartaches. Now I know what drew us together. And we both never even knew it.

"I am so sorry. I had no idea. Lucas never told me anything about that. He said that his parents have been married—"

"My father remarried someone much younger than him and they've been together for a long time. She's the only mother I know."

Joshua was the only father Cia knew. And she craved knowledge about Chris. My heart hurts for both of them. My past and my present.

She takes a deep breath and reaches out to touch my arm. "I know about your husband and daughter, and I am very sorry for that too."

"Thank you," I answer, immensely touched by her concern.

"So anyway, that might explain his aversion to opening up as of late. He's just been dealing with so much pain, so much rejection. And when he met you, he was in the middle of ironing himself out. Of course, I'm not going to excuse his being an ass because that's just the way he is," she says and laughs lightly, with the ease of teasing a sibling even when they aren't around. "He's got such a good heart, that brother of mine, except that he hides behind this solid, blank wall to avoid getting hurt all over again."

I don't say anything. I listen to her words and take it all in. She leaves me with my thoughts for a while and then hones in with a zinger.

"Do you love him, Jade?"

"I'm… I'm engaged to be married to someone else."

"Do you love him?" she repeats.

"No. I don't. How can I love someone I hardly know?"

"He loves you."

He told her that he loves me? "He doesn't. It's a game we play with each other. Maybe a strong attraction. But it will never work."

She shrugs her shoulders as if she doesn't believe a word I'm saying. Slowly, she lifts herself off the couch and reaches out to take my hand in hers. "Come on, I want to show you something." We walk down a short hallway to what I conclude is his bedroom. The gray and black color scheme is tastefully offset by an all-glass decor, a large velvet-buttoned headboard and masculine gray cashmere drapes. My eyes come in direct contact with a black and white canvas photo reproduction of a woman with flowing hair and striking, luminous eyes. It's a portrait taken from the clear reflection of a glass window; the woman's eyes are staring straight out, her head slightly tilted as she rests her chin on her knees while she sits on the floor with her arms wrapped tightly around them. She looks childlike and vulnerable, but her eyes are strong and piercing. It was the first night he came into my office. The night that had started it all. It was the night he stole my heart.

The woman in that picture is me.

"He told me that if I wanted to get to know who you were, all I had to do was to look at this picture. That the woman he fell in love with was strong and breakable at the same time. That she needed to be set free and yet he felt the need to protect her at all times. That she was a contradiction in every sense of the word."

I furiously shake my head, disbelieving her words and abashed by the truth spoken by this picture. He never showed me how he felt; I always thought it was a one way street with the two of us. And here we are once again. At first it was too much, too soon. Now it's too little, too late. That's the story of my life.

And now it's time to know his.

FORTY-THREE

Life after Jade

AND SO, CLOAKED in the hush of a warm California night, under a bright moon and a starless sky, I bask in the words that he had written from his heart. I can almost hear his voice; I try to imagine his face. I focus my eyes on the lines of the paper and can't help but smile at the way his handwriting clumps tightly to the right. "Wow. You're a lefty too," he once said. "No wonder you're so smart."

I read his words over and over again.

Summer 2015

She's forty-two years old? How can that be? The woman who sat across from me at this swanky Italian restaurant told me how old she was. I feel the need to dwell on it, but I didn't want to embarrass her any further. Besides, I felt Taylor watching me as if he sensed my immediate reaction to her when I met her this morning. She is by far the most alluring woman I have ever met. Her shoulder length reddish brown hair framing her perfect face. Smooth skin, striking green eyes, a perfectly sculpted nose and fine pursed lips. She's one of those women who desperately tries to hide her sensuality despite oozing it. Her tiny frame is accentuated by long, lean legs. She dresses in a suit but her blouse can't help but expose her deep cleavage because of the size of her breasts. Her mannerisms are classy, her giggle is childlike. She was just promoted as the first woman Executive Vice President of a large consulting company. Her words denote intelligence and practicality. Even her fingers are long and elegant, like the rest of her. It's going to be tough staying away from this woman for two weeks, but I'm a businessman first and foremost and nothing is going to keep me from facilitating this deal of a lifetime.

The goddamn flight back to Asia is fourteen hours. I'm exhausted from the two week stay in Chicago, over served, and in desperate need of sleep. Somehow, the drinks aren't working their magic on me tonight. I can't stop thinking about her.

"One more scotch on the rocks, please," I say to the stewardess as she walks down the aisle carrying a tray of nuts.

I constantly shift in my seat, trying my best not to react to the thoughts that are taking over my head. In my hand is the pen I so slyly hid in my pocket as I left her office last night. My memento of the most erotic experience I have ever had. Her lidded eyes, the slight parting of her lips, the way she arched her body upwards to take what I was giving her. Her moans. Christ.

She's fucking forty-two years old when she looks like she's twenty-five.

Her eyes left a haunting impression on me. They remind me of the bottomless sea, calm on the surface but with a tumultuous current that increases with depth.

She's not lost, just sad.

Isabel was lost. Her husband had pulled the plug on their marriage and she didn't know where to go.

Cristina wasn't lost, I just didn't love her enough to want to find myself.

Jade knows what she wants. That is something that is so attractive to me. I'm done with whiny thirtysomethings who don't know which side is up. Jade goes for what she wants and gets it. I know because I've met the assholes she works with and promoting her into their inner circle must have taken a hundred board meetings and numerous arguments. She deserves every single thing she has. I hardly know her, but I can already tell. What I can also tell is that her success means nothing to her. It doesn't fulfill those sad eyes of hers, that's for damn sure. Maybe it even serves as a detriment to her in some way or another. Just like mine.

I was hopelessly attracted to her from the moment we met, so much that I looked forward to our nightly trips to the Pantry. I wanted to prolong those smoke breaks, to get to know her better, but she stayed pretty guarded all throughout our interaction. She finally let herself go the day before I left, when she allowed me to touch her intimately. There was a light in her eyes that was missing before, but as turned on as I still am when I think about it, I feel like I have yet to break the barrier with her.

I watched her interactions with various people, never failing to be impressed by her warmth and her genuine personality. She was professional yet amiable, outspoken yet respectful. And the men in that office. Dammit. Their eyes linger a little bit too long on her, but she doesn't know it. Or maybe she does and she's practiced enough to ignore it. Everyone had only wonderful things to say about her—somehow I can tell that they knew about the burdens she carries. I was dying to ask them about her, to find more information about her personal life, but I couldn't. It's not easy when you're trying to put up a front of utmost detachment.

When I called her from the airport and she didn't answer her phone, I felt like a giddy teenager, determined to hear her voice before boarding the flight. I called her three consecutive times, hoping that she would step out of her meeting to answer my call. When she did, it felt like Christmas. It calmed me down considerably and allowed me the luxury of knowing that our two weeks together meant something. We connected.

I don't want her to forget me too soon.

I'm drawn to her. I want to be her friend. And I admit that if this merger wasn't in progress, I would have pursued her relentlessly. But until this business deal is complete, there is nothing more for me to do but wait. Life on opposite ends of the globe certainly isn't conducive to starting a relationship. And besides, I still have open issues with the women I leave behind in different destinations.

After Isabel, I basically reverted back to my sex only rule. It's been perfect so far, since my travels don't really allow me to stay long enough in one place to truly invest in anyone. It's all for the best. I have a few years yet before I have to think seriously about settling down. So far, no one's come close to convincing me to change my lifestyle.

Holy fuck. Until her.

Fall 2015

It took me a minute or two to find the energy to drop my hands down the side of my bed to reach for the phone. It rang repeatedly, pausing only for a few seconds before going off again. My eyes were still closed as I brought it to my ear.

"Hello?"

"Hi, you. It's me."

"Jade. Hi, hold on a second." I forced my eyes open and stumbled out of bed while tugging on the sheet to cover myself. I looked to my left to find a body lying next to me. Shit. I finally realized where I was as I slid my watch off the night table to look at the time. Next to it was my wallet and a mirror marked

with remnants of powder lines. A woman with ebony hair was lying on her stomach, slowly stirring into wakefulness.

"Sorry, Jade. Hi," I whispered as I tiptoed out of the bedroom, still disoriented and hazy.

"Hey. It's 9:00 pm here and I'm about to leave work. I thought I'd call to see how you are," she said happily. "Are you okay?"

"Yes, I slept in today."

"Oh, sorry. I woke you up? I should let you go. Let's talk later." I could tell that she was unsure about such an impulsive move.

"Yeah, can I call you back in few minutes? I need to get a cup of coffee."

"Oh, no worries! Sorry to have bothered you. Just call whenever." She hung up before I could say anything.

I trudged back into the room to find Ebony sitting up on the bed, sweeping her hair into a ponytail.

"Jade, that's her?"

"Huh? What?"

"You said her name last night. While we were…"

"Oh, shit. I'm so sorry, Marie," I apologized, truly meaning it.

"It's Mindy. My name is Mindy."

"Fuck," I blurted out, totally confused. "I'm really sorry. Hey, would you mind getting ready to leave? I have a full day ahead of me," I said, aware of my own insolence.

"Sure thing. I'll be out of here in a few minutes." She leaned over to try to give me a kiss. I winced and shook my head to ward her off me. She took the hint, scooted off the bed, and made her way to the bathroom.

I remained in my study until I heard the front door shut.

Whew. The coast was clear. I didn't know what happened the night before. The last thing I remembered, we were doing tequila shots. I must have taken her back here and done more than just drink. My nose felt like it was about to fall off, my head was pounding, and I felt like an idiot. Was that what they defined as a relapse? I was doing so well until now. Then. Last night, I guess. I remembered feeling so lonely, it was almost unbearable. Leave it to me to saddle up to the first pretty girl I found.

I called my therapist to make an appointment and paced the kitchen floor back and forth, searching the cupboards for some coffee filters. I couldn't let any more time lapse before I saw Dr. Caster. I'd fallen off the wagon and I needed help. I wanted to call Jade back, but I knew that after what happened, she didn't deserve a guy like me. I wasn't worthy of someone like her. This was certainly going to take longer than I thought. I had no doubt that I wanted to get better for her, but until then, she didn't need to have someone like me interfering in her life. I intended for her to be my prize at the end of this struggle. I wanted her to fill my emptiness when all was said and done.

My therapist didn't think much of my admission.

"You what?" she asked, her face scrunched up in amusement.

"Yes. Apparently I did. I called her name out while fucking, I mean, excuse me, while in bed with another woman." I settled myself on a leather couch in Dr Caster's office, affirming my latest screw up.

"Is this your emergency?" She laughed as she crossed her hands on her lap. "Is this why you had to see me right away?"

"Well, that and the fact that I got high again last night. I was doing so well without it."

"Why do you think that is? What's been on your mind lately?"

I used to think that it was useless to see Dr. Caster as often as I did because all she did was listen to me talk, but I didn't hate it as much after I got in on her strategy. She actually made me realize things on my own, most of the time while I was saying them out loud.

"I thought I was doing so well, but last night in particular, I missed her so much. I couldn't stop thinking about her. And then I met some girl named

Mindy at the bar and thought it would be a great way to kill time, to assuage these thoughts."

"Thoughts?"

"Of her. Of what we did while I was with her. How I felt. Of a future with her. I can't wait to close on this transaction so we can spend time together without her being so paranoid about everything." Jesus. I confide in this person more than I even admit things to myself. And I was paying her.

"Lucas, do you think you're going overboard here? Jumping the gun a little bit? After all, you just met her. Tell me about her. What is it about her that you're so smitten about and why is this different from the others?"

"Hmm. Let me see. Those are all loaded questions, Doc." I let the silence overtake us while we both squirmed in our seats.

She was trying to assess my current state, I could tell by the way she stared at me. I caught her sympathetic eye and held her gaze for a few seconds to show her that I was all right. At times, I thought that her qualities embodied the mother I never had. Her approach was so honest and direct; the perfect way to handle someone as blunt and outspoken as me.

"She's broken and I want to fix her," I declared boldly. "There's something about her that intrigues me. She's accomplished and intelligent and extraordinarily ethereal."

"All the women you date are beautiful. That's nothing new. You still haven't convinced me that she's different. What sets her apart?"

I saw what she was doing. She was asking me to defend my feelings for Jade, challenging me to differentiate them from the ones I've had before. And truth be told, I was at a loss for words to articulate just why I feel the way I did.

"She's always interested in what I have to say. And my feelings for her are just..." I trailed off, trying to think of the right word, "inexplicable. I'm consumed with thoughts of her. I love being with her, spending time with her, whether on the phone or through texts. But after what happened last night, I don't know that she deserves a shithead like me."

"You're not committed to her. She has no hold on you. Don't let that guilt bring you down. You've been making so much progress." She shook her head in reprimand. "But the drugs. That one, we need to talk about."

We spent the rest of the session trying to find the reasons for my relapse. There were none. It turned out, once again through the conversation that I had with myself and where she sat there and listened, that it was just plain boredom. "You've been drifting along since your mom's death. Nothing, not even your business success, has meant anything to you." She looked straight at me, her eyes searching my face for a reaction. "What gives your life meaning, Lucas? What are you passionate about?"

"I don't know. All I know is that life isn't fair. I spend my days immersed in my work because that's the only thing that's ever remained a constant in my life. I can control that. It's my business, my policies, my procedures. The rest of my life is dictated by everyone else. You find your mother, she dies on you. You fall in love, she remarries. You try to love someone else, it doesn't happen. You meet someone special, it's the wrong time and place."

"You weren't always like this, were you? You once said that you had a pretty normal childhood."

I nodded my head in agreement. "I think it all changed for me when she passed away."

"We've never really talked about that day. Would you like to try to tell me what happened? Your counselors at the Center say that you've refused to discuss it with anyone." She leaned against the back of her chair as if getting ready to settle in for the long haul. This woman knew that she would get me to spill the beans. Right there and then.

I didn't say anything for a while. Even though I knew I was going to have to relive that time eventually, I wasn't really prepared. Nothing really earth-shattering happened on the day she passed away. It was the way she looked, her words, and her touch that I didn't want to remember. I took a deep breath, pursed my lips, and exhaled loudly, the way I did when lifting reps at the gym or getting ready for a sprint.

It was a muggy Tuesday morning. I vividly remember the sweet voices of the *choir from the nearby convent as the faithful celebrated the Tuesday Novena to St. Anthony.*

"How has she been?" I whispered faintly as I entered the room to find the nurse checking her vitals and adjusting the heart monitor next to her bed. She looked as pale as she did the day before, no change, really.

"She refused the morphine drip despite being in a lot of pain. She said she wanted to be awake when you get here," the nurse answered mildly as she continued to move around the petite figure that lay limp and lifeless in a rickety bed lined with a featherless mattress.

I waited until she left the room before squeezing in at the foot of the bed by the rusted metal rail. My mother stirred when she felt the weight of my body pressed against her feet. She attempted to open her sunken eyes and smiled as soon as they rested on my face. I slowly inched my way upward, closer to her head, and she weakly reached out her hand to take mine.

"Hi, Mom," I whispered, stretching my free arm to lightly brush the hair away from her face. There wasn't much left to tuck away behind her ears, just a few wisps of thin newly grown hair on the top of her head.

"Hi, son," she croaked. "Good morning. I've been waiting for you." She strained to lift her body higher to pull something from the stand next to her bed. I stopped her from moving any further and she pointed to a folder, motioning for me to take it. "Open it. It's for you and your sister. I signed it weeks ago and it's good to go."

I looked at her, confused, as she waited for me to scan its contents. The front page was a notarized document followed by a Last Will and Testament, accompanied by various appendices and schedules outlining a list of her assets. The total amount at the bottom of the final page was astounding. She hung on patiently for me to register everything I had seen. "Mom? What's this?"

"Take care of your sister, Lucas. Please tell her that I love her so much. You both kept me going during my darkest, loneliest times. I'm ready to rest now. You have given me the peace that I've been yearning for all these years. Please forgive me for leaving you and your sister behind. If I had to do it over again, I

would have done the same thing. Where I was, who I was… it was never the life that I wanted you to have. Your father is a good man. You are who you are because of him and I am so very proud of you." She let out a sickening wheeze that came straight out of her lungs and I was filled with horror at the sight of her. Her skin looked gray, her lips were pale, her eyelids were heavy. The smell of death was suddenly in the air. It was a putrid, heavy stink that seemed to seep out of her pores. She was making every effort to get her words out.

"Mom—"

"Please, Lucas, let me finish. I inherited every cent of that from my parents and I set it all aside for you and your sister. But this is not the legacy that I want you to remember. I want you to know that without love in your life, all that doesn't mean one single thing. Your wealth, your riches, will be in the eyes of those who love you. It will be in the laughter of your family, of your future wife and children. They are the investments that matter. Use it wisely, make a difference in the world. For me."

To this day, I will never be able to express the emotions that I felt as I gently settled her back, resting her comfortably on the raggedy pillow that held her head. "I love you, Mom. There is no need for forgiveness. I understand everything that you had to do, and I'm just so lucky that I found you again." I wasn't ashamed by the barrage of tears that flowed out of me that day. I was a child grieving for the mother who loved me in an unconventional way. "Mom, rest now, we'll talk again later. You can tell Marissa everything you want to say when you see her. I've asked her to come home; she'll be here soon to see you."

She stared at me blankly, fighting hard to concentrate on what I just said. My words no longer mattered to her, she had more to say. "Will you do an old lady a favor, my son?"

"Of course. Anything."

"Lie with me for a few minutes. Let me hold you for a while. I haven't held you in my arms since you were eight years old."

I nodded my head fervently as I stood up and carefully placed my arms underneath her frail body to inch her over to the side of the bed. I lowered myself into the tiny space next to her and placed my head on her chest. With great difficulty, she lifted her arms up and wrapped them around me, lovingly stroking my head for a few minutes until her arms grew heavy and slack despite remaining tightly wound around my shoulders.

"Good night, Lucas. I love you." She hummed feebly, knowing full well that the daylight had just begun.

"Good night, Mom. I love you too."

And then the angels swooped down from heaven to take her away to the place of everlasting repose, leaving me with a hollowness so deep that nothing, not even the contents of the ocean, could fill. And sixty million dollars.

Spring 2016

Cristina met me at the top of the Ocean Park Tower today, an observation deck overlooking the South China Sea and its surrounding islands. I was there on business and she for another modeling job.

"Thanks for meeting me here today. I hope I didn't screw up your schedule too much." She smelled the same, she felt the same, and the reaction that I had towards her remained the same. I felt nothing. I lead her by the elbow to a quiet area overlooking the park's rollercoaster ride and a clear view of the sea. After finally describing my mother's last day to Dr. Caster, my outlook resembled the view from where I stood. My life was full of possibilities and I wanted only Jade to be a part of it.

"No worries," she responded lightly. "Look over there. Can you see the silverfish in the water? I can't believe how clear the weather is today." She paused, noticing the distracted look on my face. "Okay. What's up with you? You look so serious."

I rubbed my hands together nervously. "Cristina, I wanted to see you to personally apologize for everything. These past few weeks have really made me realize how much of a jerk I was towards you. I would never wish what I did to you on anyone else. Someday soon, I hope to be able to make it up to you. You didn't deserve any of that."Maybe I should have used the word "ass" instead. Jade's special word, created just for me.

Her face turned hopeful, anticipatory, as if she expected me to tell her something that I didn't intend to. "What do you mean make it up to me?"

"I mean be a better friend from now on. I'm sorry for hurting you, for breaking our engagement."

I guess I was wrong. The look on her face was calm and relaxed. "Oh, Lucas. That was eons ago. I'm fine now. I've moved on. You were looking for something that you didn't find with me, that's why you couldn't stay faithful. I'm not making excuses for you, but I'm not one to stay where I'm not wanted."

"I'm so glad that you're finally with someone who loves you so much. I want to move on too. I'm planning to take a leave of absence to stay in the States for a month or so."

"Because of her?" She knew about Jade. We'd talked about her many times, especially after my disastrous trip to Chicago. "I thought it didn't end well?"

There were people walking up and down the sidelines, wondering why we remained standing at the same spot for so long. The truth was that Cristina and I had been here quite a few times, it was a familiar place for us. She loved amusement parks and we visited this place when we first decided to take our relationship to the next level. We weren't there to take in the sights. We were there because we recognized the need for an informal setting for such a conversation. It brought back memories of the old me.

Wait a minute. There was a new me?

"It didn't. Her boss called me shortly after that to tell me to stay away from her. I've been trying to do that, but now that the deal is closed, I'm going back to see her. I'm waiting to finish my outpatient stint—you know how I'm restricted in terms of travel."

"I know. But I'm still confused. You said that she basically told you to

leave when you were in Chicago. You know nothing about her at this point. What if she has a husband and a family?" Her words stung me unexpectedly. I was shaken by the suggestion. Up until this point, I knew nothing about her. The world we existed in consisted of a one square mile radius—her office, the corner store, the bar, and the hotel across the street.

After she realized what she just said, we both stared out mindlessly into the glass, lulled by the whirring sound of the rollercoaster contrasted by the high-pitched screams of its patrons. She broke the silence by apologizing. "Luke, I didn't mean anything by that."

"No, you're right," I assured her. And as soon as I said it, I was overtaken by an eye opening realization. "But I think I'm in love with her."

"Oh my God. What?" She laughed. "Oops. I don't mean to make light of it. I just think it's so out of character for you to say something like that." She teasingly struck me on the arm as I pretended to be offended.

"I said that about Isabel," I reminded her shamefacedly, embarrassed by that period in my life. With Jade, any thought of controlling her or hurting her for sex had never crossed my mind. It was certainly another reason to believe in what I had just confessed. Maybe this really was the real thing.

"Yeah, but I didn't believe you. You should see your face now. For some reason, I can tell you really mean it."

"Yeah, sure, because you're the expert," I teased. I began to enjoy our lighthearted conversation. It was a far cry from the drama that we had in our past.

She grew quiet and pensive and her eyes started to look like she was about to cry. "You never looked that way with me."

"Oh shit. Here I go again." I pulled her close to me and held her in my arms. "I'm sorry, Tins. I really am. For everything."

We stood together for a minute or so before pulling back to see a new group of tourists trying desperately to look over our shoulders. I took her hand and started to walk towards the exit. "I think we've been here long enough," I said as we made our way back down to ground level. Gone was the awkwardness between us that normally occurred as we stood together, engaged in our own thoughts.

She traipsed in front of me as soon as we found ourselves back by the entrance full of people. "David is waiting for me by the park benches," she said. "Take care, Luke. And I wish you the best." She stepped in to give me a quick kiss. "By the way, I like this new you. Don't lose it. Show her this side of the mystery."

I smiled back, relieved that at long last, she had given me her pardon.

FORTY-FOUR

Letting Go

TWO WEEKS HAVE passed since we arrived from Hawaii. In the most wonderful sense, the man who came home with me is the Chris I knew from a long time ago. He is tranquil and harmonious, he has a goal and a purpose. His mood has also greatly influenced the way I've been feeling since my meeting with Marissa ten days ago. I manage to cast my worries aside and concentrate on preparing for our move to the island. I notice that he has stopped taking his anxiety medication and I take it as a great sign that he is finally healing. No one deserves it more than he does. The beauty of his heart and his soul makes me wonder why it took so long for him to finally find the joy that he so merits. No one has helped more than he has during the most harrowing time of my life. He deserves all the happiness I can offer him.

Two days before the movers are scheduled to pack our things for shipment, I find Chris sitting in the dark surrounded by boxes of all sizes. His eyes are closed, his head is leaned back against a large TV carton, and his face looks like he's been crying.

"Chris?" I whisper as I walk closer towards him. I kneel down on the floor and take his hands in mine. "What's the matter, baby?"

"I've been waiting here for you for a while. Where've you been?" he asks, his tone somewhat agitated.

"I was at the Pacific Heights house with the realtor. She has a firm offer, so I thought I'd go and check on her staging. What happened?"

"We have to talk. I don't think I can do this."

"Do what?" I ask, totally confused.

"Take you away from all this. From your home. Your parents. From Cia." He bangs his fists against the wood floor repeatedly until I hold them together for fear of breaking his knuckles.

"Baby, did you miss your medication today? Let me go and get it; it'll calm you down again."

"I can't, Jae. I can't do this anymore. I know what happened."

"What happened? Where?"

"With Lucas. I know that he was here the night of our party."

My heart rises to my throat. I feel like I'm about to pass out. "Chris, please. Let me explain."

"I followed you. I saw him enter the bath—" He chokes on his words. As I reach out to touch him, he lifts his hands up to stop me. "Stop. Let me finish!"

I move back; from instinct, my body quakes at the unspeakable fear of reliving the memory of what happened almost a year and a half ago. And then I remember that I'm with Chris, my kind and gentle soul. I'm anything but afraid of him.

He starts to sob as he struggles to wring out his words. "I was too much of a coward to confront you about it because I knew you would leave me. And I decided at that time that I would rather have you with me despite your indiscretion."

"Chris, please," I beg. "It was nothing. It meant nothing. I was so caught up in the flattery of it all. It's not love. He doesn't have my heart. You do. We have a daughter together. It just makes sense that we're made to be with each other."

"Jade, don't sell your happiness short," he says curtly, a fresh round of tears spilling down his cheeks. "I see you crying at night. I watch you leave me when you think I'm asleep. You've started smoking again. You're losing weight." He sighs. "I love you so much that I can hear every word your heart speaks. You say his name while we're making love. Not with your lips, but with the distant look in your eyes. It's almost as if you're wishing it was him instead of me."

"Oh my God. No, Chris! I'm so sorry. Please, we can work this out. It's all in my head. I'm just so messed up from everything that has happened. But this doesn't mean that I don't love you. I want to have your baby. I want us to be the way we planned to be, twenty years ago!"

"Oh, Jae," he cries, "those days are long gone. I love you. But maybe that love is no longer enough. Or maybe it's no longer the love that you need. Years have passed between us. We've grown to be different people. I want you to be happy. Your happiness is most important to me." I crave for his touch, his closeness, his warmth. He shares none of that with me as we stand facing each other.

"Chris—"

"Can you honestly tell me that you don't have feelings for him?" he asks bluntly. "If you give me your word that you don't, I'll forgive everything and we'll move away."

I don't answer his question. Instead, I break down in a shameless sob. I'm shaking from the truth of what I'm about to disclose.

My reason for staying.

"I'm afraid, Chris. I'm afraid that if I let you go, it will mean that I'm letting her go."

His eyes are wet with tears. He tries to stop himself from blinking, but one flash of his cloudy blue eyes has his tears pouring down his face to match my own. "Sometimes, I get so angry at you, I can't stand to be near you. You made me believe in a lie. You were dishonest about your feelings for me. You robbed me of the chance to get to know my child and allowed another man to raise her. But most times, Jae, I'm consumed with overwhelming love for you. You're my first love, the only woman I've ever wanted. I see Cia in you, just like you see her in me. That connection with her, though, is hindering our healing. I know you understand what I mean."

"I do," I say, looking into his eyes. *I'm going to miss them, his eyes. My only light in all this darkness. I'm going to let him go. Maybe for now. Maybe for forever. In trying to repair him, I've damaged him even more.* "Fix me. Why can't you fix me?" I plead, tugging desperately at both his hands and bringing them to my face.

He affectionately caresses my cheeks, but the look on his face shatters me. It's a look of surrender. Of defeat. "You need something new," he says softly. "Something outside of your past to unbreak you. I'm your damage. I'm part of your scars. There is a mutilated part of you that won't ever be the same. And no matter how hard I try, your heart is craving to start over. We have to accept that now."

"I tried so hard to stay the same, to be the same person that you know, that you loved. But I've changed and I don't know how to go back. Nothing in the world can revive it. My heart is dead," I concede, still in tears, but with surprising belief in the words I've just spoken out loud.

He breaks away and slumps on the ground. My heart breaks at

the keening sound he makes as he continues to cry. "He fills you. He can restore you, put you back together. He can. Not me."

"No! Try harder, Chris. Try harder. Fight for me!" I demand as I shake him by his shoulders.

His head sways back and forth like a rag doll. His energy, his belligerence, his spunk—they're all gone. *I've killed him. I am poison.*

I swipe my eyes roughly with the back of my hands, desperate to convince myself to force the words out of my mouth. "You'll die too, if you stay with me. I have to let you go."

"Well then, I think I know what we need to do," he says calmly and with unexpected conviction. "Jae, letting each other go means holding on to Cia. It means finding our happiness in memory of her. This is what she would have wanted for us."

I'M STANDING BY the priority line at SFO International one week later, gripping his hand as we wait for him to board his flight. Since our talk, I've done nothing but cry and bemoan the lie that I've lived. I spent the next few days begging him for forgiveness. He tells me that he holds no bitterness in his heart. I'd like to think that it's because he too, knows that true love is out there somewhere, waiting for the chance to find him. He has the job of his dreams in a place that people would kill to live in. I know I have to let him go. The love of my life deserves so much more than my misery.

As soon as the final boarding call is announced, I stand up and pull him close to me, burying my head in his chest, refusing to let him go. "Don't go. Please," I implore him.

"Don't cry, Jae. This is for the best. And you'll come to visit once I'm settled."

"I know," I agree, "but I'll miss you. You're my best friend. What we had was the greatest love of my life and you gave me the best gift anyone can ever have. I love you, Chris."

"I love you, Jade Albin. I've never loved anyone but you. We had a great run. Think about it as the right time to quit while we're ahead." He tries his best to sound chipper, but the look in his eyes tells me that he's suffering just as much as I am. "I'll be back for Thanksgiving break. And maybe you can come back with me for a visit."

"I would love that." I squeeze my arms around him with all my might, closing my eyes and trying my hardest to memorize his face for the last time. By the time our lips meet, we are lost in the frenzy of our sobs. "Please, please," I wail into his chest. "I don't think I can do this. Please don't leave me alone." My knees give way as he holds me up by my elbows and slowly walks me back to sit down by the waiting area.

"You're not alone. You will always have me in your life. In time, we'll look back on this and know that we made the right decision." He kisses me on the forehead and reluctantly turns his back on me. Slowly, I release his hand one inch at a time until the tips of our fingers barely touch and there is nothing but air between us. He faces me one last time, his eyes filled with tears as he places his hand on his heart and tips his shoulders forward in a reverent bow. I bring my fingers to my lips before bringing them down to my heart.

I don't move. I stay rooted in place until the plane pushes back and taxis forward to take him away from the pain of his past.

His past.

That's all I am. That's all I can ever be.

A wise old man once told me that goodbyes are a part of living. You bid farewell to something every single day of your life. Sometimes, it's to something superficial or material, like a favorite pair of shoes or a dried out old pen that has seen better days. Other times it's to something more meaningful like a best friend who moves away or a loving and faithful pet whose time has merely run out. And then there are those goodbyes that you never thought you would ever have to make. The ones that make you fall, make you cry, make you die.

The loss of innocence, the loss of love. Chris. Cia.

Neither time nor space will ever heal the emptiness that they leave behind.

But before every parting is a greeting. A "Hi," "Hello," "It's so nice to meet you." Sometimes it doesn't mean anything, it's fleeting and ordinary and routine, like the people you pass on a two way street, or the person who sits next to you on the bus. No matter the manner however, it signifies the start of something exciting, fresh and unfamiliar. If you truly stop dwelling on the goodbyes of your life, you will recognize that special "Hello."

It comes in any form, on any day, at any time. And when it does, you will want to risk it all despite that impending departure.

Mine came in the form of a firm handshake, a lopsided smile, and deep, dark, angry brown eyes.

FORTY-FIVE

Spanish Eyes

"YES, YOU HEARD right. I'm in Spain. No, I just landed and am about to hop in a cab to find that doggone place."

I'm on the phone with Chris, checking in like I've become accustomed to in the month that he's been gone. He sounds happy and settled in his new life, loving his job and excited about exploring his new environment. He moved into a majestic home in Kahala, right by the ocean. The pictures he sent me boast of a sprawling 5,000 square foot home in a private beach front estate. It's a rental for now; I think he's finally coming to terms with the nomadic lifestyle that accompanies the career of his choice. I miss everything about him—his love, his protection, his face, his smell, his touch. I miss seeing my daughter in his eyes.

But I don't miss the guilt that I harbored while we were together.

Two weeks after Chris left, Marissa called to see how everything was going. I didn't tell her about Chris because I didn't think that we were over. She was closing up the San Francisco apartment and thought I should know where her brother had gone. "His friends were worried about him sitting around San Francisco waiting for nothing," she explained. "With all that temptation around him, they thought it would do him good to travel to Spain for some downtime away from everything."

So here I am, in a taxicab, riding through the winding coastal roads of Port De Soller, a city nestled between valleys surrounded by a bay that opens up into the great wide ocean, on my way to see him. Lately, I've become the Queen of Impulse, but this has to top everything I've done in the past few months. I figure that seeing him one more time will surely bring resolution to the mess I've created. Something that I desperately need, as I attempt to tie up all the loose threads that have recently come undone.

The driver takes me up a steep hill to a white, cube-shaped house replete with a style that reflects an understated sense of contemporary Spanish architecture. The white cement walls are offset by tall windows with wooden shutters. A rooftop terrace with an infinity pool can be seen from miles away, and the sound of splashing water and children's voices surprises me. *He's not alone*, I conclude to myself, as I see three identical Porsche 911s parked side by side on the driveway.

I knock lightly on the glass door, hoping that no one hears me, wishing that I could use it as an excuse to turn around and walk away. Someone comes forward merely two seconds after I lift my fingers off the knocker. It's a little person. An adorable brown-haired girl in a pink tutu and white ballet slippers, wide-eyed and excited about having answered the door all by herself.

"Hi," I say as I kneel down and offer my hand out to her outstretched fingers. "I'm Jade. I'm looking for—"

"Are you Miss Universe? You sure look like her." Her little voice brings me back to the past once again.

"Maddy, who is it?" a woman's voice calls out from the hallway.

"Mommy, she's so pretty. I think it's Miss Universe!"

I stand up as a carbon copy of the little girl appears behind her. Bright, light brown doe eyes and flawless facial features—talk about Miss Universe. The mother gives her daughter an indulgent smile, then looks up in welcome.

I laugh uncomfortably as I hear another set of shuffling feet. This time, it's a light-haired man with a cane in one hand and a chubby baby boy hooked under his arm. They make a striking couple. She takes the baby from him as he so naturally encircles his free arm around her shoulders and pulls her close.

"Hi," he whispers tenderly in her ear.

"Hi," she answers, lightly brushing her lips against his.

I want that kind of quiet love.

We all stay mum for a brief second until I nervously break the silence.

"I'm sorry. I think I have the wrong house. I'm looking for Lucas Martinez; this is the address that was given to me."

"You are?" the woman asks, turning her head towards the man standing next to her.

"My name is Jade. I'm a friend of his."

"You're at the right place. I'm Isabel and this is my husband, Alex. These two little people are our children, Maddy and Jack." She leans over to give me a kiss on each cheek. Alex does the same, while the sweet little boy giggles and kicks his feet in the air.

This is the woman who left him for her husband. "It's a pleasure to meet you all," I reply, filled with awe at the love that's clearly radiating from this extraordinary family. Such genuinely happy people; I can't help but notice how they smile with their eyes.

And then, a familiar voice.

"Jade Richmond."

I can see Leigh Taylor standing a few feet away from the door. He holds hands with a dark-haired beauty wearing a pretty white summer dress.

"Oh, hi, Leigh. My gosh. I'm so sorry to intrude on your family vacation. I didn't even think to ask Marissa whether or not he was living alone." I fish into my purse and pull out my card and a pen, scribbling rapidly with the aim of leaving as quickly as I can. I'm short of breath and fighting the urge to shed more tears. *Once again, I don't find him.* "I'm staying at this hotel, if you would please just ask Lucas to call me when he can."

Alex slowly walks away, leaning heavily on his cane as his left leg drags behind his right. I notice Isabel watching him lovingly until he is no longer within her view. She then takes my hand and leads me inside the home. The heavy wooden furniture provides a delightful contrast to the bright white interior of the house. There are no shades, and the large windows open up to the most spectacular panorama I have ever seen.

"He just went out for a run," she says. "Please come inside and join us on the patio for a cup of coffee. He should be back soon."

I nod my head absently and follow her through the living room, up a flight of stairs, and through sliding glass doors that lead to the outdoor pool and a large seating area. The rest of the family is frolicking in the water. I watch them with interest, remembering the delightful sound of laughter that filled the early years of my marriage with Joshua. Isabel motions for me to take a seat. No one else has followed us here. The two of us are left alone, and I have to convey what's foremost on my mind. I have to know.

"Does it feel awkward—I mean, the fact that L-Lucas and

you—with your h-husband and all?" I stutter through my words, trying my best not to sound offensive.

"Alex continues to take responsibility for that time in my life," she answers easily, not the least bit taken aback by my question. "He sees that there was no emotional connection with Lucas whatsoever. It's funny. Although we've all moved past that tumultuous year in our marriage, we will never forget it and the lessons we learned from it." There is such a sweet calmness to her voice, to her demeanor. She's the absolute picture of serenity. All of a sudden, I am jealous of her. I want her peace. "Why are you here, Jade?" she asks bluntly.

"I wish I knew." I sigh, looking down at my hands for a moment and then affixing my eyes back on her. I feel an affinity towards this woman whom I've just met and who has a past with the man I think I'm in love with. She brings a sense of reprieve to this conversation. A small ray of hope that Chris and I can someday be good friends. "I just had to see him. For the past eight months, I've been consumed by thoughts of him, by feelings for him. I struggle to define them and selfishly, I'm hoping that seeing him will give me that clarity. I need to understand why I was willing to throw away something special in my life for a fixation that I can't even begin to understand."

I notice that the children are starting to get out of the pool and so I turn around, curious to see what's prompting them to do so. I see Alex standing by the doorway, signaling to Isabel, and she immediately stands up to leave.

"We're so sorry to have to leave you here. I'm going to bring you some coffee and then we're all heading out to take the kids to the beach for the day. Lucas should be back any minute now." She turns her head away to address the boy still in the pool. "Eddie! Time to go!"

I bob my head up and down, trying not to panic. *I'll be fine here.*

I'll wait. I don't want her to worry about me. *I'll wait. He'll be back soon and I can get everything off my chest.*

She pauses with an afterthought and reaches out to lightly touch my right shoulder. "I hope you don't mind my giving you some advice," she starts out. "The past. Sometimes, we get so hung up about it that it prevents us from looking ahead. Trust me, I know what I'm talking about. The past can never be duplicated; nothing ever stays the same. But the mind, it tricks us into thinking that we can bring it all back if we try hard enough to do so. Let the past go. Hurl yourself into the future knowing that time waits for no one. Whatever that means for Lucas, don't look back. Step forward no matter how much more comfortable you are with your past. *Trust in your heart because it places its trust in you.*"

And then I am left with the deafening silence of an empty house.

FORTY-SIX

At Long Last

I CONTINUE TO sit and stare at my surroundings, swathed in the lull of the stillness. I can see Chris' blue eyes in the reflection of the water, Cia's purity in the stark white walls of the outdoor enclosure, my whole life depicted in the endless expanse of the mountainous view. I don't think of him until I feel him next to me. I look up into those bewitching dark brown eyes.

"Jade?" He removes his earphones, shuts off his iPod, and steps away to grab one of the towels hanging on a rack.

"Hi."

"You're here? How did you know?"

"I went over to your place to deliver your Secret Agent book. Marissa told me."

He removes his shirt and I do my best not to look in his direction. "Sorry, I'm a mess. I'm going to cool off. Be right back." He walks away towards the outdoor shower, rinses off, and then dives into the pool. He goes from one end to the other and lifts himself out of the water to walk back towards me.

"You realize that now I'm too distracted to have a conversation with you." I laugh, trying not to stare at the soaking wet Adonis in front of me.

He doesn't find any humor in what I just said. "Why are you here?" He sits down on the ground right next to my feet, a puddle of water slowly gathering around him. "Is your fiancé with you?"

I shake my head. "I wanted to see you."

"Now that's a change. I already know your good news. You didn't have to come here to rub it in my face."

"Just like you didn't have to come to my mother's party uninvited."

"Oh yeah, that. Huge mistake."

I am taken aback by his declaration. That night meant everything to me. It stole away any chance I had of working things out with Chris and launched me into a world where nothing else existed but him. I realize that I can't take much more of this. I can't break down his walls and I'm done trying. I spring myself upwards without a word and quickly dart away.

"That's it!" I hear him say loudly to make sure that I hear him despite the distance. "Run away again. That seems to be what you do best."

"You're a jerk!" I yell back as I boot it out of the house, down the steep, sloping hill, and out of his life.

I TELL MYSELF that it may not be a bad thing—the fact that the earliest flight home is not till the day after tomorrow. I decide to make the most out of it, scheduling an all day tour of the capital city of Palma and some of the historic monuments along the way. Today I take my time wandering on foot along the white sand beach that lines the resort where I'm staying. It's been a few hours since the incident at the vacation house and my mind is clearer than it has ever been. I came here to find what I was looking for and I'm leaving here with the pain of knowing that it wasn't meant to be. When you feel this strongly about someone, convincing yourself that he was merely passing by will take all of the logic you can muster in your mind.

The hotel lobby is bustling with sights and sounds that are familiar to anyone on vacation in a city full of tourists—cameras, backpacks, foreign accents—I hear them without seeing them. I zip through the crowds of people and heave a sigh of relief as soon as I get inside the car that will take me to my floor. I'm the only one in so I persistently pound on the CLOSE button out of habit. Just as the doors begin to move, an arm reaches in, followed by a body.

His body.

I turn my head away, refusing to look at him, aware of the fact that we are both scooted on opposite corners of the enclosed space. *He's getting very good at appearing out of nowhere.* A family of four steps in; their chatter a welcome respite from the strain that ensues between us. I can feel the scalding burn of his eyes on me as I stare up at the row of floor numbers that light up one by one. My stop is the first one up. I don't wait until the doors are fully open, I dash out, hoping that I can make it to the safety of my room before I decide what to do next. I hear his footsteps behind me and speed up my stride until I find myself breaking out in a run. Another pathetic move on my part, considering that room 4042 is the last one at the end of the hall right next to a dead end wall. I laugh to myself as I begin to see the pattern of my life. *Hard stops. Dead ends. Irrevocable. Irretrievable. Final.*

Things happen so quickly. I grip the room key in my fingers as he pins me to the door, taking my face in his hands and fervently rubbing his lips against my cheeks.

"I'm sorry. I'm so sorry, Jade. I love you." His lips find mine and this time, there is no hesitation, no reserve, no conclusion. I want this to be our beginning. I want him to devour me, to swallow me whole. I want to hide from the world, wrapped in his arms.

He unlocks the door without breaking our kiss and lifts me up to carry me inside. "You didn't allow me to finish," he says breathlessly. "That night was a huge mistake because it's all I can think about every fucking minute of the day. Being inside you. That's the only thing that makes sense to me," he murmurs as he sets me back down on the ground.

I don't say a word. I take his hand and slowly walk backwards to lead him towards the bed. He follows me, watching my every move as peel my clothes off slowly, one layer at a time, all the while staring straight into his dark brown eyes. And then he reaches out to touch me, his fingers so delicately stroking every inch of my skin. I bring my mouth to his and he kisses me with the kind of unbridled passion that makes me forget all of the pain I've ever experienced in my life.

"Jade," he whispers, "let me cherish you."

I lift my body up to meet his touch and guide his mouth downwards, allowing his hands to roam wherever they please. I begin to unbutton his shirt but he stops me.

"No. Not yet. Let me enjoy you."

"We have no pictures." My lips betray my thoughts.

He pauses for a moment and then stretches his arms to graze the top of my shoulders with his fingertips. "That's what you think. Look, twenty-two tiny freckles," he continues to trace a downward path with his hands, "and a birthmark right under here." He touches the inside of my thigh. "I committed them to memory on that very first night."

He spreads my legs and expertly gives me so much pleasure, I can hardly contain myself when I whisper in his ear, "I want to come with you inside me."

This prompts him into action. He tears off his clothes, giving me free access to reach out for him, to pull him closer. I let out a high-pitched moan when he enters me, my legs high above his shoulders, my hands on his thighs as he slides my body up to meet his. I feel so full, like every void in me has just been suffused. I encourage his mouth, I provoke the intensity of his touch, I spur him to use his tongue, his teeth. Pleasure and pain. Only when I'm with him do I welcome them with open arms.

The overwhelming emotion of having him here with me is more than I can take. I have to tell him how I feel, but I can't define it.

"Lucas. I want to—"

"Shh. It's okay. Don't say anything. Just feel," he instructs as he holds my legs together to tighten myself around him. "Feel me just as much as I feel you." His movements turn furious, the look on his face intense. His eyes never leave mine as he moves in and out, my moans reverberating on his lips. "Only you, Jade. Teach me how to love you. Help me to let go."

With one final thrust, he fills me with himself.

I don't think of him. I can't even remember her.

All I know is that he is inside me and I'm aware of nothing else but my desire. He's giving me what I've wanted all this time. And for once in my life, I selfishly take it all.

FORTY-SEVEN

Finding Ourselves

"ARE YOU OKAY?" he asks as he takes my hand and brings it to his lips for a kiss. We're sitting atop a double decker bus on a city tour of Palma.

"Yes, I'm perfect," I answer, leaning in to kiss him on the cheek. "I've never seen you so relaxed before."

"Having sex five times in one night will do that to you," he teases. "In fact, I'm counting the seconds until this tour is finally over so you can relax me again."

We step off the bus for a walking tour of the cathedral, the last stop in our four-hour long local excursion. Also known as La Seu, the imposing structure stands out from the seafront, its golden sandstone exterior hovering above the city's walls. We have an hour to explore on our own. After walking around for a while, we decide to sit by the side door of the church, along a long nave surrounded by tall iron columns and meticulously fashioned stained glass windows. I once read a long time ago that these windows were designed to depict life during those periods, of Christ and of medieval times, of the colors of the world and visual remembrances of every era. It's funny how they've appeared at monumental stages in my life. At junctures that represent my life story.

Fate vs. coincidence. I truly believe in that.

"Wouldn't you love to live in a place like this where the weather is warm and sunny all the time?" he asks, moving his body closer to mine. It's autumn in Chicago. Football, hockey, half marathons.

"Now what would the fun be in that? I love my seasons. With them, no sadness is permanent. There's always hope."

We lean against the stone wall, side by side, my head on his shoulder as he loops his right arm around me. The captivating beauty of these vestiges renders us deep in thought.

"Why didn't you tell me about your mom? About rehab?" I ask him discretely, making sure that I don't sound accusatory or confrontational.

"What difference would it have made?" he answers lightly. I don't sense any anger in his voice.

"A world of difference. I would have gotten to know you better. What makes you tick, what drives you."

"What drives me wild is you," he teases again. "Especially when you did that thing last night…"

"Stop joking around!" I swat his arm playfully. "I would have been right there for you."

"I just had to work things out on my own. And in a way, I am glad that I did, especially after finding out that you were going through much more yourself."

I nod my head in agreement. I never told him much either, determined to work through things on my own. I know exactly how that goes.

He stares far away into the distance before continuing on. "You and I, we're two peas in a pod. Heartless. Broken. We've both touched death and despair with our bare hands. You handled it bravely; I spun off my axis."

"I really didn't. I had an emotional affair on my husband and a sexual encounter on my fiancé. That is hardly courageous," I protest. And I feel ashamed.

"I'm honored to know that it was with the same person," he rags me jokingly.

"I know, right? Crazy times," I goad back, flashing him a warm smile.

A few minutes later, we are interrupted by the approaching footsteps of our tour guide. Lucas stands up and extends his hand to help me get on my feet. "Finally," he says, "we get to go home."

THE RECEDING LIGHT of the afternoon sun streams through our bedroom window. Lucas and I lie together on the chaise lounge facing the astounding view of the ocean. My back is flush against his skin as he entwines his arms and legs around me, his right hand caressing my neck, his nose buried in my hair. The white sand beach extends miles and miles beyond the horizon, connecting countries and people and cultures. If heaven were real and Cia was there, I would be a few steps closer to finding her.

"I always wondered what this would be like," I think out loud as I hold on to his arms and encourage their weight on me. "If the stubble on that chin was scratchy. What those hands would feel like on my skin."

He instigates my comment by lifting his head and rubbing his jaw along my cheek. "Hmm. Well, tell me. How do I feel?"

"Rough!" I laugh. "In a good way."

He tilts my head sideways and kisses me lightly on the nose. "Well, I'm here now. This is real. You don't have to imagine anything because this isn't a fantasy anymore, for either of us."

"Are you disappointed?" I ask shyly.

"Oh fuck, no! Quite the opposite! The real you is a world apart from the Skype buddy I had. You're stunning and precious, a treasure to be worshiped. Your skin is so soft and flawless. You feel like heaven to touch, to kiss. You're delicious and silky and oh so very wet. All the time. You are absolutely amazing," he whispers as his free hand travels down from my neck to my breast. His fingers work like magic. They caress and touch and pinch and tease until I want him so badly again. I close my eyes and enjoy this moment with him. I snap back to reality when I hear his voice enter my thoughts.

"Tell me about Felicia," he quietly requests.

The mere mention of her name makes me feel guilty. In that instant, I become aware that we are naked. I sit up abruptly, reach for the robe sprawled out on the floor, and cover myself. "She was my life. I was so lucky to be her mother."

He pulls me back down to him, as if trying to find a way to console me.

"I'm okay, really I am," I assure him.

"I can't even begin to imagine what you went through, losing the person you love most in the world," he says sadly. "With my mother, I had only gotten to know her for a few months. The impact to me was more contempt for lost time. For you, the world that you lived and breathed was no longer. It must have been so devastating."

"It was. Everything changed for me after that day. My life didn't make sense. I woke up the next day and didn't recognize anything around me. It was like Felicia gave that life its essence. Without her, it was reduced to nothing."

"She was so pretty, by the way. Just like her mother."

"Thank you. I think it was more difficult for Chris to handle because of the fact that she looked a lot like him."

He nods his head in understanding and waits patiently. We both know it's my turn to ask a tough question.

"And you? Tell me about your mom."

"I know you've never experienced this, but when you're a product of divorced parents, you always end up taking sides with one or the other. My father always led us to believe that my mother walked out on us. While she did leave him to return home to her country, it was because she was miserable. She was a very independent woman who couldn't take the old world culture that moving to Spain with my father forced her to accept. She was a renowned psychiatrist at the height of her career. She said that she left to save her sanity, to save us from going down with her. When I heard she was sick, I decided to move back to care for her and to try to convince her to seek medical help in the States. But by the time I found her, she was resigned to living what was left of her life in pure simplicity. She lived in a small house in the mountains close to a nunnery and she prayed and offered her pain up to God every day. She held me in her arms when she died, as if it was me, and not her, who desperately needed to be comforted and rescued. Her gesture was the ultimate act of selflessness, and she wanted to pass that on to me. She was so at peace with her world and with herself; it made me so angry that all the prayers on this earth couldn't save her. I took what should have been her resentment against her faith as my own."

"How did you get over it?" I asked, sincerely wishing I could learn from his mistakes.

"I met you."

"That's not necessarily true. You went to rehab before we met."

"But I was an angry rehab patient. After you, I was a real rehab patient—I opened myself up to the many opportunities to let go of my pain." He pauses for a moment and then laughs sarcastically. "Well, until you got engaged to Chris."

"Tell me about the night of the party. What did you want to accomplish then?"

"Honestly, all I wanted was to see you," he answered bluntly, leaning down to kiss my collarbone. "But the only time he left your side was when you took a bathroom break. I apologize for acting so savagely. Truly, Jade. I couldn't express myself in any other way. For months, all we had were words and assumptions. I wanted your touch to speak to me this time, to shock me into the realization that you were no longer mine."

"There was no going back to Chris after that," I say contritely, and a funny thought crosses my mind. "I saw you take the pen."

He pretends to smack his hand on his head and laughs, looking the tiniest bit flabbergasted. "Hey, that pen got me through all the months I spent missing you."

"You? I started requesting for those pens every time I went to the supply room!"

My mind takes me back to that backdrop—the office, the merger—everything that prompts my insecurities about our age difference. I turn to face him, crossing my arms and legs at the same time.

"Why me, Luke?"

He uncrosses my arms and takes my hand in his. "Why not you?"

"I was almost ten years old when you were born."

"Exactly."

"I was getting lost in Enid Blyton's world while you were breastfeeding."

"Precisely my point. Our age difference means the world in terms of experience and thought and goals, hopes and dreams. It doesn't mean anything in number of years. So you beat me with *Noddy and the Faraway Tree* by a few years. Same story, same words, read at a different time. Interpreted in a way that reflected our respective life situations. Big deal."

"Oh my gosh!" I cry in delight. "You read those books? I was obsessed with them. You're turning me on right now."

He laughs before leaning over to kiss me. "Jade. Do you see my point here? I'm not here to play around. I choose you because of those years. That ten-year head start is what reels me in. Sophistication, introspection, direction, fortitude. You."

"Thank you. And for the record, it's really nine years," I whisper, moving closer to him as he encircles both arms around me.

He chuckles softly in my ear. "Do you love me, Jade?"

"Oh, Luke. When we were going over whatever it was during the merger, I thought about you every single day. I couldn't go on without hearing your voice at least once a week. I wanted you so much, I imagined myself with you obsessively." I can feel my cheeks warm with my admission. "Is this love? I'd like to find this out. Does six months of infatuation equate to love? I don't know."

His expression is pained. "You don't think I love you? God, Jade. Nothing makes sense without you. My life, my career, all this—it's like walking through a dessert where there's no sign of life anywhere I turn."

"You don't know me," I remind him, "just like I hardly know you. But the little I know about you, I love. I don't want to lie to you—I want to fully own the damage that I caused Chris. I want to live in truth from now on. I've wanted you since the first day I met you and I need to understand what this means for us. Can we do that together?"

"Yes. Yes, we can. I'll stay in San Fran and we'll figure it out." His upturned eyes and lopsided smile are so gracious that I fall in love with him right there and then.

He's trying to give me space. We might actually be making some progress.

"Thank you," I hum into his mouth, playfully biting the crooked top lip that I've grown attached to. "I wasn't kidding when I told you how happy I was that you and I read the same books."

"Great," he gripes. "So much for my macho image. I hope you keep this as our little secret."

"Ours." I let the robe fall to the floor and straddle him, lowering myself onto him as he groans in pleasure. Slowly, I start to move.

"Oh yeah. Number eight?" he pants heatedly.

"Number eight," I confirm, my voice emphatic, allowing myself to get lost in this wonderful yet obscure state of contentment.

FORTY-EIGHT

Fifty

"WHERE ARE WE going, Luke?" I ask restlessly as the limo cruises along Lakeshore Drive in Chicago, past the sights that meant something to me at one point or another in my life. Lucas insisted we fly here for what he called a special meeting and I assumed it would have something to do with his business. We just landed on the roof of the Trump Towers minutes ago and already, I'm apprehensive about being back in this town.

One month has passed since we returned from Spain. Lucas has moved into the Four Seasons temporarily and we spend some time getting to know each other while he works out of a rented office during the day. Who would have known that someone as dominant and serious as he is could be one of the funniest people I have ever met? He's a completely different person now that we're out of a "work relationship" and honest with each other. He's easygoing and considerate and I know just where I stand. He still has his moods, but somehow, I've been finding subtle ways of bringing him out of them whenever they start to consume his thoughts. There's something about his arrogance that intrigues me. He's not pompous, it's his self-confidence that makes him seem cavalier at times. Success for someone his age goes hand in hand with attitude. I know. I've been there.

It's a whirlwind of activity for us, from shopping and dining to parasailing and surfing. The guy can shop—it's amazing to watch him in action, picking up statement pieces that make him look like he just walked out of a photo shoot. He chooses things for me, asks me to model them for him, and then attacks me like a mad man in the fitting room. We've tested quite a few fitting rooms over the last for weeks.

"So, how'd you rate that one?" he asked me as we walked out, hand in hand, fresh from one of those encounters yesterday.

"A three." I giggled, conscious of the fact that the salesgirls were looking at me with the utmost envy.

He shook his head in opposition. "Nah, a two. It was too small—I couldn't stretch my legs."

I guess I underestimated the appeal of a younger man.

It turns out that his favorite place in the world is Big Sur, a relaxing place where I can spend all day watching him hit the big waves or lazily paddle surf on the days when the water is uncooperatively clear and calm. Maybe one day, he will help me get over my fear of the ocean. Apparently he thinks it will happen someday soon.

I make it a point to call Chris once every week. I miss his friendship, but the past few weeks have made me understand that the love I felt for him was guided by my love for Cia. I know we made the right choice in breaking up, but still, I feel no conclusion between us. I spend my days worrying about tying up the loose ends of my life.

"He's a late bloomer," Lucas says of Chris. "He's just now realizing his dream."

I don't disagree with that assessment.

That final thought throws me back into the present. Lucas is clasping my fingers in his, trailing his free hand up the hem of my skirt. I look out the window to see tiny chunks of ice forming in the river.

"Seriously, babe. Where are we going?" I ask, distracted by the feelings he incites in me.

It appears our destination is my former office building. It looks different. Bare yet imposing, and the steps of the entranceway are cordoned off.

"Look, no flower boxes, no birds, no work people. Just us."

"You, me and the cold, wintry Chicago winds," I joke, hugging myself to keep warm.

What I just said doesn't bother him. He smiles as he slowly folds one knee until it reaches the ground. He pulls out a black box and offers it to me. Impulsively, I take a step back. It doesn't faze him; he staunchly carries on.

"Jade, during my mother's illness, the tumor in her brain had begun to adversely affect her thoughts and her actions. In the last week of her life, she obsessed about the number 50. One day, she wanted to order fifty pounds of mangoes and send them to every member of our family. The next day, she wanted me to find her fifty pairs of earrings so she could pick out what to wear to her funeral. At first, I didn't understand why she had such a fixation on such a large quantity of objects. But as she explained it to me, I realized that she was trying to compensate for the shortage in the number of days that she had left in this world by contrasting them against a seemingly considerable amount of things. She wanted to prove to me that one or fifty of something doesn't change what God has planned for you. I've had all that, Jade. I've accumulated enough material things that make people envious of me, things that make people think that my world is complete, when the truth is, I had nothing. But you… you make up for everything I've lost. You fill my life with everything I will ever need. Marry me. I want to spend the rest of my life getting to know every single thing about you."

"Luke." I take his hands, but they remain clasped tightly around the little black box even as I try to get him to stand up.

He doesn't move, but stubbornly retains his position. "You and I have been through significant losses in our lives," he continues. "I spent years repenting the past and questioning my future. But after I met you, I realized that there was a plan for me all along, that things had to happen in this order because the person that I am now was molded by those events in my life. All my doubts disappear whenever I'm with you. You make me want to live, to cherish life. I've never laughed so much with anyone else as I have with you. I want to be all that you are to me. I want to be your last love. That daily train you used to get on, the one you've memorized in your sleep. That was long gone ever since you met me. I would be honored to take this journey with you. I'm your last train, Jade. Make me your last train home."

I reach out my hand to caress his face tenderly before taking hold of both hands once again and leading him towards our favorite place. "Come, let's sit."

This time he follows me and takes a seat down on the very steps where this all started between us. I can't help myself. I take his face in my hands and pour my soul into him with a kiss. He bows his head down as soon as I pull away.

"How can you be so sure?" I ask quietly.

"You're asking me this because you're not," he confirms sadly.

"Please. Please hear me out. What we have is an attraction for each other that's out of this world. But these last few months—if there's any indication of what we've shared, I can't remember anything but the waiting, the wishing, and the fact that you never reciprocated the way that I felt. I'm still getting over believing that you were everything to me and I was nothing to you."

"That's not fair, Jade. You know that I was trying to work on myself before coming to see you." He looks at me beseechingly, his hands still gripping the tiny black box. I know he's trying to make me understand, but up until a month ago, I had no idea he felt that way about me.

"Regardless of your reasons, this is how I was made to feel."

"You're finding an excuse to run away again. When are you going to stop running?" His walls are slowly building back up. I can feel it in the iciness of his tone; his body language turns stiff and distant.

"Look, I fell for you during a crazy time in my life. I want to be able to fall in love with you naturally and not obsess about you because I'm lonely and alone. All I'm asking is that we give it more time."

"But that's why I love you," he pleads softly. "You loved me through all that, despite the fact that I was never there for you."

"I don't know if I can take having another child again," I leak out.

He looks absolutely shocked, but retains his composure. "W-We can talk about that later."

"Luke. I just want to be sure." I am suddenly terrified at knowing the effect that these words will have on him.

He stands up with his back towards me and speaks clearly,

devoid of any emotion. "I've faced my fears, Jade. When are you going to face yours?"

"You continued to sleep with other women after you met me. And now you're telling me that you felt the same way about me from day one? Call me a coward, but at least I'm being honest. I just don't believe you," I spit out indignantly. "I'm sorry."

He shakes his head disbelievingly, as if he can't fathom how I could be so emotionless, so unfeeling. "So the past few weeks have meant nothing to you?"

"They mean too much," I dispute weakly.

"What are you so afraid of?" he asks, frustration written all over his face.

"I'm not afraid. I just need time."

He shakes my hand off as I try to spin him around to face me. "You of all people should know that sometimes we don't get the benefit of time. It's now or never. Either you want me or you don't."

"There you go again! Making demands on me. I—"

He doesn't wait for me to finish. He shoves the box back into his coat pocket and backs away with a tormented look in his eyes that fills me with dread.

It's over. He's done.

"Run away again, Jade. Leave like you always do."

I don't move. This time I stay rooted in place. I don't even blink. I belong here, with him.

"The driver is here to take you wherever you want to go. I'll have someone pick up my stuff from your place. Good luck, Jade. I wish you the very best, always."

I watch him walk away from me, yearning with all my heart that he stops to look back.

He doesn't.

FORTY-NINE

It Does Mean Something

"YOU KNOW YOU can stay with me for as long as you need to," Leya assures me kindly as she pours me another cup of coffee.

I'm standing by the stove, making her a quick breakfast before she has to leave for work. It's been a week since Lucas' proposal and I've remained in town to give him time to return to San Francisco for his things. We haven't spoken at all, although he has managed to speak to Leya a few times, mainly just to check on where I would be staying in the days following his departure from Chicago.

"Thank you for your offer. I'm hoping to wrap up things here in a few days and return home shortly after that."

Leya leans against the kitchen counter, clasping her fingers around her oversized coffee cup. She looks at me with a slight smile on her lips, her eyes gentle and sympathetic, full of emotion.

I turn my head towards the living room, resting my gaze on a few things that remind me of my past. "How's Jordan doing at school? Is she liking Iowa?" I ask. My chest no longer tightens when I see reminders of Cia. Jordan was her friend. I need to be cognizant of the fact that the loss of her wasn't just all mine.

"Well, she met a boy, so she's been coming home less and less. But Brent and I plan to drive up often for the football season. She thinks she might be able to find a roommate for an apartment close to campus."

"They up grow so fast. How did the time just run away with all these years?"

Leya nods her head uncomfortably. I know she's thinking of me. I change the subject immediately, but she's still looking at me with pity. I don't do well with pity.

"That night. You knew, didn't you?" I dare to ask, knowing full well what her answer would be. I place the hot pan in a sink full of water before setting a plate full of eggs and toast on the kitchen counter in front of her.

She doesn't answer for a while. I know it's because she has so much more to say that she's formulating the weight of her words in her head. She's never been at a loss for sharing her opinions with me. This time, she wants me to take her seriously.

"I saw him, and then I saw you. And I knew." Her voice starts to crack and then her tears fall softly, one at a time. "I'm really worried about you, Jade. It breaks my heart to see you like this. Why are you doing this to yourself? You know you love him. How else do you want him to prove his feelings for you?"

I want to answer her directly, but I don't know what to say. I, myself, don't understand what it is I'm looking for.

She takes my silence as her cue to keep going. "He has this effect on you that no other man has ever had. When I saw you that night, your face told me all there was for me to know. You had the look that being with him brings out in you. He's the one you want and yet, you keep on with the denial, and this horrible self-inflicted sabotage."

"You're absolutely right."

She looks at me in sheer surprise. "I am?"

"The way I feel about him just doesn't make any sense. He comes from such a dark time in my life. I don't ever want to go there again. Things that you can't explain die a natural death. What if that happens? I need to heal myself before I can truly feel comfortable about loving someone else other than Chris. Or Josh. Or Cia."

"That is the most ridiculously selfish thing I have ever heard! Chris, Josh, your parents, Cia, me—we all love you. We all want what you want. We all want to you be happy. You've definitely lost it if you think that we're all just sitting around wallowing over what's happened in the past two years. Take control of your life and run with it. Not away from it." She holds nothing back about giving it straight to me. The tone of her voice is strict and authoritative. I can tell she holds no sympathy for anything I've just revealed to her. "Stop overanalyzing things, Jade. There has to come a point where you grab the bull by the horns and ride it out. Life will pass you by and before you know it, you'll be left all alone."

"Please understand, Ley. I need time to come to my own conclusions. Will you give it to me? Will you support me while I manage through this? I promise to make myself get better," I am crushed by her lack of understanding, it moves me to tears.

Her demeanor softens instantly as she walks towards me and enfolds me in her arms. "Okay, sweetie. I understand. Take the time you need but promise me that you will eventually open your heart up to whoever makes you happy. There's nothing sensible about falling in love. That's the beauty of all this. I know you're afraid to get hurt again, but Lucas is God's gift to you for everything you've endured in the past two years. Welcome him into your life—he wants in, Jade. Let him in. Stop Running."

I SIT IN a booth at his favorite steak place across the river and wait calmly until I see his familiar, kindly face slowly approach our table. I invited him to join me for lunch on my way to O'Hare for a flight back to San Francisco the day after Leya and I had our conversation. I stand up immediately to greet him with a kiss.

"Hi, Father Mike. I'm so happy you could make it on such short notice."

"Of course. I've been wondering how you've been," he says lightly as I slide back into the booth and he takes the seat across from me.

I call for the server, who immediately takes our order for some drinks. We take a while to peruse the menus before he starts to ask me for an update.

"Your mother tells me that you recently had a marriage proposal," he says offhandedly, as if it was the most normal thing in the world.

I laugh timidly, embarrassed to have to explain to him the outcome of that event. "Oh gosh, my mother! When did she call you about it?"

"She actually called me about organizing Cia's next service. She told me about it when I asked her how you were."

"Well, then you already know how it went down."

"Jade."

In the midst of our conversation, the server takes our meal order. I ask for a steak salad while he gives in to a 12 oz. New York strip. I try to change the subject for a bit. "How's Joshua doing?"

"Very well, actually. He and Cara have been seeing Father Joseph for their pre-marital sessions."

"Oh my! I'm so happy for him," I gush, genuinely filled with so much joy at his news.

"They're getting married?"

"Yes, seven months from now."

"I'm so glad. You see? I told you he would find true love one day. Cara is really good to him."

"And he is good to her. He loves her very much." It's a fascinating fact that this man always knows just what I'm about to say. "It's okay that you're relieved that he has finally found his peace, Jade. And it's okay to wish the same for Chris too."

I shake my head, keeping it down, refusing to catch his eyes. "I destroyed Chris instead of helping to rebuild him. I'm a liar and a cheater. My life has been one big joke."

He reaches across the table to take my hands in his. "First and foremost, it was never your responsibility to fix Chris. You lost the most important person in your life. You sacrificed 19 years of your life for her. You are kind and loving and incredibly ethical—a wonderful mother, daughter, and wife. What went down in the past year doesn't define who you are as a person. You're allowed to make mistakes." He gently holds my hands down when I try to pull away. "You've never been one to play the victim of life's circumstances. And I know that you're not about to start now. Take accountability for your actions, but move on at the same time. You're lucky that it took months and not years for you to gain some clarity."

I completely agree with his statement. "Yes, it's funny but my head just cleared up as soon as I saw him in Mallorca. After I left him at the beach house, I fully accepted the fact that regardless of whether Lucas and I ended up together, what I had with Chris could never be more than a beautiful part of my past."

"Now that says something, doesn't it?" He starts to cut through his food as a sign that it's my turn to talk and his turn to eat.

"I was hoping that we would figure things out together, but he's so damn impatient." I sigh wearily. He nods his head while chewing his food, urging me to continue. Lucas' gorgeous face quickly enters my mind and I miss him so terribly. "Yes, yes. I guess it does mean something. And I'm so afraid that I've lost him."

It doesn't matter how much you have, how accomplished you are, how well put together your life is, or that you are loved by so many people. A heartache is a heartache is a heartache. Whether you're 23 or 43, the tenderness in your heart whenever you hear his name, the time you spend each day living with your memories, the loneliness that you feel despite the love of those around you—these things don't change. They remain the same.

He takes a swig of his cocktail before staring straight into my eyes. "Forgive yourself first and foremost. And then, let go of the past. It doesn't mean that you have to throw away your memories. Keep them safely tucked inside your heart, but leave room in it to make new ones. If you find that you still want him after this, you will get him back."

FIFTY

The Dawn

THERE'S NOTHING AROUND the house that reminds me of him. And yet, I think of him every single minute of every single day. It's been more than a year since I first laid eyes on him as he watched me from the corner of a conference room. It feels like eons ago since he collected his things and moved away, all the traces of our time together are gone.

I'm on a mission to let go of my past. I immerse myself in my father's business affairs, I work and travel and piece together the remnants of my life by finding comfort in the solace that being alone now affords me. I call him when these moments of weakness overcome me. He doesn't pick up the phone and I hang up without leaving him a message. I cry tears of remorse. Of bitterness. Of acceptance. I don't even attempt to question why it is that he hasn't tried to contact me. I know him well enough to understand that this is his way of trying to move on.

Leya tells me that Chicago has seen its last snow of the season and sends me snapchats of the slowly budding cherry blossoms. I make a mental note to call her in the morning. Sometimes, when I miss him, I call her instead.

Chris and I keep in touch often. He's seeing someone, a publicist who's been touring with the team for the past few months. He tells me that it isn't serious. He tells me that he still loves me. And I tell him that I will always love him. Without Chris, there will be nothing left of my past. I hold on to him if only for that reason, although selfishly I know that saying goodbye to each other will be an inevitable part of our near future. Father Mike was right about the need for all of us to keep moving forward regardless of our incessant longing to cling to what we once had.

Chris' love molded me when I was a young girl. It made me strong and determined as a young woman and hopeful about the power of love when I was a mother with a child. I was blessed by the role that he played in my life. I don't know how to let go of that.

If Lucas hadn't busted into my life like a hurricane and swept me up at that particular time, I have no doubt whatsoever that I would still be his. The storm that inflicted chaos in my home carried me to a foreign place; adapting to my new environment will determine the next phase of this, my new life.

I NEVER STOPPED believing in signs.

Almost two months after I last saw him, I'm curled up in bed reading Olivia's latest book recommendation, a page turner that I couldn't put down despite the fact that it's two o'clock in the morning and I have a full day of meetings ahead of me. My eyelids are heavy. I'm tired and about to shut my Kindle off when I see a fluttering object right in front of me. I stare at it dazedly for a few seconds until I realize that it's a moth. This time it isn't flying in the direction of a light. It circles around and around my head, lightly brushing against my hair until it rests on the pillow next to me. As I lean my head for a closer look, I drop my Kindle through the tiny space between the headboard and the wall.

"Shoot!" I say out loud. I'm tired and irritated but know that I need to recharge my e-reader before I turn in for the night. I wedge my arm into the tiny space behind the bed and feel around with my fingers, refusing to remove my gaze from the moth that's still resting peacefully on the pillow. My fingers touch something hard and cold. I retrieve whatever it is and pull my arm back in to take a look at my new find. It's a phone. Lucas' phone. It must have fallen off the bed or night table during one of his nights here. It's dead of course, so I trudge over to the charger on the wall, sit on the floor and plug it in. It comes to life right with the Camera Roll opened up to hundreds of pictures of us—our tour in Palma de Mallorca, our days at the beach, the sun, the surf, the picnics on the sand, the colorful sails highlighted against the bright blue sky. But what makes me cry— what makes me catch my breath and clutch at my heart—are the numerous pictures of me when we were in Chicago together. There are pictures of me taken while I was asleep the night he stayed over, pictures of me on the dance floor when I lost him for a few minutes, pictures of me at the very first lunch we had at the Italian restaurant, walking slowly across the bridge in four inch heels, telling him animated stories about the river. There is one of me hailing a cab the Saturday of the signing and one of me sitting by the steps staring out towards the river with a cigarette in my left hand.

The week that meant so much to me apparently meant something to him too.

"Cia!" I shout as I drop the phone to my side and frantically search for the moth that was just right next to me a few minutes ago. It has vanished. But in its place is the heart that I thought was gone forever. Tonight changes everything. Tonight, more than anything else, Cia has reminded me of something that I knew all along.

I sit in the dark for a long time and let go of all the tears that have been bottled up inside me for so long.

I cry about the day I lost Chris to a pretty blonde in denim shorts.

I ache with the pain that I caused him.

I lament at the love that I never had for Joshua.

I wail as I mourn the loss of my daughter.

I don't hold back. I grieve and I fret until all my tears have been released and I can no longer hear the sounds of my anguish. *This is the dead end of my past. Now to walk around the breakwall, close my eyes and free fall into the future.*

"Hello?" she croaks into the phone, breathy and heavy with sleep.

"Sorry, Ley. It's me."

"Jade? What's wrong? Are you okay? Isn't it 2:00 am there?"

"Ley, do you know where he is? I need to call him. I love him, Ley. I love him. I have to tell him that I love him."

She perks up immediately and shrieks, "This is great! Call him. I don't know where he is and I don't care what time it is. Somewhere in the world, it's morning. Call him, Jade." She follows up with an afterthought. "And then call me immediately afterwards to give me the full scoop!"

I dial his number as soon as I hang up the phone with her. It rings a few times but he doesn't pick up. My heart hurts with extreme disappointment but this time, I decide to leave a message.

"Luke, you were right. I love you. I think I loved you from the first time I met you. Whatever the reasons, whatever the circumstances, you were the one that my heart chose to help me pick up the pieces of my broken soul. All this time I was afraid that I translated my loneliness into my need to be with you. It doesn't matter why it happened or how it happened. I'm just sorry I wasted so much time before admitting it to myself and to you. So I'm glad that I get to leave you this message so you can play it over and over again, in case you don't believe me." I laugh nervously before rambling on. "I love you, Luke. Thank you for lifting me up out of the depths of sadness and bringing some light into my life. I would never ever trade a single minute of the time we spent with each other, whether together or apart, for anything in the world. I will always be thankful for this rollercoaster of emotions that you put me through. It made me feel and it made me think, but most of all, it made me feel alive. I love you."

"BLESS ME, FATHER, for I have sinned. It's been three years since my last confession. My biggest sin is the sin of omission. Of pretense. Of tolerating an insipid existence filled with hopelessness and grief. I was unfaithful in mind, in thought, and in heart. For these and for all my sins, I am truly sorry."

"Jade?" he asks, despite knowing full well that it's me kneeling down at his confessional.

"Yes, Father. It's me."

"I didn't know you were in town."

"I'm here to finally close up the house. We sold it last week and I came to sift through what's left of Cia's things. I leave this afternoon for home. I won't be back here for a long time, until I see you at the memorial."

"Are you okay? How is everything going?"

"I followed your advice, Father. I gave up the past. I'm now living in the present. I'm asking for God's forgiveness so I can move on."

"You have it, Jade. God's amazing grace has always been with you. I'm so glad that you finally reached out a hand to Him. You must trust and believe that you were never alone. Know that from this day forward, your sins are forgiven. For your penance, I would like you to step into your new life without looking back. Can you do that from now on?"

"Yes, Father, I promise," I whisper softly.

"All right then, bow your head and pray for God's blessing."

I lean my head forward as he raises his hands up to bless me.

"I absolve you from your sins in the name of the Father, and of the Son, and of the Holy Spirit. Go in God's peace, Jade. You deserve to be happy."

FIFTY-ONE

Leaving it All Here

TODAY MARKS THE third anniversary of the day I died. The setting sun skates across the water surrounded by the orange sky streaked with alternating layers of blue and white and yellow. The water is still and calm with only tiny rolls of waves washing upon the shore. If I looked far enough, I can see her standing at the end of the universe. I can feel her presence close by. I can hear her sweet singing voice next to me. How many times have I imagined what it would be like if I saw her again? Soon, now. Soon.

I walk sideways along the shore where the water meets the sand, farther and farther from any sign of life. Away from judgment, from condemnation. From things that remind me of the mess I've made. My hands are full, my steps are heavy. But my heart... it's open. It's free. I've done what I could to apologize for all the hurt I've caused them. I've said the words to tell him just how much I love him. Without me, I know they will all be forced to move on.

I stop in the middle of nowhere, ready to finish what I came here to do. In my left hand is one single flower. A calla lily. Simple and understated, but meaningful. In my right hand is a little box with breathing holes and a chirping sound emanating from it.

Let me sit down for a while, I say to myself. Collect my thoughts. Remember why I'm here. I sit for what feels like hours, but in the scheme of things, I know that it's only for a minute. Slowly, I open the box with the bird in it. The swallow, so tiny, but whose wings are strong and powerful, cowers along the edge of the box, shaking and afraid. I take a deep breath and touch its head with my little finger. Is that what a feather feels like? I'm shaking. I'm sick. I don't think I can do it. How can something so small scare me so much? How can something as docile, as insignificant as a bird, cause me to change my path every time I come across it? Another deep breath as I lift it gently, my fingers lightly enclosing it before I place it on the palm of my hand. Its scraggy little feet feel like pin pricks on my skin.

There. That wasn't so bad now, was it?

I laugh out loud as I raise my arm up in the air, tossing the bird up high, watching it fly far away from me. *Ha! Take that!*

The tide creeps up. The tiny box washes away as I stand up to complete my journey.

The water is dark. My feet feel cold. With the flower clasped in my hand, I move forward. Slowly, surely. I step upon the sand until I can no longer see my feet.

I flinch and jump up in surprise. Something rubs against my legs. Seaweed wraps around my toes. I close my eyes and keep moving. My last fear. Fear of the bottomless unknown that is part of every life. This will be over soon.

Beyond my comfort zone and into the ocean I go. Deeper and deeper until the tide pushes me forward and my feet can no longer anchor themselves on the sand.

I close my eyes and pray. I pray for forgiveness, but most of all I pray for those who will be left behind.

As the tide carries me further away, I delight in the numbness that the cold brings to my skin. The muffled sound of the water in my ear. The overwhelming, heartfelt feeling of closure.

Floating, floating, floating away filled with so much peace.

The fact that I'm moving away from the security of the shore doesn't bother me. I bask in the quiet solitude for a few minutes. I hear it in the distance, a sudden roar that starts from its depths and pushes itself outward towards the sky. I'm not afraid. I'm excited to feel the rush of a huge wave conceal me from the world, leading me to wherever, making me feel helpless enough to accept whatever it is that may come next. I feel an overbearing excitement as I lose control.

Trust in Him. Trust in signs. Trust in your fate. Live your life in honesty. Let your heart choose whom to love; you'll never go wrong that way. Live life to the fullest and know that those who leave this world ahead of you are watching over you always.

As the wave washes upon me, I am pulled down towards the bottom of the ocean in a powerful undertow. Still I have no fear because I know that he's right here with me.

And he is.

I hold my breath and allow a few seconds to pass before I flap my arms furiously in an attempt to resurface above the water.

I'm not here to die. I'm here to live.

And just as I expected, two strong arms pull me out of the abyss as he lifts my head above the water and holds me tightly, his strong legs treading water and leading us back towards the shore. My rescuer. My lighthouse. He's here.

"I've got you, baby. I'm here. You did it, Jade. You've bravely faced all of your fears. I'm so proud of you. I love you so much."

FIFTY-TWO

Rainbow

"OH MY BABY, I miss you so much!" Tears fall from my eyes as I rest on the stone path directly across from Cia's headstone. "I'm sorry you had to see all that," I weep as I cover my face with my hands.

Above me, the gray clouds sit still, listening, absorbing all the words I have to say; condensing them into rain that will fall down on me and wash the pain away.

"I'm better now. It has taken a while, but I'm better. For the first time in so long, my head is clear and my heart is at peace."

It's the day of the memorial service and all the guests have gone home. I'm spending some time alone with my daughter. There's just so much to tell her about since the last time I visited, since the last time I was truly honest with myself, and I want to say these words out loud in front of her.

"Oh gosh. What a time it's been. I don't know where to start.

I'm not sure how I just lost myself after eighteen years of being somebody else. He just appeared out of nowhere, Ci, and my world just went awry. Nothing made sense, everything was just so confusing. I tried so hard to fight it, but there was no turning back after I met him. I didn't know it would happen. But it did. I fell in love, baby. I don't know how, and I can't imagine why, but I love him. He brings so much color into my life. If you saw how happy he makes me, you would love him too." The words flow effortlessly, as if I'm addressing my best friend. In more ways than one, that's what she was to me. We spent every minute of every day together; she was the center of my life. "That night at the beach, he told me that he had a dream about you. That you asked him to follow me to the Ritz. I laughed when he told me that as soon as he barged into my hotel room, but I believed him. I am so glad that he was there with me, that you sent him to take care of me. I don't think I could have done that without him." I lapse into silence as I remember what he did for me that night. Lucas saved me from the past; I haven't looked back since. "I'm going to marry him, Ci. He doesn't know it yet, but one day soon, I will. He's broken me with his unrelenting proposals. I'm giving in." I laugh without restraint, without reservation.

A flash of wind stirs me from my thoughts as the leaves and branches of the trees around me start to sway lightly. I feel a cool breeze on my skin and a sweet, refreshing calmness washes over me. Out of nowhere, the same tiny moth flits around briefly and settles on her tombstone. This time, it looks different. Its wings bear tiny tinges of yellow and orange along its edges.

It was never a moth. It was always a butterfly.

I move closer as it placidly rests on the granite top so that I'm almost face to face with it. "Everything is as it should be, baby girl. Your dad is fine. He's getting married soon. If you could see how happy he is—he looks like a completely different person. And Chris.

He's fine too. He's touring around with the best college basketball team in the country. I'll be attending the awards presentation for Coach of the Year next month. Can you believe it? Chris is Coach of the Year! And those boys, he treats them all like they were his sons. They are so all so fortunate to have him in their lives." I stretch my arm out and reverently brush the tips of my fingers against the neatly polished carving on her tombstone before continuing on. I swallow my words painfully because I never thought that I'd be strong enough to let her go. "We've all come full circle, Ci. And we all miss you so much. But you need to rest now, my love." I look straight into the butterfly's antennae. "Enjoy your peace. You don't have to worry about me anymore. And thank you so much for watching over me. I will live my life for you. I will make you so proud to be my daughter. I won't be afraid to love him with all my heart, because he deserves nothing less than that. I love you, Felicia Albin Richmond. You will forever be the biggest part of my heart."

With all the strength I can muster, I dry my eyes and wipe my face, resolved to replace my tears with delight. I extend my arm out as the butterfly takes off and gently settles itself on the palm of my hand. It lingers for a brief second before circling around my face and fluttering against my cheek before flying away forever. I giggle at the thought of being kissed by an insect. No one will believe me. Well, maybe Lucas will. Or Leya. Maybe even Olivia. They've listened to my stories, they know about these signs. I kneel down on the concrete ground to say a final prayer, unraveling the scarf from my neck and tying it around the stone cross above the headstone as I do so. There's no longer any need to hide my scars. I wear them with pride, knowing that I survived through the darkest of days. I have love now. No matter what happens, I am not alone.

And as I lift my head up from where I am, I see them. One by one, the vivid colors of the flowers around the grave—bright yellows, pinks and blues. A rainbow of light that catches my eye for the very first time. I smile at myself and turn away towards the road ahead of me. He is there. Leaning against my car, watching me, waiting for me.

There he is. My rainbow. My bright palette of life.

I lay a bouquet of flowers on the ground, but not before choosing the brightest pink peony and clutching it tightly between my fingers. I spin around excitedly and search for his eyes, breaking out into a smile so filled with the promise of a future together. Slowly, he holds his hand out to me, beckoning me to walk towards him. I hold the flower up to him as a beacon of light, a signal to him that I'm no longer afraid.

Here I go, I say to myself as I hurriedly make my way into his arms. Walking towards my light. Heading into a lifetime of color.

EPILOGUE

Lucas

"GET AWAY FROM me! I hate you! I can't believe you did this to me! Why, Lucas? Why?" she asks me with tears in her eyes as I maintain a firm grip on her hand.

"She doesn't mean that," her mother counters, silently consoling me through what has been an eighteen-hour ordeal for all of us.

Her father sits in a chair on the corner of the room, relaxed and composed while reading a newspaper.

"Oh yes, I do! I do! Lucas, why? It hurts so much I don't think I will ever recover from this."

"I'm sorry, baby. Please try to calm down."

"No! Get away from me."

I release her hand and begin to back away, giving her what she wants.

"No! Lucas. I didn't mean it. Please come back. I love you.

I love you, baby, please."

Those words, those eyes. They belong to the only woman I have ever loved.

It's been a year after she left me that voicemail message. The one that had me catching the next available international flight back to the States with nothing but my wallet and cell phone with me. My life started two years after hers ended. And here we are, as husband and wife. In a private hospital room where the most beautiful woman in the world has her legs hoisted up in a medieval torture device the doctor calls stirrups.

She is having our baby.

"Jade, I think it's time to start pushing," Dr. Vierling announces as he steps into the room, mechanically donning a pair of gloves and gesturing to the nurse to stand next to him. He rolls the stool over so that he's right smack in the middle of her legs.

"No, it's not. I can't. I'm going to die if I do," she argues adamantly. "I'm too old for this."

"You're not going to die and you're not too old. On the next big contraction, you're going to have to push," he says sternly.

"I ca—Owww! Okay, I'm pushing! Aargh. Honestly, whose idea was this?" she spews out in between shallow breaths.

I continue to squeeze her hand while wiping her forehead with a damp cloth. Her father remains glued to the chair in the corner reading the financial news.

"Baby, you came third in your age group at the Big Sur marathon last year. This is nothing. You can do it," I encourage, guiding her through her breathing exercises.

"Age group, Lucas. That's the key. Age group." She pushes as another contraction hits her.

"That's it, baby, you're doing really well. Just a little more and we're there."

"The last time I did this, I was asleep. Knocked out. Why couldn't we do it that way again?" she pants, swatting my hand away, amusing Dr. Vierling, who nods at me like he's already seen it all.

"Why did you move your hand? Luke. I need your hand!" she snaps.

Our conversation is stopped short by a whimper and then a shrill, melodious cry.

"Here you go, kids. While you were busy arguing, your baby decided to come out," Dr. Vierling says sarcastically.

And that's how this story ends. Or begins.

Francis Lucas Albin Martinez was born on a bright September morning, a healthy little boy with brown eyes and bushy dark hair. From that day on, we've shed many happy tears, Jade and I. And as our love continues to flourish, we look back on the past as a reminder that life is precious, life is short.

Fight for it. Fight for true love. No matter the time and place, no matter the circumstance. It may drown you in the depths of the ocean or push you into that rough, cascading sea, but once you have it, it will keep you afloat. It will be your buoy in the middle of nowhere, the anchor that won't let you drift away. It will fill the seasons of your life with hope, for every change signifies a new beginning.

And so, as we leave you here today, listen to what a wise old woman once said:

Fate is a friend and not a foe. Sometimes, all it takes is one hello.

ACKNOWLEDGEMENTS

As I WRITE the final words of this book, I think back to the year that has passed. My heart is filled with love and gratitude for everything that you have done for me. THANK YOU so much for being here, for reading this book, for your love and support throughout this journey.

To my Street Team—without your kind words and constant encouragement, I couldn't have made it through this time. How fortunate I've been to have you all in my life. Thank you for always being there for me. Due to the limited amount of space, I won't be able to name all of you—I hope you all know who you are.

To the people who have touched my life in one way or the other—*Tammy Zautner, Gabri Canova, Krystle Zion, Marivette Villafane, Erin Spencer, Tray Davis, Suzanne Wendolski, Cynthia Mae, Melissa Jones, Stephanie Johnson, Miranda Howard, Hali Gibson, Wen Cast, Angela O'Brien, Anna Green, KC Chavez, Robin Stranahan, Jaime Iwatsuru, Misty Canada*

Devotie, Nessa Rebel Book Babe and Stacy Hgg among many others. You are all so dear to me.

To *Barbzy Murray, Alisha Rosey Jackson, Kissa Mil Xu and Emma Fernandez*—you're all still here! What an honor it is for me that you stuck around.

Megan Simpson, Serena Knautz, and Robin Segnitz—your friendship means so much.

Nelly Martinez de Iraheta—my life changed when I met you.

To my beta readers and friends, *Lisa Rutledge, Tosha Khoury, Laura Wilson*—you remind me that love and loyalty go hand in hand.

For the best book cover yet and for the light that you bring into my life, I love you, *Lindsay Sparkes.*

To *Janna Mashburn* for all your support, and to *Melissa Brown*, because I never forget.

And to *Erin Dauer Roth*, editor and friend. You are the reason why I never gave up.

Angela Cook McLaurin of Fictional Formats—this one is for you. You helped save this book at the last minute. Never mind that you kept sending me pictures of the beach in the dead of winter.

To *Christine Estevez* for believing in me.

To *Denise Tung* for always, always holding my hand.

To *Trisha Rai* for your faith in my stories.

To *Rick Miles*, who never stopped urging me to plug along and who treated me as a friend despite the fact that I was really just a client.

To *Becca Manuel* for so eloquently giving life to my book with your trailer.

And to all the wonderful blogs who signed up for our Blog Tour. I am honored that you are taking the time to read and review my story.

To my Brutus, my Butsy, faithful friend for ten years. I still look around the house for you every single day.

To my friend **007**. Don't read this book.

Thank you, **Willow Aster**, for trusting me enough to share your big reveal with me.

If I were to describe the year 2014, I would sum it up as The Year That I Left. Not only was I running around the country on business trips, I was lost in heart and mind and soul. For those of you who loved me relentlessly, who pulled me out of the fog, who listened and cried and told me to get my head out of my ass—you are my heroes. **Tarryn Fisher, Lori Sabin, my sisters, Gerri and Tessa**—I couldn't have survived this time without you.

This book is dedicated to the **Loving Memory of Mary Ogarek (1981-2014).** Thank you for being proud of me. I only wished that we had more time to talk (and laugh) about this book.

Last but most certainly not the least, to my husband, **Bill** - Thank you for never giving up on me. For letting me go because you knew I'd be back.

And I am back. Suitcases in hand, stronger, happier and truer to myself.

This is going to be the best summer of my life.

XO

Connect with Christine Brae:

Facebook:
facebook.com/pages/Christine-Brae/251960864949578?fref=ts

Website:
www.christinebrae.com

Goodreads:

goodreads.com/author/show/7076627

Email:

christinebrae@gmail.com

And now, a sneak peek into Willow Aster's new book,

Maybe Maby
Coming July 13, 2014!

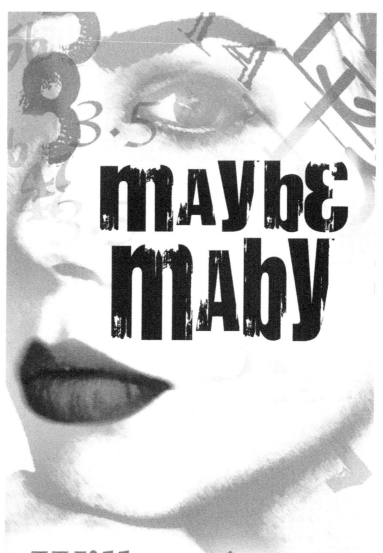

mAybE mAby

Willow Aster

1

not just blue

I BARELY MAKE it to the subway on an early Monday morning and sit beside a smelly old man. It is the only open seat. I can hold my breath. Maybe I'll die that way. My obituary will read: *She held her breath trying to avoid inhaling body odor.* It doesn't work. I have to keep sneaking quick breaths and the old man asks what my problem is. It kills me when people who haven't bathed in weeks have the audacity to think I'm weird.

I ignore him and when another open seat is available, I hop up and take it. Old smelly man shakes his head at me and I wave. I can be much friendlier from afar. I smooth down my corduroy skirt and try to subtly yank up my tights. It's December in New York and cold.

My stop comes and I rush to get off, along with dozens of other people. I count to 127 as the crowd pushes and nudges and smacks their gum around me. I will never get used to all these people in my space, but the alternative is worse: the thought of driving in the city is terrifying. On the 128th step, I turn to the right and take the 17 steps to my destination. I rub my finger through the ribbing on my skirt with each step. *14, 15, 16, 17.* Unlock the store.

Whatnot Alley is a gifts and furnishings boutique owned by Anna Whitmore. She used to be a friend of mine, but ever since she had a baby—and became the owner of her flourishing shop—she doesn't have time for anything as quaint as friendship. I came to work for her as a favor and have now run the store for 3 years. She comes in at least once a week, and my skin is on edge the entire time. Whenever she engages in conversation, it's to moan about how she never has time for anything. But she would like to have one more child, just one more… as long as it's a boy. She's already run ragged, but let's throw another in the mix for good measure. That's what nannies are for!

I lock the door behind me. We won't be opening for a while yet. Unlock. Lock. Unlock. Lock. Okay, I can move on. Moving to the back of the store, I hang my coat on the hook to my right. My gloves go in my purse, which I lock away in the bottom drawer of my desk. Unlock. Lock. If I'm going to have a good day, it takes 28 steps to do all of the above before I start the coffee. If I'm going to have a bad day, it takes 29. It's a 44 steps kind of day. I have to go back and redo my first steps because it just didn't feel right.

My grandmother, Mabel, who I'm named after, also had OCD. Speaking of leaving, she sure left me behind with a couple of doozies. Between the disorder and the name, I feel like she should have stuck around longer than my 11th birthday to make sure I survived.

Before I do anything else, I put my earphones in and begin playing my ocean sounds mix. Music is too stimulating. I find it hard to concentrate on anything but the music. The crashing waves calm me. It feels nice to know that somewhere it is more tumultuous than in my mind. Once the store opens, I will have to take off my earphones, but when it's just me, I keep everything turned off. When

Anna is in the store, she plays Top 40 radio. Some days it's bearable; other days I'm certain I will break every trinket within close range. I usually stay behind the counter on those days, where I can only do damage with the cash register.

I take a sip of the coffee I pour in my smoky blue Zojirushi stainless steel mug, rated highest on Amazon for quality. It doesn't leak, and it keeps the coffee hot for 6 hours. I've tested it and found it to be true. I chose smoky blue because it suits my moods more than the cheerful lilac or the completely soulless black. Smoky blue maintains mystery but still has the touch of melancholy. I wish I were a lilac person, but I'm not.

I made my list for today before I left on Friday and I take a look at it this morning. I can already check off 4 things, so I immediately do. I then add to the list all of the vendors I have to call today and check which shipments might be coming in. I tidy up the throw pillows on the few pieces of furniture we carry and straighten the pictures over and over again. Symmetry is a requirement. Anything else is… evil.

At 8:30, I set my phone alarm to go off at 8:53, so I will have plenty of time to gather my notes for the monthly meeting in the small side room. Anna and a couple of part-time employees come to the meetings before we open. I'm the only full-time employee, so Anna asks that I'm always ready to give input if she needs it.

But at 8:37, I begin to get the unbearable urge to wash my hands. The hand sanitizer behind the front counter doesn't get rid of the dirt. 1, 2, 3, 4 times. I have to wash with water and soap. I take off my headphones and rush to the bathroom, forgetting my phone. I lose track of time in the bathroom washing my hands over and over again. It's getting worse. I'm not sure what to do.

When I finally get back to my desk, I have just a few minutes left. I take a deep breath, pick up my phone, laptop, and coffee mug and make my way to the back. I'll be the first one there. It's hard working with other people who are slow, lazy… normal.

I haven't even started working yet and I'm already exhausted.

Connect with Willow Aster:
Facebook:
https://www.facebook.com/willowasterauthor

Website:
http://willowaster.com/

Goodreads:
https://www.goodreads.com/author/show/6863360.Willow_Aster

Made in the USA
Coppell, TX
26 October 2021